A BROKEN VOW

A BROKEN VOW

CHRONICLES OF AN URBAN DRUID™ BOOK 5

AUBURN TEMPEST

MICHAEL ANDERLE

DISRUPTIVE IMAGINATION®

Copyright © 2021 LMBPN Publishing
Cover by Fantasy Book Design
Cover copyright © LMBPN Publishing
A Michael Anderle Production

LMBPN Publishing
PMB 196, 2540 South Maryland Pkwy
Las Vegas, NV 89109

Version 1.02, January 2022
eBook ISBN: 978-1-64971-439-8
Print ISBN: 978-1-64971-440-4

THE A BROKEN VOW TEAM

Thanks to our JIT Team:

Dave Hicks
James Caplan
Dorothy Lloyd
Daniel Weigert
Kelly O'Donnell
Micky Cocker
Debi Sateren
Deb Mader
John Ashmore
Thomas Ogden
Diane L. Smith
Rachel Beckford
Larry Omans
Paul Westman

Editor
SkyHunter Editing Team

IRISH TRANSLATIONS

a ghra - my love, a romantic endearment

Dia dhuit - a greeting for hello

Maith go leor – all right, good enough

Go raibh maith agat - thank you

CHAPTER ONE

"Tell me everything, duck. I've been dying to hear how it's going with the two of you. Does the reality live up to expectation? Do his talents and attention to detail translate into other—more important—areas of life?"

I laugh at the sheer delight dancing in Myra's stunning, cat-slit eyes. "I'm not sure bedroom skills are technically more important than saving lives, but I get what you mean."

Sitting in the hanging wicker swing that mirrors mine, Myra kicks off her winter boots and crosses her feet beneath her. It may be the second week in November everywhere else in Toronto, but we spelled our sacred grove to keep our fae toasty warm and comfy.

"Maybe not but you didn't answer my question."

"And by *him* you mean..."

My boss lets out an exasperated huff and grabs a handful of her lopsided, electric blue hair. "Don't make me pull this out. I've been more than patient. He moved into your bed almost two weeks ago, and I haven't gotten one juicy tidbit."

I collect Mopsy from where he's hovering in the air in front of me and settle him onto the blanket on my lap. While I stroke his long velvety ears, he folds back his shimmering purple wings and wriggles his little whiskers at me.

"What do you think, honey-bunny? Should we put her out of her misery?"

"Yes, you should."

Her impatience is too funny. I lean back in my chair and swing beneath the canopy of trees. "You know I'm teasing. Yes, it's been wonderful. Sloan's attentive and perceptive, and it's been two weeks of perfection."

"Two weeks of perfection," she repeats, leaning deep into her swing with a smile on her face. "I like the sound of that. Please continue."

I chuckle. "What kind of details are you looking for? I'm not getting into the nitty-gritty with you."

Myra bursts out laughing. "No. Please don't. I meant, is he a passionate and giving lover like you deserve? Is he creative? Is he adventurous?"

"He is."

"And you're having fun together?"

"In and out of the bedroom, yes."

"Good. I'm glad to hear it. You both deserve it."

I spot Pip peeking through the branches at me, and I open my arms. My little fae brownie descends the tree and climbs into the swing with Mopsy and me. "This is Pip," I say, making sure she's comfy. "She's one half of the sweetest little couple I know. Her mate Nilm is around here somewhere."

Brownies, or *brunaidh* as they're known in the fae world, are the size of toddlers and have the cutest globe antennae bobbing over their cherubim faces. I can't speak to them and they don't understand me, but we make do. If there's ever an issue, Emmet rescues us.

He can speak woodland chatter.

Pip settles under the blanket with me and presses her little hand against my cheek. It's warm and soft, and she's telling me she loves me. Who needs words? We make do just fine.

So freaking adorable.

"Sloan's doing okay here? You said he left home under the shadow of a dark cloud with his parents."

I consider her question and sigh. "He's quiet about the things bothering him. I'm not sure if that's a man thing or a personal thing or if he simply doesn't want to bring down the high we're on."

"Likely a combination of all three. So you haven't discussed it at all?"

"His parents have texted him but other than that, I don't know what was said."

"Except that he's set on sticking around, right? He's not going to convince you to move back to the Emerald Isle with him and steal you away from us?"

I shake my head. "Never gonna happen. I'm a Toronto girl through and through. I have my family, my friends, and my beautiful grove. I'm home here."

"What about the deal you made with your grandfather? One day you have to take up the family post and be the Shrine-Keeper, don't you?"

"That was the arrangement when he was dying. He's fixed now, and druids can live a very long life—centuries, a millennium even. I refuse to think about it. For right now, it's enough that I'm learning my skills and my place in this life and I'm home with my fam jam."

Myra lets out a long exhale. "Well then, I wish your grandfather a long, healthy life. And I wish your Irish heartthrob hottie good fortune in finding his place here. Is he thinking about a job?"

"Honestly, I don't know. We haven't got that far."

Myra's pinched lips imply she's not satisfied with that answer. "Everyone needs their roots firmly planted if they expect to grow to any height. If you want him to settle, you should help him plant those roots as quickly as you can."

I hadn't given it any thought. It makes sense, though. He can't be a visitor in my world and build a life. He'll have to start making inroads. "He doesn't need the money, so maybe a passion project."

"He's a history buff, and he's well-educated, right?"

I chuckle. "Yeah, he's ridiculously smart. He can rhyme off dates and facts and legends like he has a reference library jammed in his cranium and he's flipping through texts."

Myra nods. "Let's start there. I'll put out some feelers in the empowered community, and you ask him if he has any plans. Maybe we can lock him down, so you don't have to worry about him leaving."

I lean back and my seat swings beneath my weight. "I wasn't worried about him leaving until now—thanks for that."

Myra waves that away and smiles at the canopy above. "You did well here, duck. This is a lovely grove. I'll come back in the spring and help you introduce a few ground plants to feed your soil, but other than that, I can't see any improvements necessary."

Coming from a hundred-and-ninety-four-year-old ash tree nymph, I take that as high praise. After hugging Pip, I slide out of the swing and shift Mopsy onto her lap. "Put your boots back on. Lunch should be ready."

"Excellent, I'm starving."

The two of us head inside and are welcomed at the threshold of the back door by the savory scent of colcannon.

"Oh, hotness, that smells amazing." I lean over the stove to get a better whiff. My tummy rumbles in agreement. "It smells like Gran's."

Sloan steps around me to grab bowls out of the cupboard and set them on the counter. He's in his element in the kitchen— which suits me fine—and it looks good on him.

He kisses my cheek and pulls out the cutlery drawer. "It should smell like Lara's. She taught me how to make it."

I love that my grandparents practically raised my guy. He has a connection to them I don't and never will. I love to hear the stories about how they nurtured him as a boy.

It makes me feel closer to all three of them.

Sadly, despite him being handsome, smart, honorable, and remarkably skilled at all things druid, his parents seem incapable of giving him the love and affection he deserves.

"Yer lookin' especially lovely today, Myra." He flashes her a playboy grin. "The fresh air agrees with ye."

Myra dips her chin and smiles. "Not half as much as love does. Garnet has a great deal to do with the color in my cheeks and the smile on my lips these days. It seems love is in the air. Our fair Fiona filled me in on your grand affair of the heart. I'm pleased for you both."

Sloan arches a curious brow, and I blush. "When she says filled her in, she means I gave her the broad strokes. Very PG, vague, broad strokes."

He chuckles and sets the bowls on the center of the stove. "What the two of ye privately discuss as girlfriends is yer business. I'm simply happy yer happy."

My cheeks ache from all the smiling. "I am. Hopefully, it's not only me, and it's a two-way street."

"Och, it definitely is." He stirs the pot and turns off the burner. "Would ye like me to serve or would ye like to scoop yer own?"

"You take yours. We'll grab ours."

He nods, fills his bowl, and makes his way over to a seat at the kitchen table.

Myra and I serve ourselves and are settling down at the table when Emmet barrels down the stairs. "Dayam, Irish. That smells amazing."

"Help yerself."

"Thanks, man. Are you trying to butter us up or something? 'Cause if you are, you're killing it."

Sloan winks at me and lifts a steaming spoonful to blow on it. "I figure it's better to make myself useful than to be turned out as a freeloader."

I chuckle. "I don't think there's any threat of that. Although Myra and I were talking about what your plans might be moving forward. I'm going back to work tomorrow at the bookshop, and Auntie Shannon needs me to work at the pub tonight, so real life is beating down our door."

He eyes the creamy potatoes and cabbage on his spoon and smiles. "What? Do ye think I need ye here to keep me entertained?"

"No. I was more concerned with what you might want to do for your sake of self-interest."

He smiles. "I have a few thoughts about that. A few irons in the fire, as they say."

Emmet chuckles and sits to join us with a heaping bowl of lunch. "That sounds mysterious. Care to share?"

"Not yet. Let's wait to see if anything comes of it."

I eye him up and down, and his expression gives me nothing. "It's not like you to play things close to the vest, Mackenzie. Everything okay?"

He swallows what's in his mouth and sips his water. "It's not like *you* to play things close to the vest, *a ghra*. I've always tended to keep my own counsel."

I tilt my head back and forth. "Yeah, I guess that is me more than you. Okay, keep your secrets. You'll tell me when the time comes, right?"

"You'll be the first to know."

"Excellent, then good luck with your secret endeavors."

Sloan scoops the creamy goodness from the bottom of his bowl and stands to take his dishes to the sink. "Emmet, have ye heard from Sarah about how the Blarney witches are handlin' the changes there?"

Emmet lights up at the mention of Sarah. The two of them have been texting every day. I've never seen him fall so hard, so fast for a girl. It's too bad it's with a girl who lives so far away but hey, life's full of twists and turns.

"She says they're good. With only seven of them surviving Moira's black magic reversal, they're looking into how to expand their numbers to a full coven and still ensure the dynamic of their group remains the same."

I swallow and use the last bit of my bread to clean the bottom of my bowl. "Good point. The witches in her coven seemed lovely and of a like mindset. I'm sure that's rare."

Myra finishes her lunch and hands her dirty dishes up to Sloan when he offers to take them. "Finding people who match and complement your core intentions is tough—"

Myra's words cut off as a horrible wail sounds in the backyard.

"That's Manx!" Sloan races out of the kitchen and is gone in a split-second. I push to my feet and round the corner as Emmet flings the door open wide.

Launching off the porch in my socks, I curse at the scene unfolding ahead of us. "Janine! What are you doing?"

Janine is standing on her back deck next door with a pellet gun propped over our fence. She waves the barrel at me, her eyes wild. "Get out of my way, idiot!"

I look over my shoulder to where Sloan is standing, holding Manx in his arms, giving her his back. My heart stutters in my chest. "You shot Manx?"

"I shot the wildcat in your backyard."

"Why would you do that? We don't shoot wildlife!" The sudden surge of emotion makes my eyes sting, and I turn away as my ice-blue fae eyes burn through the glamor that hides them from sight.

"I'm doing you a favor," Janine shouts. "If I'd been better prepared, Skippy wouldn't have been taken by a coyote."

Emmet sees my freaky fae eyes and swaps places with me to stand between Sloan and Janine. He raises his arms and becomes the only target she can point her weapon at. "Sloan, get Manx inside and assess the damage. Janine, put the gun down. Manx isn't a wild coyote. He's Sloan's cat."

I reestablish the glamor on my eyes and join Emmet in the wall to block Manx from my batshit neighbor.

"No. That thing is much bigger than a cat."

Mark rushes out the back door of their house and frowns. "What's going on?"

"She shot my fuckin' cat," Sloan shouts over his shoulder as Myra ushers him inside.

Mark's expression drops as he takes in his wife poised with the pellet gun. "You shot his cat?"

"It isn't a cat," Janine shouts.

I shake my head. "Manx is a lynx. He's...trained and..."

Emmet meets my gaze and takes the lead. "Sloan does movies and commercials with him. He has all the permits. There's no danger. Janine, you shouldn't have shot him. He's a great cat and a member of our family."

Janine's face pinches as Mark cups the barrel of the gun and lifts it up and away. "Christ, Janine. Go back inside."

When his wife retreats into their home, Mark shakes his head and sighs. "I'm incredibly sorry, guys. She's having trouble getting over the trauma of losing Skippy. With the stress of getting the house ready for sale and finding a new place...she's not herself."

"Not good enough," I snap. "I feel bad about Skippy too, but she can't just shoot my boyfriend's cat. They're guests in our home."

Mark nods. "Understood. Thankfully, it's a pellet gun. We'll take responsibility for all the medical bills. Please, come over later, and we'll talk it through. I'm sure we can fix this without it going any further."

We certainly don't want it to go further either.

Emmet was quick to come up with the animal actor idea, but despite what he said, we don't have any permits. "All right. We'll check on him and let you know how he is later."

Mark nods. "We'll be here. Sorry, guys."

I follow Emmet inside and pull my wet socks off at the back door. "Janine's lost her freaking marbles."

"Who are you kidding? They were misplaced before Skippy got snapped up as an afternoon snack."

"True story."

The two of us hustle into the house and find Sloan and Myra tending to Manx in the dining room. Manx is lying across a towel on the table next to Sloan's black medical bag. Myra is shining her phone light at his hind end, and Sloan is shifting through his lush, gray coat dropping bloody pellets onto a candle plate.

Tink. Tink.

I rush in to join them and decide not to stroke Manx's head when I see his canines bared. Sloan's animal companion is normally quite amiable but not at the moment. "Oh, Manx. I'm so sorry, puss. Are you okay?"

The low-throated growl vibrating through the air is my answer. That would be no.

"How bad is it?" Emmet asks. "I dated a vet assistant in the spring who will come help if you need her. She's good people. She won't ask questions or jam us up."

"We can handle this." Sloan curses and drops three more metal pellets onto the plate. "That woman is a feckin' menace. She coulda put his eye out. And why? Because he was groomin' himself in a sunny spot in a private backyard? Lynx enjoy crisp weather. He was mindin' his own."

I groan, feeling useless. "I'm sorry. Both of you. It shouldn't have happened."

"What shouldn't have happened?" Da asks while descending the stairs. "What's the shoutin' about?"

I fill Da in on the excitement, and he moves in to look at Manx's hindquarters. "Och, that'll be sore, fer sure, but between Sloan and Emmet, they'll have ye fixed up in no time. Yer right though, Fi. It shouldn't have happened. I'll not have any neighbor of mine shootin' into my yard. What if she'd done real damage? What if the wee monkeys were here? I'll go next door and speak to them."

"Good," I say. "Give her hell, Da."

"No," Sloan snaps, looking up from his medical ministrations. "I'll take care of it. I appreciate yer right to protect yer property and yer grandchildren, Niall, but Manx and I are the offended parties. I'll go over once I'm finished and speak to them myself."

"Not on your life," I snap. "If you're not letting Da go rip a strip off them, I'm going."

He casts me a look of frustration I'm getting used to. "Fine, but ye'll let me do the talkin'. I don't want more bad blood between the two households. They're already blamin' the empowered incidents they've witnessed as the reason fer movin' away. I don't want it to escalate."

I roll my eyes. "You make us sound like it's the battle of the Hatfields and the McCoys."

Sloan arches a brow. "I mean it, Fi. I'm not startin' a war with yer neighbors."

I hold up my hands. "Whatevs. I was digging in on your behalf. Far be it from me to fight your fights. You do you, Mackenzie. I figured you'd be fired up and ready for heads to roll. You should be. So, why aren't you?"

Sloan frowns and goes back to tending to Manx. "Hush now. Let me focus."

As it turns out, Manx has only a few pellets that dug deep into his hide and otherwise nothing that Sloan and Emmet can't tend to. The poor boy's tushy will be sore for a few hours, but Sloan is certain that by tomorrow night, he'll be up and ready for our evening of adventure, out in the wilds of the Don Valley.

"I'm sorry Manx got hurt." I slip into my sneakers at the front door an hour later.

He holds my jacket open, and I slide my arms in and shrug it on. "It's not your fault. It happened. He'll be all right. I'm sorry I snapped."

"Totes understandable. You were upset."

"It's maddening that she thought it was their right to harm him. What's wrong with people? Animals are part of our natural world. They should get the same respect we'd give another person."

"I agree. You have every right to lose your mind."

"Perhaps, but I won't. This conversation will be civil, Fi. I meant it."

"Why are you so reticent about voicing your outrage with Mark and Janine? You don't have to make nice with them on our account. They're moving anyway."

"It's simply how I want to handle it."

Myra and I talked when I walked her to the bus stop. She thinks he doesn't want to bring undue attention to the fact that Manx is, in fact, an illegal exotic within city limits.

"I called Kevin. He's working on forging us the paperwork to prove that Manx is a licensed and pedigreed actor cat in case we need it. I also asked Dora if she'd spell the papers to throw off any objections and she said she's happy to."

"That's good thinkin', Fi. Thanks."

I follow him out onto the porch and catch his wrist when the door closes. "Hey, we're alone now. Tell me what's going on. Are you sure you're okay? Whatever's going through your head, you can tell me."

The smile he offers me is warm but sad. "I'm fine. Honestly, let's have our say and get home. You need to change before you leave for your shift at the pub."

"I don't have to go. Under the circumstances, I'm sure they can manage without me."

Sloan frowns. "No, ye gave yer auntie yer word that ye'd help out. I'll not have ye break that because an unstable neighbor shot my cat in the butt with some pellets. Tonight, ye work. Tomorrow he'll be up and about."

"If you want to move our plans for tomorrow night, we can. We don't have to do the Don if it's too much too soon for him. The forest will be there the next night and the night after that. There's no rush."

He pulls me into a hug and kisses the top of my head. "Tomorrow night as planned. I'm lookin' forward to it more than ye know and everyone's set to come. I'll not have that ruined."

I smile, my excitement for tomorrow night bubbling to the surface. When my brothers and I found out that Sloan's never played a real game of hide-and-seek, we agreed that sitch needed immediate rectification. "It'll be epic. We'll play again in the summer, but it's not too cold yet. It will be tons of fun."

He steps back and takes my hand to help me down the front steps. "Savage craic, I'm sure."

"You bet your frost-bitten bippy. Savage craic for sure."

Mark opens the door as we crest the top step of their porch. Their home is the same era and style as our old Victorian but is a mirrored layout with more modern fixtures and finishes. The houses show the difference between my family and the past two hip, metropolitan couples who have lived here in the past ten years.

When we arrive on the porch, he steps back in the doorway and invites us inside. "Thanks for coming. How's your cat? Manx, isn't it?"

Sloan purses his lips and forces a smile. "He'll heal. It could've been worse."

"Please, come in. I have a fresh pot of coffee brewed, or we have tea or soft drinks if you prefer."

"The coffee smells amazing, thanks." I try to follow Sloan's lead and go the mature and diplomatic route. For me, that's the path less traveled.

Look at me. I'm adulting.

I didn't bother buttoning up my jacket, so it's the work of a moment to slide it off my shoulders and hang it on a vacant hook. "Oh, wow, you had the floors refinished since the last time I popped in."

Janine comes to the open doorway of the kitchen. "That was our July project. I'm surprised you missed the trucks. Oh, right, you vacationed in Ireland for the summer."

It was less a vacation and more about me running to find out about our heritage and being held against my will in the lair of the Wyrm Dragon Queen, but yeah, that was in Ireland.

Close enough.

"We were telling Mark that Manx will recover fully," I say. "Thankfully, you didn't catch his eyes or anything vital. He's a bit ornery, swollen, and is nursing some sore spots, but nothing that won't heal."

Janine doesn't look at all concerned. "That's all well and good but really—"

"We couldn't be more thrilled to hear it," Mark says, cutting off his wife with a hostile glare. "It's wonderful your cat will make a full recovery. We don't want any hard feelings."

Too bad, so sad. My feelings are *very* hard.

I'm in solid granite territory.

"No." I smile saccharine-sweet. "I don't suppose you want it brought to light that your wife discharged a firearm into our private property and caused bodily harm."

Mark swallows. "Fi…I understand how bad this could be for Janine and that your whole family is in law enforcement. I'm praying the fact that we've been friends and neighbors for years plays enough of a part in things so we can smooth the waters until we find another place."

Janine huffs. "Well, if this is all *my* fault, how is it not *her* fault that Skippy's dead?"

My jaw drops. "Exsqueeze me? I didn't kill Skippy. He got away from you and ran loose to the tree line. That wasn't my doing. I didn't coax a coyote out to snatch him up and run off into the woods with him."

"It was the fight on your lawn that upset him and caused him to struggle loose!"

"Or maybe he saw his chance to make a break for freedom and took it."

"You think he wanted to get away from me? What are you saying?"

"Nothing," Sloan snaps. He grabs my coat back off the hook and opens the door. "On second thought, perhaps emotions are too high tonight to discuss things. Fi, would ye give me a moment alone with Janine and Mark?"

It isn't a question. My jacket is thrust at me as he reaches around me to open the door and practically shoves me out onto the porch.

"I'll meet ye back home straight away."

The door closes, and I'm left wondering what the hell happened. How do I find myself out in the cold on this one—literally and figuratively?

"Well, fine." I don't bother putting on my jacket. I tromp off the porch and storm back to my house next door.

The *crunch, crunch, crunch* of my shoes crushing the frigid and frozen grass sounds violent, and I like it.

There's a patch of ice on the front walk, so I have my focus on the shiny ground when something scurries across the lawn to my right.

I turn to see what it is, but it's small and fast and swallowed up in the shadows of the trees across the side laneway. Ours is the last house on the street, then there's a dirt laneway that runs alongside the tree line and beyond that is an access point to the Don River system, a 200-hectare landscape connecting Toronto's downtown core.

Wildlife happens, which I love.

I stare after the dark shadow and wonder what it was.

Too big for a cat. Too quick for a raccoon. A fox maybe? I straighten and stare toward the trees. Two glowing amber eyes catch the light of my front porch and reflect at me from the depth of darkness. I reach out with my druid gifts to sense the animal and bid him a good night.

Nothing.

Either I'm too wound up from fighting with Janine to make the connection or the little thing is snubbing my efforts. Either way, those eyes keep glowing from the darkness, staring at me without blinking.

I take a step closer, and a low, warning growl spans the distance between us. "Cranky pants."

I shiver as a gust of wind tunnels up my shirt. Groaning at the assault of cold, I clutch my jacket to my chest, abandon my phantom stalker, and stomp up my front steps.

"That was quick." Emmet looks over at me from the couch in the family room.

"Ughhh, men." I stomp my feet on the mat, hang my jacket, and toe-off my shoes. "So annoying."

"What happened?" Da steps into the hall from the kitchen

looking alarmed. "Ye've barely been gone five minutes. Where's Sloan?"

"He gave me the bum's rush and shoved me out of Janine's and Mark's front door. He said he'd handle it."

Da's lips quirk as he fights to hold back a smile. "Why's that, do ye think? Were things gettin' heated?"

"Not heated enough by my account. Janine implied she had every right to shoot Manx because I killed Skippy."

Emmet makes a face. "I take it that didn't fly with you?"

"Why would it? *I* wasn't the one who dropped the dog. *I* wasn't the one who snapped it up for lunch. I feel bad about it, sure, but she can't point her bony little finger at me and expect me to smile and take it."

Da rests a hand on my shoulder and pegs me with a calming look. "Simmer down. I expect Sloan felt he could best handle the issue without the inflamed passions of two women. Ye both have strong emotions on the matter."

"Ha! I'll show him the inflamed passions of a woman with strong emotions."

Da casts a glance over his shoulder to Emmet. "Ye best hide the knives and other sharp objects. It will look bad if we have to call in a domestic stabbing in our home."

I tromp toward the stairs to get ready for my shift at Shenanigans. "Hide whatever you want, Emmet. I have Birga."

"She has a point, Da. If it's his time to go, it's his time."

Da's amusement follows me up the stairs as I storm off. "Och, that's too bad. I liked this one, too."

CHAPTER TWO

I've been picking up shifts at Shenanigans since I was fifteen. Being a busy Irish pub, at first, I legally could only work the day shifts and dinner hours. Once I was sixteen and seventeen, I worked as the hostess and manned the coat check. By the time I turned nineteen, I could wait tables and work the bar.

When I needed extra money, I picked up shifts. When I didn't want to work, I simply didn't put my name in.

Now, I only work when they need me.

"Can I say how much fun it is to work as Team Trouble behind the bar tonight?"

I reach in front of my bestie and grab the glasses coming out of the dishwasher. "All you gotta do to make that happen is ask. You know I'm always here for you."

Liam laughs and taps the next order on the screen. "Says the girl who's been to Ireland four...or is it five times in the last five months?"

I set up the next tray of drinks. With a knock on the bar, I catch Kady's attention and point at her drink order. "Hey, when you take out the travel expenses by portaling, it's like going uptown. No biggie."

He pulls two draughts and busts up laughing. "The fact that you ended a sentence about portaling across the world with 'no biggie' is crazy. You know that right?"

Now it's me laughing and pulling up the next order. "It's amazing what you get used to."

"True enough."

The two of us have always been a well-oiled team on the bar so the night flies by before we know it. By the time last call rolls around, my spirits are high, and the needle of my inner joy meter is deep into the green.

"Gawd, it never gets old." I set the lemons, limes, and cherries we didn't use into a container and tuck them into the fridge. "No matter what life throws at me, I can spend a night back here with you and feel like it's righted my world axis again."

"That's good because you know we love having you here whether you're picking up a shift or enhancing the décor."

I do. For a brief period—while I came to terms with my empowered status and what that meant—I wondered about my place in the world I knew before being a druid.

Yes, some preternatural people and creatures hate me simply because of who I am and what I stand for, but I can't only be Fiona the druid. I'm this Fiona too.

Somehow, I have to shrink the gap between my new life and my old life and simply make it—my life.

And if everyone involved is safe and happy, s'all good.

"Speaking of enhancing the décor." I pull out the weigh scale and the liquor logbook for later. "Have you had any passionate moments in the walk-in storage lately?"

Liam casts me a wild look and checks to see if anyone can overhear. They can't. I made sure before I asked. I love to razz him, but I would never jam him up—especially about him seeing Kady.

It might be super-secret, but I knew the moment I saw them together and adore them both.

"Things are good on that front. Thanks for asking."

I grab a bar towel and start wiping down the bar. The crowd thinned out when the Buck and Doe party left, and now we're down to our late-night regulars. "I'm glad to hear it. I want you happy."

"We are." He nods, focused on loading the dishwasher. "What about you and your Irish sidekick? Calum says he's moved into your bed and all signs point to the two of you making a go of it for the long haul."

I roll my eyes. "My brothers shouldn't be speculating about longevity. The truth is, we were dating casually for a few weeks, and yes, we stepped it up a couple of weeks ago, but we're still in the honeymoon phase. Relationships take time before you can throw around words like 'long haul.'"

He straightens to give me his full attention. "Well, the honeymoon looks better on you than it does on him."

"What do you mean by that?"

He gestures across the bar to table twenty-six in the back corner. Sloan is tucked into the back and is sitting alone nursing a pitcher.

"He got here about an hour ago, and I haven't seen him smile all night. A guy in a suit sat with him for a while and left. He doesn't look thrilled with whatever's going on. What's that about?"

"No idea. We had a difference of opinion earlier, but that was before I came to work. He *poofed* me here, and things were fine. At least, I thought they were fine."

He nods. "Why don't you finish wiping the bar and check in with him to see if he agrees? He looks like someone kicked his puppy."

"Shot his cat, but close enough."

Liam scowls. "Someone shot Manx? Is he okay?"

It takes me a second to put Manx together with Liam being saved by Wallace at the clinic last month. Man, in my mind, Liam and my druid side are separate. Or at least I'd like them to be. I don't want to think about vampires shooting my BFF. I don't want those lines blurred again.

It almost cost him his life.

"Yeah, Janine blasted the poor guy with a pellet gun thinking he was a wildcat encroaching from the Don."

"Little Janine next door that quilts and loves those yappy frou-frou dogs?"

"Yep. Her."

"Manx is okay?"

"Yep. You can see for yourself tomorrow night for hide-and-seek. You're coming, right?"

"For a little. I told Mam I'd be on the bar by ten."

"That works. We're heading out after supper. By nine we'll be cold and tired." I finish wiping things down, wring out my cloth, and wash my hands.

"I can't believe he's never played before." Liam pulls down three of the more rare and expensive liquor bottles we won't use before the end of the night and starts weighing.

"I know right? There's a lot he's never experienced in a family setting. I want to show him what he missed and make up for that a little."

Liam smiles. "Well, there's no one better qualified to teach him about family than you guys."

"True story."

As I head past him, Liam blocks my path and hugs me. "You're an amazing person, Fi. He's lucky to have you, and I'm happy for you both."

I hug him back even tighter. "Thanks. I love you too."

Sloan spots me when I'm halfway across the dancefloor and his demeanor changes. As he sits up straighter, the dark storm cloud he's under sweeps away and is replaced by a smile I see whenever we're together.

Is he fronting? What the hell?

"Hey there, hotness." I climb in the booth opposite him. "Sorry, I didn't see you until Liam pointed you out just now. I would've come over or had you move up to the bar so we could chat."

He leans across the table and kisses me. "Not a problem. I didn't want to disturb ye when yer busy at work."

"Yeah, wedding parties are always a good time." He offers me his glass of Guinness, and I sip it. "Hey, Liam mentioned you had company sitting with you earlier. A guy in a suit? What's up? Who was that?"

"I met with a solicitor about a few personal matters. Nothin' to worry yerself over."

"A solicitor…like a lawyer?"

"One and the same."

"Why do you need a lawyer? Are we suing Janine? As much as I love the idea, is it wise? Won't that shine unwanted light on Manx?"

He smiles. "No. We're not goin' after yer neighbor. I told ye, I don't want a war. We came to an understandin'. That's old news. I met with Mr. Singh on another matter entirely."

"Which you won't tell me about."

He sits back, and the storms are back in his eyes. "Believe it or not, I've handled my affairs all my life. The man in the suit was here to answer a few questions about finances, foreign assets, and how Canadian taxation laws work if I should decide to start a life here and lay roots. Like I told ye at lunch, I have a few ideas in the works. I'm simply getting the lay of the land."

The fact that he doesn't want or need my opinion on things regarding his future rings loud and clear.

It also hurts my heart and my pride.

Fine. I can take a hint. "I noticed you looked a little down when I headed over. Did everything turn out all right?"

He reclaims his glass and takes a long sip. "Fine. Nothin' to worry about."

Liar. "You *do* know my father taught us how to read the cues of interrogation when we were kids, right? Facial tics, body language, fluctuation in voices. How about you try that one again, and this time, with less bullshit."

His fake smile fades. "Do we need to get into it now?"

"I'm thinking we do because I'm starting to feel like an outsider in your life and I don't like it."

He grumbles and scowls. "All right, if we must...I'm not havin' a great time of it at the moment. My parents and I are estranged. For the first time in my life, I'm not sure of my purpose. My animal companion was shot. I haven't got my bearings in the city yet. And I don't want to be underfoot, so I'd like to figure out my place here both in yer life and not. Fer a person who's accustomed to order and direction in his life, it's a lot to take on at once."

I reach across the table and take his fist. I tap it and coax his fingers to uncurl so I can hold his hand. "Much better. Thanks for telling it like it is. I told you before. Honest, always. Don't shine me on."

He sits back in the booth and shakes his head. "I wasn't shining you on, Fi. I was being an adult. Believe it or not, I'm not like the men in yer family."

"What's that supposed to mean? You don't think they're adults?"

He lifts his hands and flexes his fingers. Now that he's letting his stresses show, it's obvious how worked up he is. "Don't put words in my mouth. I meant I've never had people in my corner to help me work out a problem. It's not my instinct to express struggles and expect others to help me or cheer me up. I'm not that guy. I handle my affairs."

I sit back and knock my knuckles on the surface of the table. "Okay then. I'll leave you to your problems and go back to work. You handle your affairs however you want, and I'll see you in an hour when I get home."

Shifting out of the booth, I get my groove on and wonder when things went off the rails for him. Did I miss something?

"Fi, wait."

I turn and hold my hands up when he reaches to grab my wrist. "No, it's fine. Believe it or not, I don't expect you to be Mr. Right twenty-four-seven. I've lived with six men my entire life. I understand all the phases of men: macho, pissy, broody, and proud. You're having a day. So, when I check in with you, say 'Fi, I'm having a shit day and need a minute.'"

He pinches the bridge of his nose and curses. "Fine. Fi, I'm havin' a day. The only thing that helps is yer smile. I didn't want to take that away from either of us, so I glossed over my mood. Ye do it all the time with me, and I let it slide because I trust ye to share with me when yer ready."

True story. I exhale a wave of frustration and tamp down my hurt feelings. "Okay, point to you."

He runs his fingers through his hair and sighs. "I didn't say it to get a point, Fi. I also didn't mean to come to yer workplace and upset ye. I'm sorry about that."

"Me too. And you're right. This is me backing off to let you work through your shit. Finish your beer or take your walk or *poof* home and check on Manx. You do you, and I'll be here, looking forward to you taking me home once we've finished the close."

He looks at me as if assessing my words. "We're all right? Yer not cross with me?"

I roll my eyes and close the distance to hug him. "Oh, broody, you don't give yourself enough credit. One bad night doesn't erase all the others. We're fine. Promise me though, when and if you need a sounding board, you'll include me in whatever it is that's bothering you."

He nods. "I promise."

"Myra's Mystical Emporium." I press the bookstore phone to my ear and trap it with my shoulder as I finish unpacking the morning delivery. "Fiona speaking."

"Hello, Fiona. This is Gregory." The man gives me his name like I should know who he is, so I take out Myra's leather ledger and flip through the list of repeat clients. I find his page quickly enough.

Gregory. One name, like Cher or Madonna.

Wow, he orders a lot.

"How can I help you, Gregory?"

He rattles off a couple of book titles and describes the ritual he's planning for Yule. I take down the information and verify the names. "Can Myra contact you at the four-one-six number we have on file here for you?"

"Yes. The sooner, the better."

"I'll be sure to tell her. She stepped out for a couple of hours, but I'll have her call you back once she's had a chance to look into your titles."

The brass bell jingles over the door at the storefront, and I take a last look at the message pad to ensure I haven't forgotten anything. "Wonderful, I'm set. Have a great afternoon."

After sticking the message on our computer monitor's screen, I hang up the phone and look up to greet the incoming customer.

Tall, dark, and devilishly handsome to begin with, in a calf-length, black trenchcoat, Garnet Grant has the whole Van Helsing bad idea for a fabulous night vibe going on.

If you're into that sort of thing.

Thankfully, the Moon Called mate for life, and his lion long ago gave his heart and soul away to my boss.

"Garnet, hey! How are you?"

"I am well, thank you, Lady Druid. Are you holding down the fort?"

"Yep. Myra stepped out, so you're stuck with me."

His grin is warm and genuine. "Stuck with you doesn't do it justice. It's always a pleasure."

"Ha! Please."

"And when it's not, it's at least entertaining. How were your two weeks of Fiona unplugged?"

"Wonderful. Sadly, it's time for real life to resume. I gotta pay bills. A girl can't live on love alone."

He arches a dark, manicured brow. "Love? That was quick. Is that what you and Mr. Mackenzie are talking about?"

I laugh. "Geez, Dad, it's an expression. Don't get your boxers in a bunch." I grab the boxes of new Tarot decks from the pile and head toward the doorway into the store's back reading area.

The new age divination supplies are inside the door on the first floor, and I set to work pricing them and sorting them onto the display shelves.

"So, where's my girl?" he asks, following me to the other section. "Is it her turn for the coffee run? That female has an insatiable hunger for sweets. I swear she should own stock in Tim Horton's."

"She should." I set the cost on the pricing gun and click and stick. "I'm not sure where she went. She said she had an appointment, and it might take a couple of hours. It's been that now, so I assume she'll be back shortly."

"An appointment for what?"

I shrug and repeat the click and stick process. "Sourcing out new stock, getting her nails done, mamba dance lessons…no idea. With Myra, guessing is futile. There's no telling."

"Truer words have never been spoken." Garnet pulls his

phone out and swipes his screen a few times. "Never mind, she's out front. Mystery solved."

The brass bell over the door chimes again and I try not to weigh in on the fact that he has his female LoJacked.

Not my monkeys. Not my circus.

"We're in here, Myra," I shout.

"Okay, girlfriend. When you say 'we' you mean…" She rounds the corner, sees Garnet, and freezes like a deer in the headlights. "Garnet…hey, babe. What a nice surprise."

I drop my gaze and focus on shelving Tarot decks.

Myra is an abysmal liar.

"What brings you by our little piece of heaven?"

"I came to talk to you about Yule at the compound. Zuzanna called me half an hour ago wanting a headcount. I wanted to check with you ladies to find out your plans. Fiona, you and your family are, of course, welcome to join us."

I nod. "Thanks, that's very kind, but the Cumhaills have made our plans. Since it's our first year without Brendan, we decided we'd all stick close to home and focus on family. It'll be harder still because his birthday is coming up before then."

"My condolences again. That's understandable. Maybe drinks then. There will be a drop-in for a few drinks the night before, and maybe that might suit better."

"That sounds fun. Myra can fill me in when you know more, and I'll field it with the fam."

He nods, and his long, ebony hair brushes his broad shoulders. "Good. That's settled. Now, about—" His phone goes off in the breast pocket of his trenchcoat, and he frowns. "That's Anyx's ring. Excuse me, ladies, sorry."

When he steps away, I lean in and whisper to Myra. "Everything okay? When you saw Garnet, you looked like a kid caught with her hand in the cookie jar."

She sighs. "Don't say anything to him. I went to a doctor to talk about the chances of us ever having a child that could survive our mixed races."

I cast a glance to ensure he's still busy with his call. "He didn't want you to?"

"No. After losing Grant and suffering the years that followed, he doesn't have any interest in a repeat. As much as we loved being parents, he won't even discuss children."

"And? What did the doctor say?"

She shakes her head. "He did his tests and said the odds are solidly against us."

"How solidly?"

"He said Garnet's shifting gene will overpower my nymph genes ninety-nine times out of a hundred. The recessive nature of my physiology won't support a physical metamorphosis like changing form."

I grip her hand and squeeze. "I'm so sorry."

"That's life, I guess. After all the pain and loneliness the past decade, I'll have to be content with being blissfully happy with my soulmate for the next century and lump it."

I hug her and pat her back. "Poor you. Loved beyond measure by a tall, dark, elegant, and wealthy hottie."

"It's a sacrifice, I know." She eases back. "Speaking of tall, dark, wealthy hotties, can you ask Sloan if he would mind spending a couple of hours with me one day soon? I have some ancient texts coming in from a private auction later today, and I'd love it if he could help me with them."

"I'm sure he'd be fine with that. What do you need—"

Garnet strides back in, and one look at his expression has me biting my tongue.

"What's wrong, babe?" Myra asks.

"There's been an incident. Fiona, you're with me."

His brusque manner sends up a flare of alarm. "Is everyone all right? My family?"

"Your family, yes. I don't believe you know the victim other than in passing."

"What? Oh, okay…" I hand Myra the pricing gun and give her a chance to argue. She doesn't. "I'm sorry to bail on you midday."

She waves that away. "No problem. You kids have fun."

Garnet frowns. "We're investigating the murder of a wizard. I'm not sure how much fun it will be."

Myra waggles her brows. "You don't fool me, Gar. I know how much you love a good crime mystery."

Garnet points at the store proper. "Do you have a jacket and purse you need to collect?"

I finish my text to Sloan explaining the change in plan for my afternoon and rush to the front to grab my things. "On it. Ready in two."

CHAPTER THREE

All those sayings about the power of making a lasting first impression are true. The only wizards I've encountered since becoming a druid were the men who were performing a ritual to rip the fabric of the earth plane and release a high-level demon from Hell. I'll never forget them or what happened in that basement.

Garnet flashes us to his home's driveway, and his right-hand man Anyx is waiting beside his big black Navigator. The engine rumbles a beefy welcome, and I smile. The vehicle suits him. It would be hard to picture Garnet Grant scooting around town in a Kia.

Garnet opens the passenger's side back door and helps me inside. Da might have grounds to complain about a lot of things Garnet does, but even he acknowledges the guy has impeccable manners.

It might have something to do with living a long life.

From what I gather, Garnet was a young cub brought up in the post-war era and was raised to treat a lady like a lady. Despite what I know he's capable of, he dresses well, opens doors, and picks up the tab wherever we go.

It's quite charming—deceiving too.

"So, is it Salem's coven causing trouble again?" I ask as Anyx slides into the driver's seat in front of me.

We buckle up, and Garnet shifts sideways on the wide, plush leather bench to face me. "Yes, although not in the same way they caused trouble before. This time, instead of unleashing death and destruction on the plane of humans, one of his members turned up dead."

"Right. Far less dramatic."

"Thankfully, yes."

We drive along in silence, and I watch my city pass. The wizard community is warded in a magical web of protection along the Bloor Street corridor.

Garnet explained to me a couple of months ago that if we try to transport into their territory, we could either get thrown back out, or we'd be allowed entrance but have to walk for blocks. It's easier and safer to drive.

"Can we begin at the beginning and cover Wizards 101 for those of us new to the class?"

Garnet smiles. "What do you wish to know?"

"Is a group of wizards called a coven?"

"They can be called a coven or a cohort, or I've also heard of them called a convocation."

"Do these cohorts of empowered men combine powers to bolster one another?"

"What do you mean?"

"Well, the dark witches we battled in Ireland were a unit and grew stronger by pooling their skills and spells. The white witches did the same thing. They worked as one to strengthen their spells. Is that how wizards work too?"

Garnet shakes his head. "The structure of a wizard's cohort is more every man for himself. Sometimes there are events where they'll work together—"

"Like summoning a Greater Demon from Hell."

"Like then," Garnet agrees. "But as a rule, they conduct themselves as individuals."

"Is that why High Priestess Drippy Face on the council is so high up on the power hierarchy compared to where Salem was? She uses the power of her coven to pad her numbers?"

Garnet shrugs. "That's one way to look at it. However, Janeera possesses that level of power to call upon if and when she needs it. There's nothing false about that."

"But wizards are measured based on their merit."

"Yes. Wizards build their strengths as individuals to become true powers."

"Was Salem a true power?"

"He was magically powerful, but his greater skill was in leading and uniting the others. He had charisma and vision."

I make a face. "Convincing your peeps to release a demon from Hell is less visionary and more insanity."

"Yet he nearly succeeded in summoning Asmodeus."

"Mozart?"

"I'm sorry?"

"Asmodeus Mozart, the composer?"

He chuckles. "Amadeus was the composer. Asmodeus is the Prince of Demons."

"Oh, big difference."

"Yes. A very big difference."

I think about that as we make our way through Saturday afternoon traffic. Bloor Street is one of the main east-west corridors north of where I live and work down by the Toronto Harbourfront. It doesn't matter what day of the week it is or what time of day, it's always busy.

"So, who's in charge now? Since I took out Salem, who's been driving the crazy train?"

"There's been a power vacuum over the past weeks. Two men rose to claim the top position and have been pleading their cases.

The wizarding community is divided and has suffered for backing their favorites."

"Is that what this is? Are we looking at a political assassination and retaliation?"

Garnet frowns at a text coming in on his phone. "Possibly," he says, still reading. When he's finished, he turns to me and scowls. "You said you didn't know where Myra went this afternoon."

"Correct. I didn't."

"*Didn't.*" His gaze narrows. "But you do now? She told you when I stepped away?"

"She did, but she also asked me to keep it to myself."

Garnet growls. "I backtracked the signal on her phone, and I know she went to see a fae fertility doctor. What I want to know is why? She's not pregnant, is she? I've been really fucking careful and really fucking clear on the subject."

Awkward. TMI.

"Maybe you should talk to—"

"Tell me." Garnet's eyes flash from their usual amethyst purple to a glowing gold as his animal ascends.

I weigh the situation and decide I'd much prefer to ask Myra to forgive me for overstepping than be trapped in a truck two feet from a man about to burst into an angry lion.

"Um, no. She's not pregnant. She went to talk."

The relief in his stormy gaze is profound. I experienced the depth of his pain when I cleared it a few weeks ago. I don't blame him for not wanting to go through that again. It takes a moment, but after a few deep breaths, his eyes begin to morph back to purple.

I press a hand against my chest and start to breathe again.

Garnet takes a deep breath too and gathers himself. "What did she want to talk to a specialist about and why didn't she talk about it with me first?"

"That's *really* a convo for you and Myra to have."

The growl that rips from his chest isn't aimed at me, but it's no less intimidating. "But she's not pregnant."

"No."

He considers that for a moment and lets out a long breath. "All right, back to the wizards."

Thank you, baby Yoda. "What about them?"

"When we get there, I want you to tell me what you observe at the scene. Let me know if anything seems off or familiar or rings any bells for you."

Weird. "I'm happy to help but why exactly do you want me there? You and your teams handle this stuff all the time. I hardly think I have anything to offer in an investigation of a dead wizard I didn't even know."

Garnet drops his chin. His eyes have fully returned to being vibrant purple, and that makes me feel a great deal safer than I did a moment ago. "When Anyx assessed the scene, he found a message for you."

"Me? What did it say?"

Garnet sits back in his seat and meets Anyx's gaze in the rearview mirror. "Go ahead. Tell her."

Anyx shifts his gaze to meet mine. "It says, 'Get ready to play, Lady Druid. The game has begun.'"

I stare out at the midday bustle of the city as that sinks in. Dropping my head back, I let out a breath. "Awesomesauce."

I'm not sure what I expected the home of a West Village Wizard to look like, but hey, it's nice when life surprises you. After the demon ritual battle in the basement of a funeral home, I guess I imagined a much more theatrical backdrop than a brick, two-story semi a block north of Bloor Street. The place is urban normal, nondescript, and a carbon copy of all the other houses on the street.

"What's happening there?" I point at a crowd of puzzled people in front of the next house, clustered around the trunk of a tree. I follow their gaze into the skeletal branches above and frown. "Why is there a refrigerator in that tree?"

Garnet takes hold of my elbow as we pass the crowd of lookie-loos and urges me toward a line of glowing blue caution tape.

I allow his touch without argument.

He explained to me once that having the Alpha of the Moon Called, who also happens to be the Grand Governor of the Guild of the Empowered Ones, as my escort sends a clear message that I am not without powerful friends.

I protested at the time.

Live and learn. These days, I'll take any edge I can get.

One of Garnet's regular men, Thaos, meets us at the edge of the lawn. He lifts the glowing blue ribbon dividing the scene from public access, and we pass under it.

Breaching the barrier brings a bite to my skin. When we move inside the boundary, the sizzle of magic slaps me like a cold wind. "Ouch. Is that caution tape enchanted to repel?"

Garnet releases my elbow and places a hand at the small of my back. He gestures for me to take the lead and smiles. "Of course. We don't want to draw more attention to ourselves than necessary. Erecting an aversion perimeter ensures only those empowered with some form of magical ability are aware of what's going on."

I stop on the lawn and scan the crowd again.

By all accounts, it's a regular, mundane neighborhood. It has mature trees, two-way traffic, and kids on bikes skidding on the sidewalks' icy patches.

Other than a refrigerator in a tree, there's nothing out of the ordinary going on here.

No one is looking at us.

No one realizes there's a dead wizard inside this house.

The wind shifts and I stop to reassess. The smell coming from inside the house isn't the acrid stench of decomp one might expect at the crime scene—it's musky.

I take another look. The windows are blacked out, the dusting of snow is melted off the roof but not melted off the other side of the semi, and yep, that rancid musk odor gets stronger as we stride farther up the walk.

"Is this a grow op?"

Garnet raises a dark brow. "That didn't take long."

"I'm a cop's brat. It's how my brain works." I take another look around and put the pieces together. "It's a perfect setup. Only personal use of cannabis plants is legal, but a wizard could grow a huge crop, hide it with magic, then sell it. If he has any entrepreneurial spirit, he likely owns a legitimate distribution license and a convenience store or someplace he uses as a front."

"Very good. Yes, Endor and his community run an intricate cannabis operation in Toronto and the surrounding area."

"Endor? As in the home planet of the Ewoks?"

"Or the dead wizard inside." I'm still giggling about that when he points at the front door. "Shall we go inside?"

"Yub-nub."

He shakes his head. "It's a miracle you've survived as long as you have."

I'm about to respond when a patrol car pulls along the curb and parks. "Jinkies, who called the po-po?"

Garnet pivots and we wait to see who's getting out of the cruiser. "Do you have men in the Eleventh?"

"I've told you before. I don't have men in the police department. I'm not the kingpin of corruption your father pegs me for."

I chuckle. "I wasn't thinking about corruption. I thought it would be handy to have people in the different patrol divisions so you can have them respond to incidents and keep things under tighter wraps."

The officer gets out of the car, and I wave. "Never mind. It's my dad. Hey, wait, what's he doing here?"

"I called him."

"What? Why?"

Garnet looks down at me and offers me a patient smile.

"Because you gave him an oath of honor to notify him whenever something involving me comes into play."

"Full points and on the first try. Well done, Lady Druid."

I roll my eyes and wait until my father makes his way past the crowd and up the yard. I can tell he's upset because he doesn't even notice the refrigerator in the tree.

When he ducks under the magical blue caution tape, I nudge Garnet and point at the door. "Let's go inside. We're not all going to fit on the front stoop."

We leave the door open behind us, and Da joins us a moment after we step into the entrance. "Thanks for the call, Garnet." Da lifts his chin in greeting. "So, what kind of murder and mayhem are we lookin' at today, *mo chroi?*"

I shrug. "Too early to say because we just got here ourselves, but it seems a dead wizard left me a message."

Garnet frowns. "I don't think it was the dead wizard who left the message. I think it's the alive killer of the dead wizard who left you the message."

"Oh, yeah, I guess that makes more sense."

Anyx points the way. "It's in here."

"Get ready to play, Lady Druid. The game has begun." Da scowls at the missive written across the wall as he reads it aloud. When he swings around to look at me, he has all kinds of disapproval going on in his expression. "Why does this person have ye in his sights?"

"Is that a real question?"

"Yes, Fi, it is. How do ye find yerself in yet another fix?"

I don't have an answer for that. "Da, I was minding my own. I was at work with Myra flying low on the radar. I didn't do a thing to encourage this." I point at the dead wizard slumped over his plate. "I certainly didn't do that."

"Yet, here we are again. Ye can't keep pointin' yer finger at the Fianna mark and claimin' innocence. At some point, whoever did this crossed paths with ye and thought it would be fun to challenge ye to a bit of murder and mayhem."

I shrug and stare at the dead guy. "The only wizards I crossed paths with were at that funeral home. You were there too, and Garnet, and Anyx. Why is it only me getting singled out? Do I know him? No. Could he be one of the guys from the battle to close the rift to the Hell realm? Maybe."

Garnet frowns. "Who are you talking about, the victim or the perpetrator?"

"I suppose either of them. The funeral home battle was a bit harum-scarum with thirty men in robes and the whole rip in the fabric of the realm going on. I could've come into contact with this guy or the killer or both. There's no way to know."

"So, why announce there's a game underway?" Anyx asks. "If he has more planned, why not let it play out with the element of surprise on his side?"

Da snaps a picture of the message with his phone. "Because the person orchestrating this thinks it'll be more fun to play the game if Fi's in on it."

I look at the dead guy—mid-thirties, fit, a day's scruff on his jaw, gray t-shirt, and jeans. Nothing that hints at why he would be made a pawn in some sicko's game. "What is the game? Am I supposed to know? Do I have a move to make?"

"At this point, I'd say no, not yet."

I hear the hesitation in Da's voice and get where he's going with this. "But I will once he makes his next move, and we have more to go on."

Da nods. "I'd say that's a fair guess."

I don't like that. Not one bit. "So, what now? I sit around wondering and waiting for him to kill again, to leave me another bloody missive? That will drive me bonkers."

"I think that's part of the fun for him."

I look at Anyx. "Have you cleared the rest of the house?"

"We have."

"Can I wander and take a look around?"

"Do you want a shadow?"

"No. I'm good. I need a minute to think." I start my exploration in the guy's bedroom and work my way down. He was a decently tidy guy, nothing shocking. He didn't make his bed, but he tossed his dirty clothes in the basket by the wall.

His wallet is on the ensuite counter, so I snoop.

"Endor Avery, thirty-three." I flip past his license and check out a few of his cards. The most interesting thing is a stamp card for the Oasis Aqualounge, an adult lifestyle club. "Who did this to you, Endor, and why?"

I place his wallet back where I found it and continue my wander.

The second bedroom is set up as a fitness room, the third as his home office. The main bathroom on the top floor is pristine white and likely never used. By the time I get to the main floor, I'm convinced there can't be any connection between Endor and me other than the day at the funeral home.

It's weird. This guy seems as normal as can be. Other than his parents making a really bad choice with his name thirty-three years ago...

And his basement being stuffed full of pot plants.

And him being a wizard.

"What is *she* doing here?" a man with dirty-blond hair snaps as I descend the stairs. His long-sleeved knit hangs loose on his bony frame as he shifts his glare from me to Garnet. "Hasn't she done enough? First, she kills Salem, and now she kills Endor?"

Harsh. "No. The only thing I ever did was stop your maniacal plot to summon a demon."

"And kill Salem. And leave us with no fit replacement."

I shrug. "It's not my fault your community is lacking in leadership skills. Have someone join Toastmasters. Or raise the bar on recruitment."

Garnet looks at my father, and Da holds up his hands. "This is yer rodeo, Grant. I'm here as an observer."

Angry Wizard strides over to get a closer look at the body. After taking a long moment to assess Endor's state, he turns his attention to Garnet. "How did he die?"

Since I went upstairs, they'd moved Endor's body. Instead of slumping down onto his dinner, he's now sitting upright. Aside from the putrid gray overtaking his skin tone and his eyes being glazed over with death, there are no obvious signs of what ended his life.

"Yet to be determined," Garnet says.

"Who found him?"

Anyx answers that one. "He employs a couple of nymph youths who tend to the well-being of the plants. They let themselves in this morning as usual and found the body."

Endor Avery was a smart man. Having fae with nature gifts nurture his cannabis forest downstairs was a great idea. He had quite an enterprise going on here.

"She has something to do with it or else why would she be here? She flat-out killed Salem and now Endor's dead. I don't care that she's your pet, Grand Governor. She needs to be held accountable for her actions the same as the rest of us."

Da saunters across the room so he's standing beside me. I don't mistake the gesture for a second. He's expecting this guy to take a run at me.

Rude. Why does everyone want a piece of me?

A wet, gloopy noise has us all shifting our attention to the dead guy.

I make a face. "What was that? It sounded gross."

Garnet looks more puzzled than freaked out, so I try to notch down the creepy scenarios bursting in my mind. At least the body isn't moving, so zombie resurrection and demon possession are likely off the table.

Still, I take a step toward the couch behind us and tug Da with me.

Garnet strides over to take a closer look and my shield flares to life. "Garnet, no. I don't like this."

My shield amps up to full fiery fury. "Garnet, get back!"

I grab Da by the waist and pull him as I launch us both over the back of the couch. The force of our momentum tips the three-seater over, and it follows us to land on the floor.

We hit hard, my shoulder shouting in protest as the ride comes to a full stop.

We're under the cushioned tent of the couch, and I take a beat to read what my shield is saying now. "I think we're good. My mark has gone quiet again."

Da lets out a grumbled *harumph* and pushes at the couch's back cushion to reclaim our freedom. "Was a full-bodied tackle necessary?"

As the legs of the couch crash back to the hardwood floor I stare at the plasma-bomb shrapnel dripping off the ceiling, light fixture, table, and walls.

"Um…all signs point to yes. My shield did not want us to get slimed."

The sight is bad enough. The smell is worse.

The reek is a cross between fire-roasted rot mixed with the cloying sweetness of baby powder. I swallow against the gagging pressure pushing at the base of my throat.

"Anyone interested in what I ate for lunch? There's a good chance you're in for a look-see."

Endor Avery is all but unrecognizable as human from the waist up. His shoulders have flipped inside out over the back of his chair, and his head hangs upside down from his back skin, looking at the floor.

Angry wizard friend stands beside the carnage wearing Endor's insides as a thick layer of splattered grossness.

Garnet peers around the wall to the kitchen and Anyx comes in from the front porch.

"Did you guys flash out?" Focused on fleeing the source of my shield's warning, I lost track of the two lions.

Garnet grimaces at the scene. "I may question your sanity at times, Lady Druid, but I'll never question your survival instincts. When you shout to clear the room with a voice like that, we'll always listen."

I'm pretty sure there's a compliment in there somewhere, so I take it as it's meant. "What the frickety-frack does that?"

We all stay well back from the two bloody wizards.

The one still standing must be in shock because he's gone stiff, eyes wide, and looks horrified.

I climb onto the soft, gray couch, tromp to the end, and jump over to the club chair to get a better look.

Garnet looks at me like I've lost my mind.

"Hey, I've played enough 'floor is lava' to know when not to touch the ground. I kill at this game."

"Would you look at that?" He points at the blood spatter covering the top of the table.

The plasma pool seems to have given up outward expansion and is now in reverse. Hunks and bloody chunks rejoin and collect across the wooden surface as they puddle back together.

"That is *so* wrong." I swallow and focus on not barfing.

"It certainly is interesting," Garnet says.

"Screw interesting. Can you say, *The Blob*?"

Garnet's and Anyx's blank faces stare back at me.

"Steve McQueen? No? Okay…it was a terrible B-movie where everyone gets dissolved and digested by an alien amoeba. The growing red puddle of death seemed innocuous at first—*until* by

AUBURN TEMPEST & MICHAEL ANDERLE

the end, everyone is gobbled up and dead. Do you see where I'm going with this?"

Garnet frowns. "You think a sentient alien race that will try to consume us infected this wizard?"

Wow, it sounds even worse when he says it out loud.

I groan. "We deal with magic races and opening up rifts to the Hell realm. Are you saying you draw the line at sentient homicidal blood goo?"

Garnet frowns and reaches toward the blood.

"Please don't touch it." I hold my hand out to stop him. "If not for my sanity then for Myra's sake. I don't want to be the one who has to tell her you turned into a plasma bomb and exploded."

Garnet scowls at me, but before he can argue, Anyx comes forward and raises his hand. "How about we err on the side of caution?" He scowls at the moving blood. "I'm with Fiona on this one. Until we know what it is and what it's doing, I vote we keep our distance."

"Thank you, puss."

Anyx pegs me with a glare. "Call me puss again, and *I'll* consume you and make you into the next puddle of blood. Me adopting caution doesn't mean you're right. It only means we need to know more."

"Mrowl. Point taken."

Despite his initial protest, Garnet steps back and gives the living puddle of blood a little space.

Angry wizard friend lets out a baleful groan and thaws from his frozen state. He looks down at himself, at us, and the Endor body husk hanging on the back of the kitchen chair.

Despite hearing crime scene stories from my father and his fellow cops my entire life, nothing could've prepared me for this kind of explosive end.

I imagine it's so much worse to be the one wearing it.

Endor's hater friend makes a beeline for the stairs. A moment later the shower comes on upstairs, and I think about the pristine white bathroom. I wonder what it'll look like when that guy gets all the Endor goo off him.

"What do you suggest we do with it?" Anyx points at the shimmering puddle. "If we can't touch it, how do we clean it and clear the scene? If we don't clean it, what exactly will it do once it regroups?"

I shudder to guess. "Vampire blood burns in the movies. Maybe poison alien blood does too. If not…maybe he has a shop vac? Or mason jars in the pantry? Maybe we could use spatulas to scoop it and seal it into something for testing."

Garnet grunts and nods at Anyx. "Look for jars or something we can use to seal it up. If we capture and contain it, perhaps we can learn how to destroy it."

"Good plan." The rising tide of plasma thoroughly grosses me out. I think this is a good time for me to get outta Dodge. My only problem now is how to get out of here without touching the floor. "Garnet? A little help?"

CHAPTER FOUR

"So, was the Ewok wizard killed by a demon that slipped through the cracks maybe?" Dillan asks after Da and I get home and fill them all in on our afternoon of excitement. "Could the blood weirdness be a Hell thing?"

"No idea."

Emmet sets down the winter storage bin I sent him to retrieve from the downstairs closet. "If this has something to do with you and the wizards, the only collision you've had with them was them summoning a Greater Demon, the *Euchair Prana,* and what they did to Myra."

I crack open the container of snow pants, scarves, and gloves so we can get outside and get our game of hide-and-seek underway. Right. I forgot about the fight at Myra's bookstore. "I didn't kill anyone there. Everyone else killed their guy, and Mr. Tree took my guy and sucked him into the ground beneath the store."

"Maybe this isn't about the Greater Demon or their summoning nonsense."

"What does Garnet think?" Sloan asks.

"It's too soon to guess," Da says, "but the man's instincts about this not feeling like demons are sound."

"What makes you say that, Da?" Emmet asks.

"A demon released from Hell serves its master when summoned. Yes, it will fight to break that tie, but the break is more likely to come when the master is either killed or ensorcelled."

"And the puppeteer becomes the puppet," Emmet adds.

"Exactly. The message to Fi and the weird blood didn't feel like the work of a demon. It's not about power. It's about toying with her for effect."

"It's still messed up." Dillan stares at the picture on Da's phone. "I'm forwarding this to the family channel so we can all think on it. We have an unsub fixated on Fi who thinks blowing up wizards is a good sport, and blood grossness is part of his MO."

Emmet checks his phone and frowns. "He has nice penmanship. I'll give him that."

Emmet's not wrong. "I noticed that too. It kinda creeped me out. In the paranormal horror movies, the whole note in blood thing is wild and drippy. My guy's writing is neat and intentional."

"Can we not refer to him as yer guy, please?" Da snaps.

"Maybe that goes to the character profile," Aiden offers. "Dillan, didn't you fool around with a girl on the profiler team from the Special Investigations Unit when they did a joint investigation last spring?"

Dillan's face breaks into a wide smile. "Michaela Machado. Be still my heart. She shall forever have a place on my list of the top ten."

I snort. "I don't think Aiden is suggesting we have sex with her. I think the interest is geared toward how good is she at her job?"

He shrugs. "I think she's good. She gets loaned out to the Mounties and Ontario Provincial Police and other law enforcement branches when needed."

Da nods. "We don't have enough information to start generatin' a profile yet, but we'll keep Michaela in mind if we need help in that department going forward."

I glance at where Sloan is scowling in the corner. "You're awfully quiet."

"What's the appropriate level of engagement when a killer challenges yer girlfriend to a game of homicidal fun?"

I lift my hands and shrug. "I'm not sure. This is my first invite to a game of homicidal fun. It's new to me too."

Da grabs a fresh beer from Liam as he arrives in the family room with his arms full. After he sips, he casts a disapproving glance at me setting out everyone's gloves. "If any of ye had a lick of sense, ye'd cancel yer game and stay inside for the night."

"Not a chance." I scowl. "My murderous admirer might not strike again for days or weeks or months. I'm not sitting locked up in the house because some weirdo has a beef with me. There are already at least four races and dozens of people who hate me. This new guy needs to haul his murdering ass to the back of the line."

Da rolls his eyes and scans the room. "Watch yerselves out there. I mean it. If any of ye get into trouble, I want ye to sound the alarm and call for the fuckin' cavalry."

"It's only a game of hide-and-seek, Da. We'll be fine."

He pegs me with a look and takes another swallow of beer. "Famous last words, Fiona Kacee. For once in yer life, just do as I say."

We're quite a troop as we pile out the front door and head for the forest where we used to play as kids. It's five-thirty on a November evening, so the sun is setting and it will be dark in fifteen or twenty minutes. With the loss of sunshine comes a nip of winter cold. It's nothing like what we'll suffer through in a few months, so we bundle up and are thankful.

It could be worse. Ha! Who are we kidding?

It *will* be worse.

When we arrive at the old oak tree that holds the remains of our childhood fort, my siblings and I all give the tree a pat and say hello.

Funny. We grew up not knowing about our druid side, but always talked to our tree and held a reverence for nature.

"Okay, listen up." Dillan raises his arm to point. "The game boundaries are Rosedale Road to the north, the river to the east, the houses to the west, and our laneway to the south. For the sake of keeping things fair to those who don't have powers, no powers are allowed. No flashing. No invisibility. No night vision. It's pretty much a full moon. That's all you get."

Aiden nods. "Because there are so many of us, we're breaking up in teams. Since this is Fiona's and Sloan's night, they're the captains, and since Bruin senses Fi and Manx hears Sloan, we'll keep them matched with their companions. Also, there are eleven of us, so I'll be the judge and oversee the shenanigans. That makes it an even five on five."

"You think you can keep us in line, bro?" Emmet teases.

"I know I can, little boy."

"Oh, challenge accepted."

It doesn't take long to break up into two teams. I have Bruin, Dillan, Kevin, and Liam. Sloan has Calum, Emmet, Nikon, and Manx.

"Okay, boys, what's our team name?" I ask as we scrum up and huddle in.

My brothers and I have our favorites, and we start pulling out the top picks. I nod when we come up with an agreement, and we break from our huddle. "Okay, we're going with *Not Fast, Just Furious* for the win."

Dillan pumps his fist in the air. It's his favorite, and he's on my team, so life is good.

I look at Sloan and smile. "Okay, broody, lay it on me. What are you boys going with?"

Sloan rolls his eyes. "We are *RazzMyTazz*."

I laugh. "A solid choice. Okay, since you're our hide-and-seek virgin, we opt to let the *RazzMyTazz*'ers hide first."

Aiden nods. "Fi's team, bring it in and start counting. Sloan's team, off you go. You have until the count of one hundred Mississaugas."

Sloan frowns. "Isn't it Mississippi?"

I snort. "One of Toronto's burbs is Mississauga—named after the native band that originally lived there. Emmet made the Mississippi-slash-Mississauga mistake once when we were kids, and we went with it."

"It's a tribute to our first Canadians," Emmet says.

"Are we ready?" Dillan asks.

Cue the nods around the circle.

"Pitter, patter, time to scatter," Aiden says.

Everyone does just that. I watch as Sloan runs off with Emmet and Calum and my chest expands. This is good.

"Eyes on the tree, Fi."

I laugh and join the rest of my team with the count. I raise my forearm to save my forehead from the rough bark.

Dillan is counting us off, and I realize this is about as perfect as life can get.

"Thanks for coming guys," I say into the sleeve of my jacket. "I wanted to show Sloan what it means to be part of our family. You guys came through for me big time."

"It's a great idea, baby girl." Aiden pats my shoulder from behind. "After the stress of the past few months, it's nice for all of us to get back to basics."

It is. "Speaking of the stresses of our lives. How's the house-hunting coming?" I lift my gaze off the tree but don't look anywhere but at Aiden. "Any prospects?"

He shakes his head. "We haven't found a place I'd settle with my wife and kids, no. Being a month from the holidays, I'm not holding out much hope of finding anything good. We might end up taking over the basement for a while after all."

I grin. "You say that like it's a bad thing. It would be awesome to have you guys full-time, especially over Christmas—no, I guess we're celebrating Yule this year."

Aiden chuckles. "The kids will be excited. Same family fun, four days sooner."

"Or maybe we combine and celebrate Yulemas for four days straight," Kevin says.

I laugh. "I like the way you think, boyfriend."

Christmas has always been a celebration of food and family. It doesn't matter what the name of the day is or when it falls on the calendar. This will be our first year without Brendan, so shaking it up is a good thing.

"We should decorate the grove with tons of lights and sing carols out with our fae."

Aiden nods. "That sounds perfect. Jackson loves the grove and Meggie won't even know a life without druid influences. It'll be exciting to watch them grow into things."

"Ninety-nine...one hundy," Dillan shouts into the night. "Ready or not, suckers! We're coming for your asses."

An hour later, I'm guarding the home tree and waiting for my team to scare up Sloan from wherever my druid dreamboat has found to hide. They've been at it a while now and the rest of his team—the loser captives—are getting restless.

"Give it up, Red," Nikon taunts from above. "You might as

well call it and give us the win. Irish is ghosting your team. You'll never find him."

I chuckle and point up at where Nikon, Calum, Emmet, and Manx watch from the railing of our fort above. When they went up there after capture during the first game, I wasn't sure the old fort floor would hold them.

Aiden gave Sloan and Calum special permission to use their powers to solidify the tree and the twenty-year-old construction so that no one would fall to their death.

Movement in the trees to my left has me shifting around the wide trunk for a better look.

Where are you, hotness?

As the guard, I'm the last line of defense to ensure our opponents don't touch the tree before getting tagged.

I won't fail them.

A shift in the shadows has me focused on the space between a fluffy spruce and the trunk of a birch tree. "Who goes there? State your business."

No one answers.

If it were someone on my team, they would answer.

I move out a couple of feet to cut off the angle of approach. The sound of running footsteps behind me has me cursing and turning to round the old oak. I run out to intercept Sloan, but he has momentum and surprise on his side.

I lunge to tackle him, but he evades, laughing.

I catch my footing, pivot, and take chase. With my arms and legs pumping, my breath comes out in white clouds of condensation. Calum, Nikon, and Emmet are shouting from above, cheering him on.

Right before he gets to the tree, I make a Hail Mary flying leap and…fall short.

It isn't enough.

Sloan tags the tree and turns in time to catch me as our bodies collide. There's no stopping our crash to the forest floor. I call on my body armor and roll in the cage of his arms to take the collision with the frozen ground.

We tumble in the brittle scrub, rolling on the snow-dusted ground until we come to an uncoordinated stop. In a tangle of arms and legs, he lifts his head and flashes me the most amazing smile I've ever seen.

This.

This man could steal my heart. Who are we kidding? It might already be a lost cause. Gazes locked, we both catch our breath and take in one another. The energy between us shifts. The sheer joy of the moment sparkling in his dark eyes turns to something deeper.

Lying over me, it's the work of a moment for him to lean closer and claim my lips. Gone is the cold chill of the ground at my back. In the racing beat of my heart, there is only heat.

"Get a room," Nikon shouts from above.

"They have a room," Calum retorts. "It's right beside mine. And let me tell you, they've been making up for a slow start. I've taken to wearing earplugs."

I roll my eyes as Sloan helps me up and I throw them a dirty look. "You're full of shit, Calum. We cast a silence spell before we do anything. Something, I might add, you boys might consider doing going forward."

"All right, children," Aiden says as the rest of the gang jogs in. "Sloan tagged home. Point to team *RazzMyTazz*. Switch it up and away you go."

We're into the fourth round and the night is winding to a close the next time I pause to reflect. The tips of my fingers are numb, and my cheeks have long ago stopped being cool and are now freaking cold. I have, however, tucked into the best hiding spot *evah* and am going to win.

I'm going to force them to give up.

Thundering footsteps crash past me and by the sounds of the laughter right before the weighty *thud*, Nikon tackled Kevin to the ground.

That only leaves me to be caught.

I hold still to avoid detection. It takes a while before they finish tussling in the scrub and move off, laughing.

I settle in for the duration.

If I exhaust their search, *Not Fast, Just Furious* takes it three games to one. If they find me, it's a draw.

"Poor Fi," Emmet taunts, from about fifty feet to my right, "you must be *soooo* cold. Don't you want to head inside for hot chocolate? Nom-nom, baby girl. Nikon brought us a specialty Baileys. Didn't you, Nikon?"

"I sure did," Nikon says about thirty feet to my left. "Salted caramel. Mmm, doesn't it make you want to groan with delight, Red?"

I press my lips together to keep from laughing.

Okay, that was funny.

"Groan with delight?" Sloan shouts from a distance. "Really, Nikon? Are ye tryin' to seduce my girlfriend again?"

I smile at Sloan's annoyance. He protests Nikon's flirtatious ways, but he's not the least bit threatened.

He knows I heart him hard.

"Over here," Calum says. "Manx picked up a scent on the wind. Sloan, come see if he's tracked her down."

Since Calum is calling them in the opposite direction, I guess that's a big fat no.

I hunker down and check the night sky. In a few more seconds, a cloud will pass over the moon and diminish visibility. From where I am, I can see the clubhouse tree. In the old days, I'd take advantage of the straight shot for a mad dash. I'd wait for Emmet to take Calum's suggestion and check out what Manx found, then I'd run.

Mature me has more patience.

Let them explore what Manx found...because it ain't me.

With my sights on the clouds, I adjust my position in the crevasse I've wedged myself into and applaud my strategic growth. Light footsteps rustle the leaves by my head.

Shit. Who is it? How did anyone get this close without me knowing? I slow my breathing and focus on not giving away my position.

Another rustle and I relax.

The footsteps are too soft for any of the men. Maybe if one of them called on their powers for *Feline Finesse* or *Silent Stealth.* Nah. That would be cheating and bad form.

I dismiss that idea and listen.

I'd love to heighten my senses or commune with nature to figure it out—but then I'd be the one cheating.

It's likely a forest animal.

I've almost convinced myself of that when my shield flares and I smell it...a rancid ode to brimstone and baby powder.

Shit. In a rustle of panic, I out myself from lying exposed on the ground, activate my armor and call Birga to my palm. Standing in plain sight, I turn in a slow circle, searching for my stalker.

"Who are you? What do you want?"

Adrenaline pumps through my veins at a dizzying volume. The glamor burns off my eyes, and for the first time, I welcome the weird fae sight I developed a few weeks ago.

Where is this creep?

Where's his aura against the darkness of night?

"What's the game? Why did you kill the wizard? What does it have to do with me?"

"A nightmare for some, to boredom I come. Gamers might choose me to chat with a friend, but conflict collides and fails to blend. Who am I?"

I hear the voice but can't place from which direction it's

coming. The whispered threat comes from everywhere and at the same time nowhere. That sounds impossible, but it's the only way I can describe it.

I spin, Birga's staff braced under my arm, her tip poised to defend. Yeah, this guy is a barrel of laughs. There's no one around...not even my family. Where is everyone?

Piercing panic lights me up inside.

"Don't you *dare* hurt anyone I love. I'll never play your stupid game if you do."

"Not Rumpelstiltskin but the task holds true. A death each time you get a clue. Not your loves, your boundary lain. Innocent deaths and strangers' pain."

What? No. "I didn't say that. *No* deaths. I don't want anyone to die."

Laughter rises around me, and I catch the reflection of two glowing amber eyes. They're ten feet in front of me and low to the ground as if they belong to an animal—or at least someone in an animal form.

My fae sight flares and I see the dark intentions of the creature before me. He isn't wholly malevolent like the Unseelie prince I met on the eve of Samhain, but he's not pure and good like the white witches either.

This guy's aura is different.

As I scan him, a sickening fog washes me. I swallow and try to shake it off, but his laughter bounces around in my head making things fuzzy.

"The fun is in motion. The game has begun. By the feast of Yule, your life is undone."

His eyes gleam with amusement as his form shifts and rises before me.

"Screw that." I grip Birga and launch at the aura before he can make a move on me. "The game ends here."

My hands are shaking with adrenaline as I engage. "Die, you twisted fuck."

The world is dark, but Birga's spear tip hits true. My tormentor throws his shoulder back and pivots at the last minute. I adjust and catch him square in the chest.

The momentum of my strike knocks him off his feet, and he hits the ground in a satisfying *thud*.

I'm tackled hard and fast from my left.

Hitting the frozen earth is like being tackled onto a concrete floor. My shoulder and hip take the worst of it, then my head cracks against the ground.

With my *Tough as Bark* in play, I barely feel it.

I flail, fighting the hold. I'm being held from behind, but a lead weight pins me down from the front as well.

I fight.

Life is undone, my Irish ass.

Shouting male voices penetrate the fog from a distance. Brilliant white light flares in front of my face and obliterates the mist holding me down in a piercing instant.

I freeze, and the world shrieks to a stop around me.

Bruin is snarling wildly close by.

Dillan's eyes are wild, and he's screaming in my face. "For fuck's sake Fi, it's us. Wherever you are, it's not real. Someone's fucking with you."

I swallow. My entire body trembles. Are the shakes from the cold, the terror of meeting my stalker, or the adrenaline of the fight? I can't be sure.

There's so much to pick from.

"I'm good." I scan the panicked faces staring down at me and turn to meet Aiden's gaze. He's called forward his druid gift and has his armored arms wrapped around me like a python. "It's me, bro. I'm back."

Emmet nods then turns and rushes away. "Fi's back. How bad is he?"

The question hangs in the air for a split second before my hamster gets back in his wheel and Dillan's words replay in my head. *It's not real. Someone fucked with you.*

Ohmygawd...I speared someone.

"Who? Who'd I hit?" I'm scrambling out of Aiden's hold and trying to get around Dillan when I realize Sloan didn't check on me. "Sloan!"

Dillan catches me around the waist and hushes me. "Not Sloan. Irish is trying to heal him."

"Heal who?" I take inventory of who I've seen and who I haven't. "Liam? Kevin?"

My heart hammers hard against the cage of my ribs.

"No, Fi. Relax." Calum pushes in close to my face so that his eyes cyclops in front of me. "It was Nikon. He's immortal, remember? It could've been much worse."

A wave of relief takes me over. Luckily, Dillan has a hold on me because my legs give out. How horrible am I that I'm relieved it's Nikon? I shouldn't celebrate hurting anyone...even if he is immortal.

"Let me see him. Is he okay?"

"No, baby girl," Calum says. "He's far from okay. He's been pierced through the chest with an enchanted spear."

Oh, it sounds so awful when he says it like that.

"I need to see him."

"Not a good idea," Dillan says. "It's grisly, Fi. You don't want that image."

Rage burns hot in my veins, and I sense as my ice-blue evil eyes start glowing. "It's my image to bear. Let go of me."

Dillan holds up his palms and steps back fast. "Fuck, I hate it when you do that."

Calum swallows and shifts out of my way. "Take it easy, Fi. Don't hulk out on us here."

"The sun's getting real low, big guy," Dillan says.

I ignore the peanut gallery's comments and storm over to where Emmet and Sloan are working on Nikon. Birga still pierces through his chest, and his body is rigid and tremoring against the forest floor.

All the rage inside me dissolves in an instant, and I drop to my knees. "Oh, Nikon." I lose sight of the blond hottie behind a wall of tears. "I'm so sorry."

Black splotches mar his youthful face. He coughs, and I realize why. He's choking on blood. The moon's silver light spares us the vibrancy of the scene, but I see it.

He gasps, his breathing a hitched and labored wheeze.

"Why isn't he healing?" I ask Sloan.

His hands are glowing with the healing, and his lips are moving in a steady ramble of casting I can't hear. "Call yer spear back to yer arm. I didn't want to pull it through and risk more damage."

I do as he says, and Nikon's body slumps still.

Tears fall in hot runnels down my cheeks and drip off my chin to land on his face. "Is it because of Birga's enchantment? Is this real? Have I killed him?"

I grab his cheeks between my palms and ease his gaze over to meet mine. "You're going to be all right, aren't you? Nikon, you have to be. I can't kill you. Please."

With a final exhale of breath, Nikon's body sighs to a stop, and his eyes lose focus.

"No!" I scream. "Nikon, don't you die on me."

I'm grabbed by the shoulders and pulled away from Nikon's lifeless frame. Sloan sits back on his heels looking wrecked as Kevin and Calum grab hold of one another.

How can this be happening?

I double over, the agonizing pain in my chest too much to breathe through. I'll die here too. Honestly, at this moment, it would be better than living through this.

Sloan meets my gaze and scrambles to his feet to gather me into his arms. He squeezes me hard, crushing my bones and making it hard to breathe.

At least I don't feel like I'm about to blow apart.

He holds me for a long while, and the world seems to stop around us. How could such a perfect night end this way?

"Irish? What's happening?" Emmet is on his knees beside Nikon's body and is pointing.

We stop and watch while Nikon's body disappears.

It doesn't move or glow or heal…it's just gone.

CHAPTER FIVE

"So, is he dead, or isn't he?" I sit on one of the wooden kitchen chairs and search the faces of my family and friends, hoping for someone to have the answer. "Did Birga negate his immortality? Because from where I was sitting, he died."

Da turns from the counter with a tray of hot chocolate and hands me the mug. "We don't know enough about his gift to decide either way, *mo chroi*."

"We don't know much about him at all," Dillan adds.

Emmet holds up his phone. "Has anyone ever Googled him? It says here, Nikon could either be a version of the name Nike who was a Greek god or there's another mention of Nikon who isn't a god, he's a Telchine."

"Which is what?" I ask.

"Some kind of sea spirit native to the Isle of Rhodes that was worshipped as a god."

Calum frowns. "Nikon isn't a sea spirit, and he's not a god. He told us who he is...was...is. Dammit, I hate this. He's not dead. I know it."

I sip at the lip of my mug and taste the sweet decadence of

salted caramel Baileys and fight not to cry again. "I don't want him to be dead either, but if he's not dead, where did his body go?"

"To the Isle of Rhodes." A stunning woman steps into the doorway from the hall. She has hair that looks like spun gold and is elegant in jeans and thigh-high boots and a cute ivory bomber jacket with a fur-trimmed hood. The room scrambles, but it's obvi she intends us no harm. "Sorry, folks, I knocked, but no one answered. My brother sent word I needed to get over here and tell you all he's not dead."

I sit up, my heart pressing at the base of my throat. "He's not? You're sure?"

She nods. "I spoke to our papou ten minutes ago, and he gave me the message. It'll take Nikon a couple of days to recover his strength enough to communicate and flash back, but he is and will always be immortal."

"Thank the goddess," Sloan gasps.

"Amen."

"Hallelujah."

Dillan arches a brow and offers her a winning smile. "Your family's factory reset is returning to the homeland?"

"Something like that."

"What's your name, resplendent sister of Nikon?"

Her mouth quirks up at the side, and she offers him a smile. "Dillan, right? Nikon warned me about you."

I catch the disgruntled surprise in Dillan's expression and burst out laughing. "Oh, I like you."

"You're Fiona?"

I set my hot chocolate mug on the table and get up to greet her. She's gorgeous and well put-together, and I'm covered in blood and have puffy eyes and a runny nose from blubbering about killing my friend. "Sorry. I'm a mess. It's been a night."

"Not to worry. When you live as long as we have, you see people at their best and worst. I find you learn a lot more about people from the moments when they face their worst. Your heartbreak and concern for my brother are unnecessary but well received. He's very fond of all of you as well."

"He's a welcome addition to the family," Da says. "Can we get ye something warm to drink or offer ye a seat?"

She waves that away. "No, thank you. I came specifically to deliver the news about my little brother's well-being. I should get back to my plans."

Da steps forward to escort her toward the front door. "Well, thanks again, my dear, for comin' to tell us. Ye lifted ten hearts in ten minutes simply by takin' the time to do it. Much appreciated."

When the door clicks shut, Dillan flops against the frame of the doorway and sighs. "I'm in love."

I chuckle and reclaim my hot chocolate. "If she's Nikon's older sister, she's *waaay* too old for you."

He grins. "With age comes experience."

"So, from the top." Da scowls. "Nikon's injuries aside, what happened out there tonight?"

Liam raises his hands and taps out. "Sorry guys, unless I can be of any help, or Fi needs me to stay, I gotta change and get to work."

"No, you go," I say, the night weighing on me. "Thanks for the offer, but you should probably steer clear of me until this stalker mindfuck is over. I'm a danger to those around me and don't want to get you killed."

"Again," Emmet adds.

"Again," I repeat.

Liam hugs me around the neck and kisses my temple. "Not a chance. You can't get rid of me that easily."

I pat his back and ease away. "He said he wouldn't hurt

anyone I care about, so you should be safe. Still, please be careful."

"Caution is my middle name."

"Stephan is your middle name."

"Close enough. Text me if you need me, day or night, and either way, I'll be here tomorrow with lunch to check in."

"Sounds great, thanks." When Liam leaves, I stare at the somber crowd and sigh. "I guess there's no getting around this, eh?"

Emmet offers me a sympathetic smile. "I vote to let Fi shower and get some sleep. This can keep until the morning, can't it?"

Emmet's a softie and hates to see anyone suffer. As much as I want to take the opening and run with it, the others are right. We need to go through what happened and figure out who we're dealing with. "It's okay, Em. Let's getter done so I can collapse in my bed."

I start my recap with hearing the footsteps approaching while I was in my hiding spot and have to back up to include the weird eyes staring at me last night when I tromped home from Janine's and Mark's place.

"So, it's been watchin' ye then?"

I don't like the sound of that, but yeah, there's no sense fooling myself into denying it.

"Okay, so what did it say?"

I close my eyes and try to remember. The night is jumbled in my head. With so much emotion it's a blur. "He talked in riddles."

"Actual riddles," Dillan asks, "or nonsense circles that felt like riddles?"

"Actual riddles." I rack my brain to recapture what he said. "Gawd, I was so panicked, I barely remember. He said something about starting the game and I said I wouldn't play if he hurt anyone I care about, then he said he accepted my terms so only innocent strangers would die."

"That's no better," Da snaps.

"No, of course not, but when I argued that fact, it seemed to be moot. He'd moved on."

"What else did he say?" Dillan asks. "Do you know his name? Is he a demon?"

"He said something about Rumplestiltskin and gamers chatting and a death each time he gives me a clue."

"A clue about what?" Calum asks while jotting things down on a notepad. "What's the game?"

"I don't know. Gawd...it's all such a clusterfuck." I run my fingers through my hair and let out a frustrated groan. "Dammit, how could I forget any of it? It was important."

"You were scared, baby girl," Aiden says, his voice steady as always. "Give yourself a break."

"But if I don't remember, people will die."

Sloan frowns and holds out his hand. "No matter what happens, it won't be yer fault, *a ghra*. Come here to me and let me try something."

He takes my hand and walks me to the family room. With him, Emmet, and I covered in blood, I chose the kitchen for our debrief, but he's already *poofed* upstairs and washed up. My hands and jacket got the worst of it, but I'm still a bit of a macabre mess.

He sits in one of the chairs, opens his knees, and points at the floor. "Have a seat."

I settle onto the area carpet while everyone else files in to join us. "Now what?"

"Face out toward the room, legs extended, hands loose and relaxed in yer lap."

I do as instructed, and he starts massaging my shoulders. "Now close yer eyes and let my gift clear yer mind. The memories ye see and hear are over. There's nothin' to hurt ye now. Yer safe, surrounded by yer family. Do ye understand?"

"Mhmm..."

"Big breath in and draw clean air into yer lungs. Feel the

oxygen fuel yer cells. Release the fuel into yer bloodstream and let it circulate through yer whole body. Can ye feel it?"

Normally I'd think this is hokey bullshit, but with him massaging my shoulders and neck and with his deep, sexy voice carrying in the air around us, it's quite effective. Oh, and Spiritual is one of his primary strengths.

"I feel something."

"Horny doesn't count," Dillan says.

"Shut it off fer ten minutes," Da snaps. "Let the boy try to help her."

I draw another deep breath and try to focus. "I'm good."

"Good. Now, when you exhale, I want you to imagine pushin' all the hurt and fear and grief out. Yer aware it happened but yer steppin' back to observe from a distance."

I exhale and release the tension of the past hour.

"Now, yer in yer hidin' spot in the forest and ye hear the quiet footsteps above yer head. We know now it was the game player, but ye didn't know then. What tipped ye off to the danger? Does he say somethin'?"

"No. I smell him. It's the same rancid, smoky, brimstone stink laced with baby powder. That was the stink Endor Avery gave off when he exploded this afternoon. I recognized it and knew the killer was close."

"Another big breath. In and out. Are ye all right?"

"Fine."

"So ye free yerself from yer hiding spot."

"The best hiding spot *evah*."

"Noted. Ye free yerself and search for the threat. Do ye see him?"

"No."

"But he speaks to ye. Tell me what he says."

I let my mind drift, falling deeper into the warmth of Sloan's touch. The words flutter into my mind as if being coaxed free from a whirling wind of chaos. "A nightmare for some, to boredom I come. Gamers might choose me to chat with a friend, but conflict collides and fails to blend. Who am I?"

"Excellent. Then what?"

"That was it for the first riddle. Then he said, 'Not Rumpelstiltskin but the task holds true. A death each time you get a clue. Not your loves, your boundary lain. Innocent deaths and strangers' pain.'"

My body's getting heavy, and I close my eyes and want to curl up with Sloan in bed.

"Stay with it a little longer, *a ghra*. Did he say anything else before he left ye confused?"

I dip my chin and yawn. "The fun is in motion. The game has begun. By the feast of Yule, your life is undone." I sigh and look up at the worried expressions around the room. "That was the last thing he said."

"Well done, luv. Now, is there anythin' else, a sound or a smell or a feelin' ye remember that seems odd or important?"

I think about that. "His eyes are low to the ground, like an animal, then he straightens and takes the form of a man. My evil eyes see his aura against the darkness of the background. It's strange. He isn't evil…he's indifferent. Like he doesn't care one way or another."

"All right. Anything else?"

"No, that's when things got foggy, and I attacked him—only it wasn't him."

"We're not going there, Fi. It was a mistake. Yer mind was bein' manipulated. Ye made a mistake." He leans forward and gathers me in his arms and kisses my temple. "Ye did well. Now, how about I take ye upstairs and run ye a hot shower? The boys and I can start on the riddles and see what we come up with."

I nod. "That sounds perfect. Thanks."

Once the tension of me killing Nikon is over, I can breathe again. I take my time upstairs in the shower to not only wash off the trauma of the night but to send the goddess every vibe of thanks and gratitude I can muster. I know she's not sitting around influencing my life and making things happen, but still...Nikon's life is a big win.

I've never been a religious person, but I give credit when it's due. Before becoming a druid, I believed in family and the strength of conviction to do the right thing.

Even after meeting the goddess, I can't say my belief system has changed much.

I believe in my family, in love, and in our code of doing what's right. That's what works for me.

Still, I send my gratitude out into the world.

Tonight could've ended so much worse.

Thinking about it gives me the quakes. I wrap a towel under my arms and sit on the closed toilet seat. Dropping my head into my hands, I shut my eyes and thank the goddess. If me attacking someone was truly beyond my control, at least it was Nikon.

Poor Nikon. Final death or not, I saw the pain in his eyes.

I killed him.

A gentle knock on the door brings my head up. "Fi? Are ye all right? May I come in?"

"Yeah. That's fine."

The door opens, and Sloan slips inside.

I stand and meet him with my arms open. "Don't look so worried, Mackenzie. I'm okay."

He holds me tight to his chest, gripping the back of my head. "No lies, remember? Ye love yer family and friends too deeply for this not to have rattled ye to yer core."

I reclaim my independence and grab a pair of fuzzy pajamas. Giving him my back, I get dressed and fight another round of tears.

Sloan says nothing, and I appreciate it. He leans back against the edge of the bathroom vanity and lets me settle my nerves. It takes a while…and a few tissues…and a cold cloth covering my face.

When I'm ready, I hang my towel and grab my brush. "Did you guys come up with anything earth-shattering from the riddles?"

"A few possibilities. Nothin' that can't wait until tomorrow to discuss with a fresh outlook."

"You mean we can go to bed and shut out the world?"

Sloan takes me by the wrist and tugs me toward the bathroom door. "That's exactly what I mean. Come. I think my girl could use a time out for a little TLC."

"A lot," I say, the hall floorboards creaking as we make our way toward my bedroom. "Your girl could use a *lot* of TLC."

"I stand corrected. As ye wish."

I wake in the dead of night, my heart racing, the nightmare that tormented me slipping away from memory. I don't have to remember what it was about. I feel the agony of loss to the marrow of my bones. Nikon. Brendan. And always, my Mam. I hate death.

Whether or not Nikon is immortal, tonight he died at my hand. I killed him. It's only through a miraculous fluke of magic that he's not truly dead.

To be responsible for the loss of someone I care about is my worst fear. If that had been Liam or Dillan or Emmet or Sloan, I wouldn't be able to survive the guilt. I clasp my hand over my mouth to keep Sloan from hearing.

"Are ye all right, *a ghra?*"

I sweep the sheet under my eyes and draw a deep, steadying breath. "Fine. Go back to sleep. It was a bad dream."

"Do ye truly think I'll drift off to sleep while yer upset? Come here and let me ease ye." He wraps his arms around me, and I snuggle in tight.

When we first got together, I was pleased with how well we fit. All of his chiseled and toned next to my soft and curvy. It's a true complement. I'm not as soft and curvy as I was four months ago, but that's good too.

It's pitch black in my room with my blinds pulled, so there's nothing to be done but feel my way around.

It's a hardship.

"Any interest in easing me with more than a hug?"

His chest bounces beneath me as he laughs silently into the darkness. "I'll erect the cone of silence."

I prop up on my elbow, reach into the bedside table, and smile as my fingers sink into the two hundred condoms filling my drawer. My brothers thought they were such smartasses bombarding us with a gag gift.

The joke will be on them when we tell them we've used them all up. TMI evil, I know, but hilarious.

"Do you want to take the lead or shall I?"

Warm hands splay at the base of my spine as he wraps me in a hug and claims my mouth. "Lady's choice."

Noice. I like being in charge.

CHAPTER SIX

The next two days are spent with the men in my life hovering, and each of us mulling over my murderous stalker's riddles. One thing about the Cumhaills is we value intelligence and are extremely competitive about outsmarting one another. I suppose that's two things, but the point is we're determined to figure out who and what my mystery riddler is.

"I, for one, won't argue that they're keeping a close eye on you, girlfriend." Dora lifts the tattoo gun off my shoulder and brushes my skin clean. She has her fuchsia wig on, her eyes done in gold glitter, and her nails done in zebra print.

When I first started mastering the spells that Gran, Granda, and Sloan taught me in Ireland, I was horrified at the thought of marking my skin. Now, it's become a point of pride. I carry my proficiency on my skin, and with the ink infused with fae magic, I can access those spells readily.

Non-empowered folks can't see it, and those who can understand what it means. The more I have, the more they should take notice.

"I know better than to argue. After what happened in the forest, I understand the impulse, but considering what happened to Nikon, I'm not sure I want them so close. What happens if I get brain-fogged again and spear someone who's not immortal?"

Dora swipes the *Ice Dagger* spell with the cooling gel and covers the symbol with gauze. Sloan thought it would be prudent to master a few more weaponry spells so I have options if cornered again.

Ice Dagger and *Sleet Storm* seemed like two sensible skills to master considering it's the third week of November and we live in Toronto.

"Has the Greek returned home?"

Dora is one of the cherished new friends I've made since discovering the secret world of the empowered within Toronto. Considering who she lived her life as before, I'm forever humbled that she finds value in being part of my life.

"No, but his sister said it would take a few days before he's able to return home."

"Was it Andromeda or Politimi who delivered the message?"

"She didn't leave her name—tall, blonde, and regal, with the same look about her as Nikon."

"That's Andromeda. She's a power lawyer and a force to be reckoned with. Politimi has dark hair and dark eyes and was born to Nikon's father, Helios, and a wife much later in life than Andromeda's and Nikon's mother. As far as I know, those are the only three of them who chose to live here."

"How many are there?"

"Oh, goddess only knows. When a Greek god of a man like Helios Tsambikos is immortal, he doesn't stay single for more than a few decades before another wife comes along and bears him another couple of kids. I know there are at least a couple of dozen."

Wow. I never would've guessed that.

"He's always so eager to hang out with my brothers and me. I kinda thought he was in the same boat as Sloan and didn't have siblings of his own."

"I don't think he's close with many of them. It's hard to find things in common with people two thousand years younger and living on another continent than you."

"I guess so."

I close my eyes and listen to the buzz of Dora's inking gun while images of Nikon and two dozen siblings bounce around in my head. When he first talked to me about being immortal, he didn't seem to be all that excited about it.

I suppose it's hard...knowing that any wife he chooses will die and leave him alone with their children...

"Wait. If he's that old, does Nikon have kids?"

"I expect he has a great many."

Huh. Why haven't I thought about his life?

"You're all done, girlfriend." Dora straightens in her chair. She sets the gun down and pulls off her latex gloves. "I'll give you the room to put your shirt back on. No bra for today. Sloan can heal the skin for you tomorrow but not until the magic in the ink takes hold."

"Got it." I sit up from where I'm lying face down on the tattoo table and clutch my shirt to my chest. I intentionally wore a bulky sweatshirt so that it would be easy to slide back into afterward. "Hey, Dora?"

"Yeah, baby?"

"You'll be careful, right? I don't know who or what this thing is that decided to make me a player in his game, but I don't want anyone to let down their guard."

"Don't worry about me. I may be dusting off the cobwebs, but I've got game no one in this time has ever seen."

"I have no doubt." I free my hair from the back of my sweatshirt and join Dora in the living area of her loft above her nightclub.

"All set?"

"Yep. Lead the way." I grab my coat and purse while Dora picks up her keys.

When we originally made our arrangement for Dora to be our ink spell artist, our payment was time spent helping out in the soup kitchen she runs for the homeless out of the other half of her Queen Street building. Even without needing to settle up, it's something my brothers and I are game to do.

"Fiona!" someone says from the back of the cafeteria-style room.

I step behind the serving counter, hang my purse with my coat over the top, and wave. "Hey, Sarge. How's things?"

"Same as every other day except better cause I'm still here to see it."

"Glad to hear it."

I lift a few stainless steel pot lids and smell what's cooking for lunch today. "Nothing like chicken noodle soup on a wintery day to ward off the chill."

Walter, an old Asian man who lives in the alley up the block, holds up his bowl. "Dora's soup is amazing. Two days ago, I had a cough so bad I spat up blood. I thought I might have to go to the hospital. I came in for a bowl of Dora's chicken soup, and now I'm better."

"That *is* amazing." I smile at Dora. "One might even think this soup is magical."

Dora pulls the neckband of a full-length apron over her fuchsia wig. "Everyone knows the healing properties of chicken soup. I happen to make one that tastes good too."

Walter sets his bowl on a tray, and I get him a roll and some butter to go with it. "Nice to see you, Walter."

"Nicer to see you, pretty lady."

I smile and turn to help the next person in line. I've never seen her here before. Not that I know everyone. "Hello, what can I get for you?"

The woman in front of me struggles, and I shift closer to figure out what the trouble is.

Her pupils are shot, and she has the shakes. A little girl clings to her leg, which I don't think is wise for either of them because the woman is about to go down.

"Dora! A little help." I get around the counter in time to catch her elbow and ease her to the floor.

Dora gets there a few seconds later.

When the mother starts to thrash, I scoop up the little girl and take her over to look at the food. "Are you hungry, sweetie? What do you think would fill your tummy?"

The little thing looks like a modern-day Shirley Temple. Round cheeks, beautiful golden-brown ringlets, and a look about her that seems more than a little familiar.

Oh, dear.

I look back at Dora tending to the mother. She's struggling, but hell, Dora's stronger than she looks. She bends, scoops the woman up, and takes her into the back.

Crap on a cracker. I think I know what this is.

If I'm right, that woman is high as a kite and Moon Called. Tonight's the full moon, and not a good time to lose control. Well, she can't shift here.

With the little girl on my hip, I ladle her a bowl of soup, grab some cutlery and a roll, and set it on a tray. We go over to the tables, and I set her up with Sarge and Walter. "Hello, gentlemen. Do you mind if we join you?"

"What's to mind?" Sarge says.

"We always have room for lovely ladies at our table," Walter agrees.

"Excellent." Setting the little thing down, I help her with her soup and pull out my phone. The first person I text is Garnet.

Might have a Moon Called incident in progress at Dora's soup kitchen.

The second text goes out to Sloan.

How close are you to being finished? Dora might need some help with a strung-out shifter at the soup kitchen.

When I've sent those, I check that the little girl is eating her magical chicken soup. "What's your name, sweetie?"

"Imari Rose."

"Well, now." Sarge smiles. "Isn't that the most beautiful name for a beautiful girl?"

The front door opens and Anyx strides inside.

"Excuse me, gentlemen." I rise to my feet. "Could you two keep Imari Rose company for a moment?"

I don't wait for an answer before I jog across the dining hall floor and meet Anyx. "She's in here. I don't know if it's drugs or if she's suffering from moon madness or who knows what but there's something very wrong, and it's about to spill out onto mainstream civilians."

Anyx follows me into the back kitchen, and we go on the hunt for where Dora took Imari Rose's mother.

We find them in the room nearest the back door. Dora has the woman closed in what looks to be an intake room of some kind and has a foot braced against the wall, holding the doorknob.

"She's a strong one." Dora grunts as the woman screams and yanks the door for her freedom. "One of yours, I presume?"

Anyx looks through the fire glass window and frowns. The six-by-six-foot room is empty except for two chairs on opposite sides of a little table. It's a good thing there's not much more in there because she's already destroyed what little there was.

"By the looks of her, I'd guess she's a bear. I can tell you for sure if I smell her."

Dora chuckles. "Well, I'm not letting her out, so if you want to flash in there, be my guest."

Anyx does just that.

He goes in there, and Imari's mother spins. With her arms up, her fingernails expand past their nailbeds, and long claws extend. With a lunge, she goes for Anyx's throat. He grabs her arm and keeps the deadly attack at a distance.

Sloan arrives and rushes to stand behind me. "What did I miss?"

"A bear shifter has lost her mind."

"If the woman wants out so badly, why doesn't she flash out and gain her freedom?" Sloan looks at me, but I have no answer, so he looks at Dora.

"A shifter in this state of madness can't focus enough to flash. When I saw her eyes, I knew there was a good chance I could contain her in there."

Anyx evades being sliced and diced twice more before he flashes out to join us.

"What's wrong with her?"

Anyx smooths his flaxen hair into place and leans against the wall to catch his breath. "The first problem is that she's psychotically altered."

"Is it drugs?"

Anyx shrugs. "I've never seen anything like it. It's like she has a hurricane trying to bust out of her."

"You said that's her first problem. What's her second?"

"Well, you were right. She's Moon Called, and the pull of the night has overwhelmed her. I've never seen anyone over the age of puberty have this much trouble controlling a shift."

Sloan has a hand on the glass, shaking his head. "Can we knock her out? She's liable to have a heart attack if she continues like she is."

The words are barely out of Sloan's mouth when the woman lets out a shrill scream and drops to the floor.

Dora snarls a string of ancient curse words I've only ever heard Fionn use. Before I have time to ask what they mean, Sloan and Anyx both *poof* into the holding room and bend to check on her.

"Is she dead?" Dora releases her hold on the door and opens it a crack.

Sloan nods. "She is."

I remember the little cutie patootie out front and my heart breaks for her. She's about the same age I was when my mom died. "What the hell just happened?"

Sloan and I leave Anyx and Dora to deal with the death of Imari's mother. Sadly, because of the situations that bring people to her establishment, Dora has dealt with more than one death here at the soup kitchen. She has things in place. While that's going on, Sloan and I return to the cafeteria to check on the woman's baby bear, Imari.

We find her right where I left her, sitting at the table with Walter and Sarge. "Hey, guys. Sorry that took so long. How are we doing out here?"

Sarge tosses me a look. "I led troops into battle, taught in training schools, and raised four kids and nine grandkids. Having lunch with an angel is no trouble, is it beautiful?"

I smile at the angel in question and hold out my arms. "Hey, do you want to go somewhere fun? I know two very special kids who would love to play with you for a while."

"Is Mommy better?"

Sloan frowns. "Your mam got really sick, angel. We tried to help her—"

"—but she was worried about you being left out here alone. She wants us to make sure you're happy and safe. So, while my friends figure out what made your mom sick, we're going to take good care of you as your mommy wants."

"I'm not supposed to go with strangers."

Aiden comes in the front door right on schedule. He's in his uniform, and when he sees me holding Imari, he heads straight for us.

"Drat. It's the cops." Walter looks guilty. "What did you do now, old man?"

Sarge flashes him a middle-finger salute and scowls. "He's not here for me, knucklehead. That's one of Fiona's clan. It's as plain as day. They all have the same look, and that one is the spit of her."

It's true. We all look quite a bit alike, and Aiden and I are the two with red hair and blue eyes.

"Hey, Fi." Aiden joins our little gathering. He has his full daddy persona on when he bends to speak to Imari. "Hello there, Imari Rose. Fiona told me your mommy's not feeling well and you might like to have a play date at my house with my little boy and girl while people try to help her."

She looks at me, and I nod at her. "It's okay. I'll come with you, and we can ride in the back of Aiden's police car and everything."

"Will Mommy be mad?"

"No sweetheart. When there's trouble, police officers help you. This policeman is my big brother, Aiden. He's very nice, and his wife Kinu is even nicer."

Aiden chuckles. "Well, thanks for that."

I smile at Sloan. "Can you grab my coat and purse from the hook behind the counter and maybe tell Anyx and Dora where we're off to?"

"And Mommy," Imari says. "Make sure."

Sloan swallows. "I'll take care of it. Back in a flash."

While Sloan takes care of our exit preparations, I carry the little bear over to grab a cookie for the road. "Sometimes when I'm sad, I like to have a treat to make me feel better. It must've been scary when your mommy collapsed, eh?"

"Mommy falls sometimes. It's okay."

Nope. Not this time. "I don't want you to be scared of coming with me. Do you know what a pinky-swear is?"

She shakes her head.

"It means when two friends hook their little fingers and make a promise, it has to come true. There's no lies or tricks or breaking your word." I link my finger with hers and smile. "I pinky-swear that I'll take good care of you and that it's what your mommy wants. You can trust me."

After we pinky-swear, she places her hand on my forehead, and my skin tingles. "I know, silly. You're a bear girl, like me. I see him."

I check over my shoulders that our conversation is our own. "You see Bruin?"

She nods. "I have a bear too."

"I know, but it's a secret, right?"

"Yep. But not with you. You have one too."

Right. I suppose that makes sense. "How about a cookie for the road?"

"Yes, please."

"Do you like chocolate chip or oatmeal raisin?"

"Yes, please."

I giggle. "A girl after my own heart. Both it is."

CHAPTER SEVEN

A iden drops us off at his place but doesn't stay. Instead, he leaves us in the capable hands of his wife, Kinu. Before she had the kids and decided to stay home full-time, Kinu was an intake agent for Toronto Children's Aid. She worked with the police and dealt with children in bad situations. That's how they met. She knows what to say and how to handle things better than I ever could.

"The introduction of the kids went as well as I expected." I giggle as the three kids ditch us to run off and play.

Kinu rounds the breakfast bar and pulls a couple of apples from the fridge. "The fact that she engaged immediately is a great sign and also terribly sad."

"How so?"

"It implies that what happened today isn't unusual or frightening to her. She's been down this road before with her mother, or she'd be more shaken up."

"That's sad." Sloan stares down the hall.

"You two go do what you need to do. She's fine here until you know more."

I steal a wedge of green apple and munch it. "Anyx got the

mother's name from her ID, but she only had a health card. No license so no address. He'll track down any family or next of kin she might have. I think being here is better than her sitting in the soup kitchen or getting shuffled off somewhere."

"Definitely. Does the empowered community have children's authorities the same way we do?"

I shrug. "No idea. I'm still a noob."

"Well, it's not a problem. The poor thing is welcome to stay and play with the kids."

"You're sure a third won't be too much?"

Kinu pegs me with a strange look and sighs. "I can handle a six-year-old girl."

"You think she's six? I figured four."

"By the size of her, you'd think that but her vocabulary and cognitive strengths say she's older. She's probably tiny from being underfed and not properly cared for."

"Poor monkey."

"Not to worry. She's fine here and will keep the other two busy and out of my hair the rest of the day. My only concern is what I'm supposed to do if she turns into a bear. There's a no-pet clause for the building, and our landlord's already looking to clear out the tenants early so he can spruce up the building before the sale."

Sloan tosses a balloon at Jackson as the three kids come squealing down the hall. They giggle, bobbling it in the air, then capture it and retreat to the bedrooms as quickly as they came. "Moon Called don't begin to shift until puberty." He chuckles. "Imari will remain a little girl like any other for years to come."

Kinu finishes with the apples and sets them on a plate, then grabs some cheese strings. She sets up snack time at the Japanese low table in the center of the living room. "Then we'll be fine. Don't worry about us."

Her eyes tell a different story. She's tired. "What aren't you saying? Is it the apartment hunting? Do you need an hour to yourself? I can stay and help."

She captures a strand of brunette hair and traps it back in her ponytail. "Nothing's wrong. I'm good. We're good. It's all good. You go figure out what happened to the mom and who's missing her."

Sloan catches my eye and shakes his head.

Okay, fine. Maybe I need to work on letting people work through their stuff without prodding. In my defense, I only ever want to help.

"All right. Your pants are totally on fire, Kinu Cumhaill, but contrary to what some people think, I *can* mind my business. When you're ready to talk about what's stressing you or need a sounding board or a shoulder to cry on, I'm here."

Kinu chuckles and rubs a hand over her face. "Thanks, Fi. You're one in a million. I'll let you know."

I pop into Jackson's room, give everyone a round of hugs, and check in with Imari. "Are you okay to stay and play while Sloan and I pop out for an hour or two?"

She barely has time to wave goodbye before she's distracted by the monkey hijinks.

I laugh at myself. She totes doesn't care I'm here.

Sloan is waiting for me in the kitchen with my coat.

"If she needs me for anything or is too much, let me know, and we'll pop back."

Kinu finishes tidying the kitchen and hangs her dishcloth over the side of the sink. "We'll be fine. Aiden's off in an hour and is bringing home a bucket of chicken. No cooking for me tonight. Life is good."

I hug her. "Excellent. Enjoy. Love you." I shout down the hall on my way out. "Love you, monkeys."

When we round the corner to the entrance hall, I pull on my winter boots and zip up my coat. "That went about as well as it could have, I think. Considering."

Sloan arches a dark brow. "Considering ye didn't tell her that her Mam passed. Do ye not think it best to be honest with the wee girl?"

"No. Trust me from personal experience. This news shouldn't come from a stranger. Let Anyx figure out who her next of kin is. It should be her daddy or her grandma who breaks it to her. Once he finds out where she belongs, he'll reunite her with her family for support."

"Are ye forgettin' ye met them in the soup kitchen? If they have family and a support system, why were they there for a hot meal?"

I frown at him. "Do I look like I have all the answers? I'm making this shit up as I go along. Geez, work with me. For right now, Imari has a roof over her head and new friends to play with. Can you give me the freaking win?"

Sloan laughs and pulls out his phone. He swipes the call off the screen and takes my hand. "I'm sorry. Take yer win. Where to next?"

I sigh. "How about back to the bookstore? You haven't made time for Myra with those books she wanted you to look over, have you?"

His dark eyes widen. "What books are we talkin' about?"

Oh, crud. "The ones I forgot to tell you she wanted your help with. Okay, definitely to the bookstore. I have to fall on my sword to save your reputation. You're really late on getting back to Myra on this. Rude."

Sloan rolls his eyes. "Yer ridiculous."

Sloan *poofs* us into the lounge area of the bookstore, and I press my hand on the ancient ash. "Hello, Mr. Tree. Have you had a good day?" I look up at the full, green leaves spread out under the glass ceiling and take that as a good sign. "Looking good, dude. Keep it up."

"Are you sweet-talking your man to keep it up in my store? Inappropriate."

I burst out laughing as Myra hangs over the second-floor railing and grins at us. "No. I...oh, you know exactly what I was saying."

"Yep, but I got you. And look how cute our Irish lover looks all flushed and flustered."

Sloan flashes her a bewildered look. "Black men don't get flushed."

"Says you." I pat his cheek. "Whether or not your cheeks flush, you get flustered."

"With you around, it's a certainty. Now, wasn't there a reason we came here?"

I straighten and make a face. "Sloan Mackenzie reporting for duty. In truth, I forgot to tell him about your books, so the slow response is on me."

Myra giggles and walks around the mezzanine toward the metal ladder over by the far wall. "Not a problem. The books I brought in are ancient. Having them sit for two or three extra days did no harm."

My phone vibrates in my pocket, and I pull it out. "It's Garnet."

Myra laughs. "I swear he talks to you more than he does to me on an average day."

"I get murder and mayhem while you get all the manly mating perks."

Myra's eyes light up as she steps away from the ladder. "Oh, those perks. I gotta say, I don't even care what side hustle the two of you have going on as long as I get those perks."

I answer his text, and a moment later Garnet flashes in and stands next to us. "I'm glad you're available. I need to steal you away for an hour. Are you busy?"

"Partner swap," Myra calls, lacing her arm around Sloan's elbow and kissing his cheek. "I'll keep your man busy if you keep mine. Have fun, kids."

Garnet missed the first part of this conversation and doesn't look amused.

The scowls on the faces of both men are too funny.

"Okay, you two work on your book project, and we'll go off and deal with death." I reach up on my toes, grab Sloan, and kiss him a good one. "Save all the manly perks for me."

Sloan looks at Garnet, then Myra and me. "They're both nuts."

Garnet must've caught up on the convo because the tension in his shoulders eases. "Yeah, but they're our nuts."

He extends his hand to me and grins. "Lady Druid?"

"What are we doing here? Did we have something scheduled I forgot about?" Garnet releases his hold on me in his private quarters of the secret headquarters of the Guild of the Empowered Ones. Twisting to grab our robes off his desk, he hands me mine. "Come to think of it, Grand Governor, where is here, exactly? It occurs to me that I don't know where this is. I've always been escorted."

He swings his robe around his shoulders and starts with the front fasteners. "Did Bruce Wayne publicize where the Bat Cave was? No. We're here for an emergency meeting. Put on your robe and assume your Governor of Toronto Druids persona. We're late."

I don't know how I can be late for a meeting I only found out about this minute, but whatevs. "Robin knew where the Bat Cave was. What's the emergency?"

"You haven't earned your place as Robin yet. I told you what it's about in the text I sent you."

I pull on my robe and free my hair. "Excuse me for coming to class unprepared. Your text was a mile long, and I've been busy with an outbreak of murder and mayhem. Go ahead. Give me the highlights."

Garnet chuckles and pulls his long, dark hair out of the collar of his robe, then checks his look in the mirror. "The meeting is about an outbreak of murder and mayhem. There, now you're all caught up."

I smile, pleased at how far his sense of humor has come. By my estimation, it's a combined influence of Myra and me. It suits him. A man can't live on blood and intimidation alone.

"Lead the way, Grand Gov'na," I say in my best British accent, which admittedly is awful.

"First, here. Take this. I keep forgetting to give it to you." He hands me a bank card with my name on it. "Your Guild pay started getting deposited monthly from the time you took your oath. Your password is 'pain in my ass' except the 'i's are ones."

I chuckle and slide the card into my purse pocket and zip it up. "I didn't know I'd get paid when I signed on. When Nikon told me, I almost fell over."

"So you were going to take this on for what—the good of the city?" He studies me for a moment and rolls his eyes. "Of course you were."

When he strides off, I follow him out of the private chambers toward the meeting room down the corridor. I've only been here one other time, but I remember the way.

That was for an emergency meeting a month ago when Xavier, the Vampire King, lost track of three of his human sheep from his feeder flock and they got picked up by a patrol car out of Aiden's station.

It's also when my fellow Guild Governors threw me under the bus as the representative to take care of it.

Ha! Sucks to be them.

The meeting room is elegant and sleek. A long, black table shimmering with a high-gloss finish runs down the center of the room. A silky silver fabric covers the walls, and the lighting from the coffered ceiling and the pin-dot LEDs makes the sheen dance.

I lift my gaze to sweep the crowd, looking for Suede or Zxata or—"Oh my gawd."

I close the distance between Nikon and me and throw myself into his arms. Hugging him tightly, I close my eyes and am so thankful when he returns the embrace.

Tears burn and brim in an instant.

"Oh, Greek. I'm so sorry," I half-whisper and half-sob into his neck. "Are you alive?"

His chest bounces as he sets my feet back on the floor and rubs my back. "I'm alive, Red. Andromeda told you that, didn't she?"

I pull back and wipe my face with the sleeve of my robe. "She did, but—" I fall against him again and go for another hug, needing to absorb that he truly is healthy and strong. "Please, don't die on me again. I can't take it."

Nikon pulls back and presses his forehead to mine. "I came to see you first thing this afternoon when I got back, but you weren't home. When Garnet called the meeting, I figured you'd be here. I came as much for the meeting as I did to allay any fears you still have that I'm hurt or angry with you."

"Are you? I totes get it if you are. I'm so sorry." My voice is more an outpouring of clogged emotion and sobs than actual words.

He wraps an arm around my shoulder and walks me to the hall. "Fi, you need to pull it together, sweetheart. I'm okay. I'm immortal remember?"

I pull back and try to rein it in. "I'm so sorry."

"Stated and accepted. I never for a second thought you were in control when you harpooned me. I only hope that now that you realize you love me, we can ditch the Irishman and run away together."

I blink and pull back. "Hubba-wha?"

Nikon keeps a straight face for all of ten seconds before he busts up and pulls me back into a hug. "Oh, Red, I'm fucking with you. It's time to laugh again. It's your sass and wit I want, not your tears. Trust me. I know your heart and know this tormented you. It's over now."

"I'm glad to hear that." Garnet sounds annoyed. I straighten and grab a couple of tissues from the box our Grand Governor is offering. "Wipe. Blow. Do what you need to get control of whatever this is and take your damned seats. Between him kissing you last time and your emotional meltdown this time, the entire room is buzzing about the two of you having a grand love affair."

I wipe and blow as instructed and kiss Nikon on the cheek. "I heart you, Greek."

He flashes me a glorious Greek god smile. "I heart you too, Red. Now, let's get in there and play the part of the reunited lovers."

I laugh and pat my cheeks dry with my sleeve. "My robe will need to be dry-cleaned, Garnet. Sorry about the snot."

"All right," Garnet says as we enter the meeting room again. "Guild emergency meeting, take two. Can everyone *please* take their seats?"

Zxata is waiting inside the door, and I hug him and assure him I'm fine and will explain later.

Where's Suede? I ask Nikon telepathically as we round the table.

He chuckles. *I took her to the grove in Ireland for a booty call last week. She and the wood elf lit quite a fire.*

I chuckle and take my seat. *Good for them. Look at you. Our soft-hearted trans-Atlantic booty Uber.*

Xavier casts me an amused look as Nikon and I settle onto the two chairs across from him. "If nothing else, these meetings have become more interesting since the arrival of our Lady Druid."

After a deep inhale, I lift my chin and give Garnet my full attention. "Ready and steady, sir."

Garnet nods. "Now, for those of you who didn't feel it necessary to read the meeting update text I sent, the long and short of things is that we have an unfortunate incident with the West Village Wizards dying and hours later, exploding into a horror show of internal carnage."

"Wizards, plural?" I ask. "There's been another since Endor on Saturday?"

He nods. "Yes. Nate DeRont's body was found this morning. From what we've been able to piece together and the state of things at the scene, we're estimating his time of death midday Sunday and his bodily detonation Monday morning."

"Does he have any direct connection to Endor?" I ask. "Did he come in contact with him when he was sick?"

Garnet nods. "He's the blond wizard who wore Endor at the first scene."

I gasp. "He touched the blood."

"In truth, the blood touched him."

I make a face and sit back in my seat. "So, it *is* transferable by contact. My Spidey-senses warned me as much."

Garnet nods. "It's only due to your instinct that Anyx and I weren't infected. I owe you one for that."

I shrug. "I'm sure, having to deal with me, you pay that price back on the daily."

Malachi leans forward looking more green than usual. "When you say bodily detonation, what do you mean?"

I consider how to best describe it. "Picture the victims as human pizza pockets that have been in the microwave for too long. One minute they're lying there, then *blam! splat!* they're scarlet muck dripping from every surface."

"Um…gross." Nikon sticks his tongue out. "Good visual though, Fi. Very visceral."

I glance around the table at the wide eyes and looks of nausea. Okay, that might've been a little too descriptive.

"What do we know about the cause of death itself?" A big guy with ram horns asks from the end of the table. "Is it a disease, a curse, or do they drop dead with it looking like another cause of death like a stroke or a heart attack?"

Garnet tents his fingers together and lays his arms on the table. "We don't know yet. We've never seen anyone at the time of death. Only post-mortem and post-detonation."

"But we have people working on the blood," I say. "Has the lab had any luck?"

Garnet opens the file folder in front of him and frowns. "The lab has never seen anything like it. They've tested the blood samples we gave them and say the cells have almost a sentient awareness."

I widen my eyes and fight not to point and say 'I told you so' but *hello*—we both know I did. It's *The Blob* all over again. "So, what does the blood want?"

"Our best guess is to actively infect others."

Rude. "Okay, so Endor gets offed by the Riddler and explodes on Nate, his angry wizard friend. Who found Nate?"

"His cleaning ladies, we expect."

"You don't know?"

Garnet flips a page in the folder. "Thaos says a mop bucket and a couple of caddies of cleaning supplies were inside the door at DeRont's house. By the bloody footprints leading away from where the mess of the man splattered, he's guessing the Monday morning cleaning women came in and found the body. They approached, and it detonated."

"Infecting them too."

He nods. "That's our working assumption. Thaos is tracking

down what cleaning company he used and who might've been there to become infected."

"Can we go back to the part about this Riddler person killing Endor?" High Priestess Drippy Face asks. "What's that about? Who is he? What does he want?"

"A bloody death toll while tormenting me." I give everyone an abbreviated version of what's happened since Saturday afternoon when we found the message on Endor's wall.

"So, once again, we're here because of you or something you've done," she snaps.

Rude. "We still have no idea why the Riddler targeted me. For all I know, one of you put him up to it. It seems more situations orbiting around me have been because of the people in this room than not."

"All right, let's stay on topic, shall we ladies?" Garnet hits a button hidden on the table's surface, and the three riddles appear on the four walls of the room, so everyone can see them without twisting to read.

"The stuff about Rumplestiltskin and people dying we got." I frown at the wall behind Xavier. "He wants me to guess who he is and he's going to take blood sacrifice for every clue. It's the other one that stumped us."

"A nightmare for some, to boredom I come. Gamers might choose me to chat with a friend, but conflict collides and fails to blend." Nikon finishes reading and looks at me. "That's an easy one, Red. Discord. It's Discord."

I have no idea how he thinks that's "easy," but hey, he has a couple of millennia on me, so what do I know? I Google the word discord and see if it fits into the clues.

It does.

"*Ohhh,* and yeah, my brothers use Discord for their gaming chat. I'm with you now. Slam-dunk, Greek. Chocolate bar for you."

He meets my palm in a high-five and grins. "My first Cumhaill Oh! Henry bar award. I'm honored. Truly."

"So, who the fuck is Discord?" Xavier gives us the stink eye. "The whole blood thing doesn't affect my people because we're already dead, but if he's tainting our food source, the assholishness must end."

The Vampire King's concern for the people detonating into chunky shrapnel is heartwarming, but his use of words is inspiring.

I smile. "I vote we add assholishness to the dictionary."

Nikon nods. "Agreed. And how about assholier than thou? That's where my mind went while Xavier was talking."

I giggle. If it were possible for steam to come out of someone's ears literally, we'd be seeing that right now.

Garnet's phone *pings* and he reads the incoming message. "Maybe our answers are here. Come in, Thaos."

The door to the meeting room opens, and Garnet's third in command joins us. He hands Garnet a few handwritten notes and waits while his boss scans them.

"All right. We have the cleaning crew nailed down and names and addresses to track. We also have another site of bodily detonation. Thaos, you take the latter. I'll take care of following up with the cleaning ladies. Would anyone like to join? Many hands make light work."

"And faster results." I raise my hand.

"I'm in," Nikon says. "Immortality has its benefits. I can't be detonated."

Garnet looks at the others. Zxata raises his hand. The gremlin man—I can never pronounce his name—raises his claw. To my surprise, Xavier joins the team.

"Very good. That's two names for three teams of two. We find the ladies on this list. If they're alive, Nikon or one of the Moon Called can flash them to the safehouse in Dufferin Grove. If they're dead, don't approach. If they've already detonated, call it in for a cleanup crew."

"A cleaning crew for the cleaning crew. Ironic," Malachi says, distracted by something on his phone.

What a douche-canoe.

"All right." Garnet rises to his feet. "Those of you involved, come with me, and I'll divvy up the names. Everyone else, we'll keep you posted."

CHAPTER EIGHT

Garnet has six possibly contaminated cleaners for us to check out, and with those names are their home addresses and a couple of personal notes their boss gave us in case we have to hunt for them. I text Sloan my first address and invite him to join. He's never been in that section of the downtown core, so he'll have to meet us the old-fashioned way—public transit.

For the sake of efficiency, Garnet pairs me with Nikon because I don't know where the Dufferin Grove safehouse is. If we find one of the cleaners, Sloan and I wouldn't be able to *poof* them there until we've been there once. Zxata goes with the gremlin, and Garnet and Xavier pair up.

"How do vampires get around? Can they *poof* or do they fly like in the movies?"

Nikon uses Google Street View to pinpoint the first address and studies the map before taking my hand and portaling us there.

Where Sloan's wayfarer portal feels like a buildup of energy and a *poof* when we travel, Nikon's method feels and sounds more like an instant snap of the fingers.

Snap. We're there.

We step out from between a hedged yard and the side of the house next door and check the house numbers to make sure we're in the right place. "Vampires don't fly. They run incredi-fast though—like Barry Allen fast—so it seems like they fly. A few vampires can portal, but only if they were made from people who already had that ability."

I picture Moose, the vampire who took Liam and me prisoner and *poofed* us first to some rich guy's home, then double-crossed rich guy to sell us to Kartak the Hobgoblin. I might wonder what he was before being made into a vampire if I cared enough to commit brain cells to the task.

He shot Liam.

Birga and I ended him.

"What about daylight?" I pull out my phone to check on Sloan's progress and check the time. "It's only three o'clock in the afternoon. Can Xavier tromp around in the streets of Toronto looking for women in the middle of the day, or is that why Garnet took him?"

"I think Garnet took him to keep an eye on him, but even if he hadn't, Xavier's age and the lack of direct sun this time of year means he's fine outside. He wears a hooded jacket and gloves until sundown, but winter is a vampire's friend. They don't feel the cold, and they can be outside pretty much day and night for four or five months."

"Well, I'm glad somebody enjoys it." We climb the front steps of a three-story triplex, and I find the right buzzer. I push it, and we wait for a response.

Nikon leans back on the iron rail and crosses his arms. "C'mon, Red. Are you telling me with an active family like yours that you don't ski or snowboard or snowmobile?"

I burst out laughing and push the buzzer again. "Da raised six kids on a cop's salary. Sure, we played street hockey and hide-

and-seek, but we didn't have the money to buy lift tickets and expensive equipment. Da's rule was that if we all agreed on a sport, he'd put out money once and we had to make the equipment last. Needless to say, by the time the hockey equipment got down to me, it wasn't fit to wear."

He sticks out his bottom lip. "Aw, that's a sad story."

I smack him in the gut and laugh. "Dumbass."

"Smartass."

"Pain in the ass."

"Nice ass in those jeans."

I point my finger at him in warning. "I'll let you get away with that only because you're alive and I'm so relieved to see your pretty, teenaged-boy face smiling at me."

He laughs and waves at Sloan striding up the street with Manx in a harness at his side. "And because you know I'm a huge fan of your hot Irish boy toy. I'm glad the two of you are hitting the horizontal. You deserve it. All work and no play makes Sloan a very uptight male."

I chuckle and lower my voice. "I don't think that had anything to do with me taking it slow."

"Maybe not, but he's a much happier man now that he has the keys to your city. Look at the spring in his step."

"Keys to my city?"

"Permission to storm your gates?"

I roll my eyes and smile at the incoming happy faces. "Hello, Manx. Thanks for joining the fun."

"Thanks fer the invite."

When I asked Sloan to come, I didn't think of inviting Manx but don't want to make him feel bad, so I go with it.

"Hey, hotness. How did the book stuff go with Myra?"

Sloan leans in and kisses my cheek. "It went well. We finished up, and I met Kevin and got the paperwork for Manx and thought we'd celebrate by strutting our stuff around the city."

He hands me the leather leash and pulls Nikon in for a manly, back-clapping hug. "Och, am I glad to see you, my friend. Ye gave us quite a fright, I'll tell ye."

Nikon pats Sloan's back in return and eases away. "You guys. I'm immortal, *and* I sent Andy to reassure you. Did you miss the point of her stopping by?"

I giggle. "The men may have, yes. They were too busy picking their tongues up off the kitchen floor."

Sloan nods. "I won't lie. Yer sister is a knockout. Dillan, Liam, and Emmet nearly fell at her feet."

Nikon chuckles. "Andromeda turns heads. Always has. Not yours though? You didn't include yourself in the list of men whose hearts beat a little faster."

Sloan waves that away. "My heart only beats faster for one special lady these days."

I laugh and give the buzzer one last push. "I wish one of us had our video recording when Dillan made his play. It was way too funny when she shut him down with 'my brother warned me about you.'"

Nikon grins. "She told me. Gotta keep the players from playin' when it comes to my sisters. Although she did say he was hotter than she expected."

"Gawd. No one tell him that. His ego is big enough."

The door opens and the man coming out jumps when he sees us standing there. "Sorry." I step back so he can exit. "We're here to see Jada. We didn't mean to get in your way. We can squeeze…"

He steps sideways on the front stoop and blocks me until the door closes behind him. Then, he checks that it's locked and throws us a look before descending the stairs.

"Okay then, buh-bye. Have a great day."

Nikon chuckles. "Okay, we better stop loitering and get in there. Do you want the honors, Irish?"

Sloan checks over his shoulder, steps tight to the threshold of the doorway, and Nikon and I close in to cover his disappearance. A second later, he lets us inside, and we're on our way to the second floor.

Jada Neil lives on the top level of an old, brick triplex off Kingston Road near Woodbine Ave. It's set up so each of the three apartments has a full floor and a staircase that winds up from the front door. The four of us jog up the steps, around the landing, and continue up.

"I'll never live on the third floor," I say absently.

"Don't tell me yer afraid of heights," Sloan says. "I've seen ye climb towering trees of the grove when yer feelin' particularly rambunctious."

I giggle. "I was thinking about lugging groceries up the stairs all the time, but I love that my boyfriend uses words like rambunctious."

Nikon chuckles behind me. "I love to watch you when you get rambunctious."

"Ye can't help yerself, can ye?" Sloan crests the last step on the third-floor landing and knocks on the door. "We need to find someone more appropriate for ye to come on to."

"What fun is appropriate?" He looks aghast. "Don't worry about me. I have a couple of very inappropriate sexy side-hustles going on to keep me in line. Fiona's virtue is safe from me."

I snort. "Fiona's virtue is safe regardless of your sexy side-hustle. I'm off the market. End of story."

Nikon shrugs. "There's that too."

My phone vibrates in my pocket, and I pull it out to check. "It's Garnet. They're onto their second name already. Shit. Okay, we gotta get something done. Nikon and I shouldn't be a team. We're like distracted squirrels."

Nikon laughs. "After you live a few centuries, the pressure of getting things done at a moment's notice kinda loses its urgency."

I suppose it would. "Okay, hotness. Let us in."

Sloan *poofs* off and unlocks the door from the inside. I take a cautious glance from the open doorway, but nothing seems out of order. "Okay, remember. If you see her and she's alive, we take her to the safe house. If she's dead and in one piece, we back away quickly, and if she's already exploded, we—"

"What the fuck!"

I jump forward and scream, launching myself at Sloan.

A thirty-something brunette with a ponytail glares at us from the top of the steps. "What are you doing in my apartment? I'm calling the cops."

I'm still patting my chest and trying to restart my ticker when Sloan drops me like a hot rock and steps around me. "Jada Neil?"

Her gaze narrows and she sets her grocery bag down and reaches into her purse. "Who wants to know?"

"Leave the pepper spray where it is," I say with more edge than I mean to. "We're here because we believe your cleaning crew was exposed to a life-threatening..." What the hell do you call it?

"This about what happened at Nate's house?"

"It is," Sloan says. "It's very important that we get you and your co-workers into quarantine until we learn if you've been affected by the virus Fiona was speaking about."

"Virus? Melissa and Chlorine said Nate exploded like a ripe watermelon hitting concrete. What virus does that?"

"You weren't there to see it firsthand?" I ask. "Your boss named you as one of the people on the crew."

She shrugs. "Yeah, but Nate's place was our second house. I get a five-minute smoke break between houses. I was in the driveway. They took the stuff and went in and, like, three or four minutes later came running out screaming and splattered in grossness."

"Did you get any of the grossness on you?"

"Fuck no. I wouldn't even get back in the van with them. I called the Guild tip line and booked it on foot."

"That, and the smoke break, probably saved your life. Whatever this is, the science team believes it's contracted by direct contact with the blood."

She holds her hands up. "Then I'm good. I didn't get anywhere near that mess."

I pull out the list of the other names and show her. "What about these ladies? We have six names on here."

"On a big day, we divide into two teams of three cleaners. One does a bathroom and dusts, one does the beds and vacuuming, and one cleans the kitchen then starts the mop. I was with Joy and Chlorine. They were the ones who got hit with that...whatever it was."

"Perfect. Thanks." I look at Sloan and Nikon. "What about the quarantine?"

Nikon frowns. "I think you're safer if you stay here and hunker down for a day or two. If you're positive you didn't come into contact, I'd rather not expose you to anyone else."

She bends and picks up her groceries. "Look, my girlfriend is visiting her parents for two days, so I was planning on eating in and reading in a quiet apartment. If it's all the same to you, I vote for self-isolation."

Nikon nods. "Me too. Give us your cell, and we'll have someone call you later tonight, in the morning, and tomorrow night just to be safe."

I pull a Wendy's receipt and a pen out of my purse and hand it to her. "Please promise not to go out in public until we're sure you're safe."

She frowns. "Oh, I know *I'm* safe. I won't be going out in public, don't worry. If there's a contagion blowing people up, I'm steering clear of everyone until it's taken care of."

"Good plan."

When we exchange places with Jada, and she closes and locks her door, Sloan picks up Manx and Nikon makes contact with us and portals us west across town to the Dufferin safehouse. Since no one is here, I text Garnet. He and Xavier appear inside the front foyer of the spacious four-bedroom home a moment later.

"All right, so you're clearing Jada Neil?"

I check with Sloan, Nikon, and Manx and nod. Then I fill the two of them in on what Jada said about the other cleaners.

Garnet frowns. "We came from the home of Joy Granger. We got there too late. Her husband found her an hour ago and had the horrifying ill fortune to trigger the blood curse."

"Is it a blood curse?"

Garnet shrugs. "I can't say for sure, but it's nothing natural, so it's some kind of spell, hex, or curse."

"Okay, so if Joy is dead and you have her husband in custody, that's one victim contained. The other three names belonged to the other cleaning team, so they shouldn't be affected. That means the only person we're looking for is Chlorine James, and if she's dead, anyone who came into contact with her."

"Agreed." Garnet looks at all of us and shrugs. "We don't all need to traipse around town. Nikon, if you can portal Xavier home, maybe you could help Zxata and Hinderschnind-ziffle finish off connecting with the other team's cleaners. It shouldn't take long if they weren't exposed."

"On it. Will I see you guys later?"

"Yeah." I meet him with a knuckle bump. "Come by tonight for a drink. I'm sure the boys will want to see you alive, and I owe you one."

"Alive?" Even curiosity looks like stern disapproval on Xavier. He scrubs a hand against his trim beard and holds me in his oddly caramel-colored gaze. "Nikon is immortal. Why wouldn't he be alive? Does this have to do with the waterworks at the meeting today?"

"Ye were crying at yer meeting?" Sloan says, touching my arm.

"Tears of joy, hotness. I got a little overwhelmed when I saw Nikon." I turn and face Xavier. "Yes, that's because the trickster, Discord, manipulated me into spearing him through his chest. Immortal or not, I killed him."

Xavier arches a brow, and I'm not sure if he's more surprised or impressed. "Interesting."

I shrug and look at Garnet. "Should we go?"

He's finishing a text and nods. "Zxata and Hinderschnind-ziffle are at the third address on the list. They're waiting for you."

Nikon nods and places a hand on Xavier's shoulder. "Got it. See ya tonight. Oh, and don't forget my chocolate bar for solving the riddle."

"I won't. You earned it."

"The woman's name is Chlorine? When Jada said that, I thought it was a nickname." I shake my head. "What were her parents thinking?" Sloan, Manx, and I follow Garnet up the narrow walk of a rundown rowhouse. "Then she decides to become a house cleaner? It's a little on the nose, don't you think?"

Garnet's lion side lets out a growl that rumbles in my chest. "How about we worry more about the blood curse killing our citizens instead of a poor choice made by the woman's parents decades ago?"

I make a face at Manx, twist my pinched fingers against my lips, and throw away the key.

Garnet proceeds to enter with a decisive knock-and-walk without giving anyone inside a chance to answer. Either he's losing his patience with the entire situation, or he's confident Chlorine James is already dead.

"Sweet mercy," Sloan gasps, halting in front of me.

I peek past the shoulder of his expensive cashmere peacoat and wrinkle my nose at the splattered grossness. "Yep. Too late here."

"That's disgusting. Manx, stay at the door, sham. I don't want ye walkin' in here. At the very least we have clothes and shoes to protect us."

Garnet sighs. "We need to get ahead of this bullshit. You two *poof* into the back bedrooms and see what else we're dealing with. Someone triggered this mess. I don't have to remind you to be careful."

I slide my hand into Sloan's and point toward the back hall. "Maybe there by the bedroom doors. That looks safe enough."

He tightens his fingers around mine, and a moment later we're standing in a dingy hallway looking into a fifties bathroom with an olive-green toilet and tub. "Speaking of disgusting."

"Is the retro decorating not to yer liking?"

I blink up at him and frown. "It's only retro if it's intentional. When it's a run down and original piece of shit, it's not retro. It's just old."

"Noted." He releases my hand and walks to peek into the two bedrooms. "Double bed, disheveled and dirty, but no bodies living or dead."

He steps farther into what looks to be the bigger bedroom and wrinkles his nose. "For a cleaning lady, the house isn't much of an endorsement for her skillset."

Agreed. While he checks out that bedroom, I head into the other. It's another example of the chaos of low expectation living. Sad. I've known people who had next to nothing in life but still had pride in what they did have.

There's no need to live like this.

Drug paraphernalia and the like litters the top of the dresser. "It seems the roommate likes recreational chemical escapes…" I curse as I notice the little clothes piled against the wall between the mattress and the dirty dishes.

I shuffle my feet to scooch through the debris on the floor and pick up a pair of threadbare pajamas. "I think the roommate is a single mom."

Straightening, I take a closer look at the clutter on the dresser. "We're in luck. There's a picture—*Shit!*"

Sloan rounds the corner, wide-eyed. "What? What is it?"

I shove the picture into his hand and race back up the hall. "We need to go. Garnet! I know where the infected roommate is."

Sloan catches me at the end of the hall and *poofs* me to the front door.

Garnet meets us in the now-crowded front hall. "Who? Where are we going?"

Sloan already has Manx in his arms and looks as sick as I feel. He hands Garnet the picture and grabs my arm. "It's the woman who died in the shelter this afternoon. We left her with Dora and Anyx."

Sloan portals us to the back area of Dora's soup kitchen and I run to look into the little intake office where we left Imari's mother over three hours ago. "Dora!" I shout, running toward the front of the building. "Dora! Where are you?"

"I'm here, baby," she says while rushing in from the servery. "What is it?"

I run straight into her and hug her. At well over six feet tall without her stiletto boots, she towers over me but bends to hug me back. "Thank goodness. Where's the dead woman?"

She straightens and looks over my shoulder at Garnet. "Your man arranged for her to be taken to the Guild morgue. We were curious about what happened."

"Oh, shit." I grab Sloan and Garnet and nod. "Hurry. It's been hours. She's gonna be ready to blow."

Garnet flashes us into a long hallway with glossy tile floors and plain blue-gray walls. "Stay here." He turns and pushes through one half of a set of swinging doors.

I run my hand over my forehead. "This is bad."

"We don't know that yet."

I blink up at him. "I feel it."

My shield starts to tingle, and I feel a pull of something drawing me up the hall. "Something's wrong."

I jog up the hallway, the opposite way from the doors Garnet went through. My instinct tells me whatever is about to happen it's this way.

Following the bizarre Fianna bat signal, I find two people in a medical room. The guy is examining Imari's mother, and the woman is about to join in.

"Help me roll her," the guy says.

The wet, gloopy noise her body makes has my shield flaring wildly.

"No. Sloan, get them out." I race to kick the doorstop out of the way and yank the thing closed. It has a slow mechanical close, and I screech and pull with everything I've got.

Sloan *poofs* in, grabs the two people, and *poofs* them out of the room.

The door clicks shut as the woman explodes.

I turn my head and wince. The sound is bad enough. I don't need the visual. Well, more of one. Her insides plaster the fluorescent lights, the table, and the floor.

"Are you two all right?" I move in to look them over. "You didn't get any on you? You're good?"

Anyx and Garnet run down the hall, and I lean back to use the wall to prop me up. "Everyone was out before she detonated."

"Well done, Lady Druid."

I hang my head and draw an unsteady breath. "It's too early for that. There still might be one person contaminated."

"Who?"

"Her little girl."

"Do you know where she is?"

I nod as tears burn in my eyes. "At my brother's house...with my family."

CHAPTER NINE

"How do I tell him?" I look from Sloan to Garnet and play with the long ebony tuft of Manx's ear. "Have I infected them by bringing her here? Have I killed my family?"

"No, *a ghra*. Ye haven't. Even if the woman wasn't the best mother, I don't think she'd let her little girl come in contact with the kind of gore we found in their apartment. Imari is fine. I know it. Besides, yer shield never tingled a warning about takin' her to Aiden's."

I draw a steadying breath. Either he's getting much better at lying, or he truly believes that.

I choose to believe the latter.

Garnet squeezes my shoulder. "If she's healthy and well after this many hours, I'm sure Sloan's right. There's nothing to worry about. You saw a little girl in trouble, and you paid her kindness in a life that hasn't been kind. Don't panic."

I swallow and knock on the door. Aiden answers a moment later and smiles. "Hey guys, come in. Mr. Grant, it's nice to see you again. Welcome."

We file inside, and I take off my boots and hug my brother.

When I pull back, Aiden's smile falters. "What is it, baby girl? What's wrong?"

I squeeze his hand and, in a whisper, fill him in on the highlights of our afternoon and how we ended up back here.

"No. She hasn't shown any sign of being sick. I'm with Garnet and Sloan on this. If something horrible invaded my home, I'd breathe my last breath before I let it touch my kids. Besides, Imari said she had a sleepover last night with her friend in the building."

Sloan exhales a long breath. "She likely wasn't even in the apartment, Fi."

Aiden nods. "It also explains why she took her to the soup kitchen. She was probably trying to figure out how to handle things."

I hug my brother again and blink fast. "I'm so sorry."

"Enough. Come in. Let me pour you a tall glass of get over it. Oh, and I'll get you a straw, so you can suck it up."

I laugh and wipe my eyes. "Okay, that was a good one."

"Everything okay out here?" Kinu comes out of the bathroom with a troop of freshly bathed monkeys. "Everyone into jammies, and we'll have a snack and a story before bed."

The kids squeal and run down the hall in their cute little towels with animal heads and ears. Meggie is a duck. Imari is a bear. Jackson is a frog.

"Everything is fine, babe." Aiden winks at me and gives me a subtle head shake. "Mr. Grant wanted to check on Imari. He runs the show for the empowered citizens of the city."

Kinu looks down at herself all splashed and wilted from her time in the bathroom, then at the toys strewn around the room. "Of course. I'm sorry. The day got away on us."

"Don't apologize. You did us a great favor by taking Imari into your home while we figured out what happened."

"And you know now?"

Garnet dips his chin. "Sadly, yes. It seems the poor thing has had a bit of a rough start. With her mother gone, we'll have to—"

"You're like me," Imari says, smiling up at him from behind Kinu's leg. She tilts her head to the side and her golden-brown ringlets hanging against her borrowed Paw Patrol top. "You have an animal inside you too."

Garnet kneels to meet Imari eye-to-eye, and his breath catches in a gasp. I've always loved to see a man flip into daddy mode, but it's especially beautiful because I know about Garnet's loss and felt how deeply it devastated him. "Yes, little one, I do. How did you know that?"

The Paw Patrol pj's she's wearing are big on her, the cuffs of the sleeves and pant legs rolled up. Jackson is a strapping, healthy four. She's a tiny, undersized six.

Imari reaches out with her hand and touches Garnet's forehead with a pointed finger. "He's right here."

"Well, isn't that interesting."

I smile. "She sensed Bruin too. She's a very special girl."

I feel the magic of his animal side ascend, and his eyes flip from purple to gold. He lets out a long, contented purr.

"Garnet? Everything okay?" I take a step closer, trying to read his body language to gauge if I should be worried.

"Everything is as it's meant, Lady Druid," he says, his voice that of his lion, not the man. "Come, angel. Thank the nice people for your play day. It's time to go."

Imari smiles. "Your animal is very happy."

"Thunderstruck is probably a better word," he says to no one in particular. Rising to his feet, he picks her up and wraps her in his arms. "Are you ready?"

She nods. "My bear is happy too. Can I play with Jackson and Meggie again?"

He looks at Aiden and Kinu and reads their cues. "Of course, angel. Another day, but very soon."

Aiden hustles off and comes back with a bag and Imari's jacket. "We walked to the dollar store after dinner and picked up a few things for fun. These were Imari's picks."

Garnet accepts the bag and jacket but isn't paying attention. His gaze is locked on the girl in his arms, and that rolling purr is still rumbling.

"Garnet? Is everything all right?" I ask.

"It is. Trust me. The universe has not only put her in my path but has put me in hers. Don't worry about a thing." He straightens and looks at everyone, his eyes still a warm gold. "Goodnight, folks."

When he flashes out, I blink at the others. "Does anyone have any idea what that was about?"

"They bonded," Sloan says. "It's similar to what Moon Called mates experience, but can happen with others. His lion claimed Imari as his cub. She is his to love and protect now. She's part of his pride."

"That quickly?" Kinu says. "What about if she has a father or other family? You can't just say 'this child is mine' and take her."

Sloan shakes his head. "We saw where that little angel has been living, and the conditions were deplorable. As Garnet says, all is as it's meant. If she has other family, he'll make it work, but she's his now."

My mind trips over that. The romantic in me loves the idea of a happily ever after for all. I pull out my phone to text Myra.

Congratulations.

For what?

You'll see.

With a grin, I hold out my hand. "Let's call that a day."

"Agreed. And what a day it's been."

It's six-thirty by the time Sloan *poofs* Manx and me into the back hall. He unbuckles Manx's harness, and the lynx shakes like a dog fresh out of the lake. "How was your first day in the streets of the city?"

"Tiring," Manx says. "If you need me, I'll be on the basement couch closin' my eyes."

I'd like to stretch my legs, Red. If yer home for a bit.

"Consider me turned in for the night, buddy. Time for you to get out and have some fun of your own." I release my bear from his home in the center of my chest and smile as he creates a breeze to kiss my cheek. "I love you too. Enjoy."

I'll take a quick spin around the perimeter before I go.

"Sounds good. Keep an eye out for any evil foxes with glowing eyes."

"Will do."

The moment I hang up my coat and finish unbuckling my boots, I sigh. *"Poof* me upstairs, will you, hotness? I want out of these jeans. Do you think, after containing a vicious plague of a blood curse and finding my friends a baby to raise and saving countless lives in the process, we deserve a little private time out?"

Sloan chuckles. "I do, but you invited Nikon over for a drink, and I have a few things to take care of."

Well, poop.

"Okay, Plan B. I change into comfy clothes, and we take a page out of Manx's book and sneak a twenty-minute cat nap before we go again."

"Sounds perfect."

"Then, after drinks with Nikon, and after you do your 'few irons in the fire private business stuff,' we get undressed and shut out the world."

"Deal."

It's eight-thirty when the back door opens, and Sloan comes inside with Nikon. "I found this one loiterin' on the back deck." Sloan flashes me a wink.

Nikon chuckles and takes off his coat and boots. "Yep. I was practicing my Peeping Tom act, but you let me down. Nothing sexy and inappropriate at all."

"The night's young." I join them in the hallway. "FYI, you're a couple of drinks behind the rest of us. You, of course, have the option to shotgun and catch up, or pace yourselves and point and laugh until the scales balance."

Nikon laughs. "Is that a real question? Door number one, Monte. Load that gun."

Sloan sniffs the air and grins. "Are we goin' all out?"

"Hells yeah. Why not?"

"It's Wednesday."

I snort. "Oh, my love. Shake off the weight of adulting once in a while and let your Irish shine through. I have a chili-chicken nacho bake in the oven, and the rest of the party platters are on the dining room table. We're in this…which you would've known if you were here instead of off doing your private business things."

Sloan frowns. "Are ye still sore at me, then?"

I sigh and take another swig of the swamp-mix Calum and Kevin came up with. The first two glasses were tough to get down, but I won that battle, and it's clear sailing now. "No. I'm not sore. That came out bitchier than I meant. I'm a little buzzed and shouldn't have said it like that."

He hugs me and slides an icy hand under the hem of my shirt and up my back.

"Ack, no!" I screech and push him away as he bursts out laughing.

"It's not that cold."

"Yeah, let's hear you say that when I stick my hand down your pants after being outside."

Nikon snorts. "Guys don't argue about cold hands if someone grabs our junk. Any contact is welcome contact."

"True story," Emmet agrees while jogging down the stairs. "Greek. Good to see you, my man. Welcome back to the land of the living."

Calum, Kevin, and Dillan come out of the dining room stuffing their faces.

"Greek!" Dillan clasps palms and pulls him in chest-to-chest to slap his back. "Good to see you."

The next incoming affection is Kevin and Calum. After another round of hugs, everyone breaks it up and heads into the dining room to get Nikon started on his catch-up.

Sloan stays with me in the kitchen and takes the oven mitts away from me. "Friends don't let friends bake drunk."

"I've heard that."

He peeks into the oven at the cheesy-chili goodness. "How long until this is ready?"

"Fifteen minutes. Why? Are you hungry? It's going to have to sit for a little before we eat it. Last time, Dillan burned the top of his mouth so bad he complained for a week. There's more food set out if you're starving."

"Nope. It's not that. I was chattin' with a man over the fence as I came in. There's an open house next door if yer curious. Ye mentioned when we popped in there last week that ye hadn't seen some of Mark's and Janine's renovations, and I thought ye might like to snoop."

I grin and clasp my hands over my heart. "You get me so well. Hells, yes. I want to snoop."

I set a timer on my phone and grab my black leather bomber jacket. "Open house at Mark's and Janine's. Anyone feeling nosy?"

"Can we take our drinks?" Dillan asks.

"Sure. Didn't you know? November..." I check my phone, "twenty-first is Toronto Mardi Gras night. Red solo cups to go."

"Sweet."

"Will there be topless women with beads?"

"Will Janine be there?"

Sloan frowns. "I don't believe so."

"You're outta luck, Emmet."

The four of them pile out of the dining room a moment later, drinks in hand.

They sweep Nikon up in the scramble, and I get out of the way so the boys can grab their boots. "Who are Mark and Janine, and where are we going?"

"Our mundane neighbors next door," I say.

"The nutter that shot Manx in the ass," Emmet adds.

Nikon steps into his boots and leans down to snap the badass silver buckles. "How is your ass anyway, puss?"

Manx is sitting like a majestic statue at the front door waiting to leave. "Fine. Thank you. How are you feeling?"

I didn't realize Manx would want to do a house walk-through, but hey, it's a party, and he's part of this crazy crew now. Sloan relays Manx's response to Nikon on the way out the door.

"Never better. Thanks for asking."

A blistering wind hits us the moment we step off the porch, and I turn, pull up the collar of my coat, and walk backward. I grab Sloan's arm with my free hand and lift my cup with the other. "Don't let me fall."

Sloan laughs. "Then don't walk backward drunk in the dark across an uneven lawn."

"I'd rather go down and get a wet ass than smacked in the face with that Arctic wind."

"The wind's coming from the south off Lake Ontario, not the Arctic."

I make a face. "You're so literal it hurts my brain."

He chuckles. "You're so mercurial it hurts mine."

"Point to you."

"Check it," Dillan says.

I tense, afraid to see a pair of glowing amber eyes in the darkness, but D is pointing at a black SUV parked up the road in front of the rental house. "Since when do the renters in the party palace drive anything that's not a fifteen-year-old compact with body primer?"

"Party palace?" Sloan repeats.

"Yeah, the owner lives in China and rents it out to university kids. There are usually four to six frat boys living there full-time and all their friends part-time. In the summer, their good times spill out onto the street. That's when Da gets his groove on."

Dillan laughs. "The street owners call him The Warden."

I smile. "Him shutting down the party palace and laying out the ground rules of how things are gonna be is kinda a seasonal ritual the whole street gets a kick out of."

"I can hardly wait to see that."

"Assuming you make the cut," Emmet says.

"You know what they say about assuming..." Dillan says, trailing off expectantly.

Sloan's smile fades, and he looks at me. I keep a straight face for all of two seconds before I crack up and push him toward the porch. "You're fine. They're screwing with you."

He holds my arm as they start up the steps to access the front porch. When we have a bit of privacy, he draws a deep breath. "Now's the time to tell me if you don't see this going forward the same way as I do, Fi. Seriously. Don't let me be the only one all-in."

I wrap my arms around him and kiss him under the ambient gold light of the porch. "You're not the only one all-in, broody. I've never been so stupidly happy with any guy."

"There was that girl a couple of years ago," Dillan says.

"What was her name again?" Calum asks. "Brianne, Breanna, Bree..."

"Would you guys shut up and go inside? Geez. Piss and vinegar tonight, I swear." I meet the bewilderment on Sloan's face and chuckle. "Why do you listen to them? I've never had a girl-friend. Not my thing. It's all you. Hands down."

"Holy shit," Dillan says. "Fi, check it."

I grab Sloan's arm, tugging him up the steps and inside. "Holy shit what, dude—oh!"

"Right?"

The place is empty—nothing but gleaming hardwood floors and hollow spaces.

"They already moved out?"

A guy in slacks and collared shirt strides in to greet us. His pointy-toed shoes make a confident *clack* on the floor, and he extends his hand. "Elliot Laurent, welcome."

He shakes everyone's hands. If he's surprised that we all blew in with drinks in our hands, he hides it well.

"Yes. To restate the obvious, the house is empty. The sellers found something they loved, and it was a time-sensitive offer. It was a bit of a rush, but they relocated and are happily settling into their new home."

"Where did they end up?" Kevin asks.

"Milton. I believe they were both pleased at the reduced commute and the rural setting."

Calum makes a face. "To each their own. A toast to Janine and Mark in Milton."

There's a rowdy repeat of Calum's toast, then we spread out and explore.

I'm still thinking about Milton when I decide it was a smart move for them. "Mark works in Mississauga, so good for him."

"Good luck to Mark." Emmet raises his cup.

Everyone raises their cups, and we drink to that.

"Can I get someone to sign a registry sheet, please?"

Sloan and I go to the kitchen while the others fan out.

I grab the pen off the counter and slide closer to the clipboard with the sheet to fill out. "Have you had many people through? We use the laneway at the back to come and go. We sometimes miss what's happening out front."

"A few. They accepted a tentative offer. I expect that will firm up in the next day or two. Are you thinking of putting in an offer or are you curious?"

"We live next door. Just curious. Buying in this market is beyond the budget." Sadly. I finished my part of the Brendan life insurance process with Mr. Mantle and even with all that plus money paid out by the TPD and the Widows and Orphans Fund, it wasn't enough.

He smiles and takes the clipboard back, reading through my answers. "Well, enjoy your look around, Jane."

I hide my smile behind my cup and take a long sip of liquid ambrosia. "Thank you, Elliot. Come, Richard, let's catch up with the others and look around."

Sloan flashes me a scowl but doesn't blow our cover.

We meet the guys in the upstairs master bedroom, and I let out a low whistle. "Dayam. Mark and Janine had it goin' on up here."

The overall feel of the house is much more modern and polished than ours, but the building's architecture holds the same basic bones. Ten-inch walnut baseboards, crown moldings, and trim lead the eye through the room.

"What do you think?" Sloan steps into the walk-in closet.

"I love all the wood, but it's too dark with rich colors. The place would look way better if the walls and accents were in warm ivory or a buttercream."

"Mmmm buttercream," Emmet says in passing.

"My sentiments exactly, Fi," Kevin says behind me. "If it were all original, then yeah, the navy and wine walls would work, but they've already updated the finishes, so update the décor too."

"Preach." I wander around and look out upon our street from

this perspective. Funny. It's the same, yet different. Trippy. "I wish Aiden and Kinu could've figured out a way to snatch this place up."

Emmet snorts. "Sorry, I left my one-point-six-million in my other pants."

Dillan snorts. "No shit. The only downtown natives that grow up and can afford to stay are the ones who inherit."

"Or are destined to rent forever." Kevin's voice echoes against the hard surfaces of the upstairs bathroom. When he comes out, he points inside. "They have a jet tub. You guys should get a jet tub."

Manx runs by, slapping his massive paws on the floor like he's a kitten. He gets to the far end of the room, spreads his legs, and slides in a slow spin before booking it back down the hall.

"Wow, Manx loves house hunting," I say.

Sloan chuckles while watching his boy prance and play. "He sure does."

The timer on my phone goes off, and I pull it out to turn it off. "Chili bake is ready. Gotta go."

Sloan shakes his head. "I'll go turn off the oven. Do you want it to cool on the counter?"

"On the stovetop with a sheet of foil over it."

"Got it. Continue your tour, Jane."

"Thanks, Richard."

Sloan *poofs* away, and Calum and Emmet start laughing. "Seriously? You're going with Dick and Jane?"

I shrug. "You know real estate people. They always call you back and are like, 'Are you ready to buy? How about now? How about now?' Hard pass."

"So, what number did you give him?" Calum asks.

"416-468-2223"

Dillan pulls out his phone and tracks the number. "Four-one-six-hot-babe. *Noice.*"

"Well played, sista." Emmet meets me for a high-five.

Calum gestures at the hallway. "Well, Jane. Shall we take a tour of the basement?"

Sloan finds the five of us in the basement standing in awe, admiring the pool table. "That is a gorgeous piece of furniture," he says.

"And they up and left it behind." I sigh, shaking my head. "No way in hell I'd leave her here."

Dillan bends at the waist, laying his upper body across the sage green felt, and strokes her surface. "I'm in love."

I don't blame him. I am too.

"Maybe they didn't want the hassle of taking it apart and transporting the slate to their new house?" Calum suggests.

"Or they didn't have room in their new house?" Kevin adds. "If they want babies, maybe this baby no longer fits into their lives."

"Don't listen, baby." Dillan pets her felt. "Mommy and Daddy might not love you, but we do. Irish. You can portal groups of people. Can you portal large pieces of furniture? Not far. Say, maybe two hundred feet that way."

Sloan grins. "I can, but I won't. Ye can't steal someone's pool table, Dillan."

"No, *I* can't, but you can. Didn't we just go over that?"

Emmet strides over, pushes his finger into Sloan's arm, and holds it there.

"What's this?" Sloan asks, looking confused.

I chuckle. "Peer pressure."

"Och, well, the answer is still no."

"You suck, Irish," Dillan snaps. "They'd never pin it on us. You're like the perfect crime waiting to happen."

Sloan makes a face. "Is that a compliment?"

I slide an arm around Sloan's hips and take another drink. "My Richard uses his superpowers for good, not evil."

"Your Richard is a Dick," Dillan pouts.

When the rowdies burst into laughter, I point at the stairs. "Okay, gather the lynx. We're heading home for the Greek's 'Glad you're not dead' party."

Dillan gets up and gives Sloan the finger. "The party would be better if we had a pool table. Just sayin'."

CHAPTER TEN

The next morning is rough. There might be something to Sloan's concern about drinking on a Wednesday night. Not that he has an ounce of sympathy for any of us—he doesn't. He's sadistic that way.

"You're in far too good a mood." I take two pain relievers and chug a glass of water. "What's that stupid grin for?"

Sloan is lying across my bed—which he made to military specs— his eyes bright and his smile sexy. So annoying. Even his ripped jeans and faded t-shirt are a rich man's attempt at casual grunge. He's so damned designer-chic. "I'm thankful for this moment in my life."

I raise my fingers to my lips. "Sorry, I barfed a little in my mouth there. Don't take it personally."

He laughs, gets up, and grabs his wallet off my dresser. "How about a little healin' touch before I go?"

"Yes, please. Do you have to go? I have a couple of hours before Myra expects me for my shift at the bookstore. We could spend an hour in the grove."

"It's temptin', but I have an appointment at eleven."

I draw a deep breath and remember all my protestations

about remaining independent and focused on establishing my life as a druid. Do I have the right to feel slighted because he wants the same thing? Nope.

Suck it up, buttercup.

"How are your life plans going?"

"Things are takin' shape." He strides across my bedroom floor, skirting around the snoring bear, and meets me by the door. "Close yer eyes."

"Are you giving me a present?"

"Of sorts."

I do as I'm told and give him the reins. He cups my jaw in his hands, and his healing touch activates. The heavy fog, nausea, and body aches ease and are gone.

When I open my eyes, he's there smiling. "Better?"

"Much. Thank you."

He kisses the tip of my nose and winks. "Drink more water before you go into the emporium. I'll see ye later."

"'Kay. Be good."

He chuckles. "What exactly do you think I'm up to?"

"How would I know? I'm minding my business like a support-ive, non-pushy, independent girlfriend."

"All right. I promise I'll try to be good. Why don't you take Manx into the grove and have a soak in the hot spring?"

I smile. "It would be more fun in the hot spring with you, but maybe."

———

An hour after Sloan left me to my own devices, I park in my usual spot on Queen Street and head into Myra's Mystical Empo-rium. It used to freak me out that someone might see me come in or wonder where I'm going, but after almost five months of coming here, I'm over it.

The store is spelled so only empowered folks know about it, and only those who need something we sell can find it.

The bell chimes over my head as I bolt through the entrance. I'm brisk-walking like an athlete, so excited to find out about Imari. "Myra. Where are you?"

"In here, duck."

I follow Myra's call into the lounge area where she and Imari have amassed a pile of books on one of the leather sofas under the branches of her home tree.

"Hi, guys. How's things?"

"My mommy is with the faeries now." Imari looks up at me with big, sad eyes. "She got too sick, and now she's behind the veil with the goddess."

I kneel on the area rug and squeeze her knees. "I'm sorry, baby girl. I'm sure you miss her very much."

She nods. "Garnet says I can have a cookie with him and talk about Mommy whenever I'm sad."

"Yum, that sounds nice. My mommy went to live with the faeries when I was your age. I was sad too. But you'll get less sad, I swear."

"Pinky-swear?"

I hold up my hand and hook pinky fingers with her. "Pinky-swear."

That seems to help her. "Myra says I don't have to be sad because Mommy can keep Grant company until we go behind the veil. Then we'll all play together."

"Myra's a smart lady. She and Garnet will take really good care of you."

"Can your bear come out? My bear wants to see him."

I blink and look at Myra for her take on that. I don't release Bruin at the store, but the lounge area is open and big enough.

Myra nods. "That's a fun idea. Yes, let's read a story to Bruin. Would your bear like that?"

"My bear isn't happy. We're tired."

I release Bruin, and he materializes on the area rug in front of the sofa seating area. He lays down, and I know he's trying to make himself seem less massive.

It's sweet. It doesn't work, but it's sweet.

"Imari, this is Bruin, my bear."

Imari slides off the sofa and smiles up at my massive grizzly. "When my bear gets sad and sleepy, Mommy lets me snuggle her bear."

"You want to snuggle with Bruin?" The tension in Myra's voice is unnecessary, but I understand where it's coming from.

"It's okay. He'd never hurt a child. Meg and Jackson adore him."

Myra nods and watches Imari get down on the rug.

Are you okay with this, buddy?

Och, of course. The little cub is mournin' her mama bear. I can stand in fer a bit.

When Bruin rolls his heaping body onto his side, Imari gets down on all fours and climbs under his front paw, burrowing into his fur. "I'm sleepy, Bear."

I squeeze Myra's wrist when she lets out a quiet whimper of worry. "It's okay. Let them rest. Bruin can tell me if they need anything."

Myra looks from the rug to me and back to them. "Are you okay if Fiona and I go into the bookstore, angel?"

Imari doesn't answer because she's already asleep.

The two of us make our way to the front of the store, and I set down my bag and hang up my coat. "So, monumental life shift for you last night. Congrats. How are you and Garnet?"

Myra blinks at me and runs a hand through her electric blue hair. "You mean, how are we handling the most perfect thing that could've ever happened to us? Honestly, we're scared as hell."

"Why? You guys are going to rock this."

She rounds the counter and pulls out the leather ledger she uses to track regular customers. "Not about being parents—we're thrilled about that. I think after being a happy family once before, we're scared of losing it again, you know? What if she has kin somewhere that want her? A father? An alpha? What if something happens and she's taken away?"

"Does Garnet think that will happen? He seemed pretty possessive about keeping her last night when he saw her."

"That's Moon Called bonding for you. It's as instant as it is irreversible. I'm sure he wished he could've broken that hold over the past couple of decades. It was emotionally difficult for us to be estranged—but it was physically hard for him. A base animal isn't always as logical as the man."

I knew that too.

You learn a lot when you clear someone of their pain.

"Nothing bad will happen. I feel it. I know the three of you are a lock."

Myra smiles. "Okay. Me too."

"Good, now, change in subject. What books do you have or how do I find out about Discord? It's been a week since he reared his foxy little head, but he told me the game would go until Yule, so we have another three weeks."

Myra goes to her computer and starts searching. "All right, grab a pen. I'll give you the reference codes."

I'm an hour into my research when my phone buzzes in my pocket. I pull it out. It's an Ireland exchange, but I don't recognize the number.

"Hello?"

"Fiona, it's Wallace Mackenzie calling."

"Oh, hi Wallace." I'm unsure why Sloan's father would call

me...unless. "Is something wrong? Did something happen to Sloan?"

"I wouldn't know. Isn't he there with you?"

I press my hand to my chest. "Yes, sorry. I worried there for a sec. What can I do for you?"

"Tell her she's done quite enough," Janet hisses in the background.

The phone muffles for a moment, and I have no doubt Wallace is trying to hush her. "Apologies, Fiona. I forgot to turn down the telly before I called."

Right. "Not a problem. Is everything all right?"

"No, actually, everything is not all right." Wallace has always spoken to me with a certain amount of formality, but now, his voice is more terse than usual. "We had an upsetting call from our family solicitor this afternoon and were informed Sloan made changes to the beneficiary of his estate."

Hubba-wha? "Sorry. I'm not following. What does that have to do with me?"

Cue another round of Janet having an Irish hissy fit in the background.

"It has everything to do with you, Fiona, since he's named you as the recipient of his trusts."

My mind blanks out on that. "This is the first I've heard of this. Sloan and I don't talk about money. Honestly, I don't want to talk about his money. It doesn't interest me in the slightest."

Janet gets colorful in the background on that one, but I try not to listen. It's hurtful, and if I ever expect to have any kind of relationship with these people, I don't want to hear this.

"I'm sorry, Wallace. I don't know a thing about this. If you and Janet are upset, you should speak to Sloan. He is, after all, independent and handles his affairs."

"I'm more than a little disappointed to hear ye say that. After witnessing the honor of yer grandparents and yer da fer over fifty years, I had hoped ye held their values close. It appears I was mistaken."

I close the book in my lap and shift to the edge of my seat. "I'm sorry you feel that way, Wallace. I respect you and everything you've done for me, but don't think for a moment I'll take your backhanded slights the way Sloan does.

"I'm sorry you're pissed, but I told you the truth. Sloan and I don't discuss his private affairs. If he made changes, they had nothing to do with anything I said or did to prompt him. I've been trying to smooth the hurt he feels toward you two so you can patch things up.

"Because yes, I do carry the same values as Da and my grandparents. I believe in honor and family and extending a kind hand to those around me. I also share their outlook on money. I have what I need so therefore I am rich.

"The fact that your bank account and Sloan's bank account have more zeroes than mine doesn't even register. Zero fucks given. If you'd taken ten minutes to get to know me, you'd know that. Consider that bridge burned. Goodbye, Wallace." I end the call and stare at the screen while shaking.

"Well said, duck." Myra's standing at the counter and frowning. "That was the in-laws, I take it."

I'm so pissed…I. Can't. Even.

I stand and look around. "I need air."

"Then off you go. Maybe you can stab someone on the way home. That would make you feel better."

"Don't tempt me." Stomping over to my things, I grab my coat and bag. After stuffing my purse and a couple of the books I found interesting into my bookbag, I sling it over my shoulder and grab my keys. Bruin's rumbling snore is going strong in the back. "Let them sleep. He can meet me at home later when naptime is over."

"I'll tell him. Take care, hon. Call me if you need me."

"I will. Love you."

"Ditto. Right back at you."

Changed the recipient of his trusts? What the hell does that mean? I'm halfway to my Hellcat when I feel the tingle of eyes on me. I'm not sure what instinct it is that tells a person someone is watching you, but we all have it. I had it before I became a druid and it's one of those things that no one should ignore—let alone a woman alone in the streets of a busy city.

Stopping in my tracks, I scan my surroundings.

Discord appeared to me as a fox twice, but from what I've been reading, it's not a form like the Moon Called. He's more like a doppelgänger. The five primary characteristics to describe him were: fundamentally ambiguous, a deceiver, a shapeshifter, an inverter of situations, and a messenger.

It's been a slam-dunk so far.

The creepy thing is, he could be any one of twenty people on the street passing by.

He could be the pigeon on the sidewalk.

"Okay, now I'm just freaking myself out."

"Is something wrong, Miss Cumhaill?"

I spin and raise my hands into a defensive position, stepping back from a clean-cut, military-type in a suit. There's nothing overtly alarming about the man's appearance. I simply sense his coiled strength ready to spring.

"No problem. If you could take a few steps back and walk away, we'll be all good."

"I'm afraid I can't do that. I need you to come with me."

When he moves forward, I match his movement. *Feline Finesse.* "Fool me once, shame on you. I know who you are now. I won't fall for your tricks again, asshole."

Breathing deep, I grasp the ambient magic from all around me and ready to make my escape.

When he steps in to cut off my access line to my truck, I take a couple of quick steps and vault over him, landing in a crouch and jogging to my vehicle.

Yes, it's broad daylight, but a girl who can do an aerial isn't technically going to tip onlookers off to magic. Maybe I'm a gymnast or a circus freak.

I round my bumper ramming my thumb into the unlock button on my fob and swing my door open as quickly as I can.

Rough hands grab my elbow and yank me back.

With my spell still buzzing in my cells, I evade the man's attempt to secure his hold, spin, and knee him square in the crotch. "Don't threaten me. Enough blood's been shed already. I'm not playing your twisted game."

Jumping into the driver's seat, I get the keys in the ignition and crank it. My engine roars to life. Pulling my shifter into gear, I put my foot on the gas and— "Dammit!"

I slam on the brakes, and my tires squeal on the asphalt.

One black SUV cuts off my front end and another blocks me from behind.

What the hell?

A split-second later my door window shatters, and I'm shot with the metal forks of a taser.

Twelve hundred volts light me up.

My body goes stiff.

My mind fritzes.

The world goes dark.

"You chose to make this difficult," the military guy grunts.

I'm facing down on the pavement with my hands cuffed against my ass and the damp cold of the city street making me shiver. "What do you want?"

"Previously stated," the guy with the sore balls snaps. "I need you to come with me."

I shake my head, but it does little to clear the cobwebs.

Even with my gray matter fried, I'm getting the distinct impression these people have nothing to do with Discord and his mindfuck game of murder and mayhem.

They're far too anal and reserved to be empowered.

They are law enforcement.

"I know my rights. State who you are and why you're detaining me right now, or I'll shove an unlawful detainment case so far up your ass it'll come out your previously broken nose."

The guy who recently had his knackers re-adjusted yanks me off the pavement and rams his face up in my grille. "Fiona Cumhaill, I am Officer Hiller of the OPP major crimes unit, and this is Catherine Lent of the SIU. You are being detained in connection with, but not limited to, several cross-jurisdictional major crimes cases, including murder and organized crime. Keep making this difficult, and I'll add assaulting an officer."

Oh, crud. "That last one will never stick. You didn't identify yourself, and I feared for my life."

A female officer opens the door to one of the black SUVs and shoves me against the side of the truck. With the slice of a utility knife through the canvas strap, she relieves me of my bookbag and shoves me into the vehicle.

"Hey. That's my favorite bag." So rude. Closing my eyes, I let my throbbing head fall back on the cushioned rest and focus. *Bruin? Can you hear me, buddy? Are you awake?*

Nothing comes back to me. I'm not sure if that's because he's still lost in dreamland or because my hamster is still convulsing in my skull.

Either way, backup isn't coming.

CHAPTER ELEVEN

Ontario runs with four unique branches of law enforcement. We have the Royal Canadian Mounted Police—our Mounties—who are best known for their red coats, riding on horseback, and standing guard at the Parliament buildings. They have national, federal, provincial, and municipal policing mandates.

Then we have the Ontario Provincial Police, which handles province-wide issues like highways, waterways, rural communities, and cross-jurisdictional problems—of which, apparently, I am one.

Our municipal and regional police force is where Da and my brothers fall into line. They're part of the policing forces that handle cities and towns.

Then there's the SIU. The Special Investigations Unit is a civilian-run law enforcement agency that holds jurisdiction over municipal, regional, and provincial police officers and investigates police-involved incidents for potential misconduct.

The fact that they're involved at all has my panic rising.

Is this about my family or me?

I stare out the window as we make our way through the

streets. Midday on a Thursday, my world is active, everyone going about their business. Somewhere out there, my brothers are doing the same thing these officers are doing—detaining and arresting people they believe are involved in illegal or dangerous activity.

Except, I'm innocent. Innocent, I tell you!

I know the drill. Once they get me settled in an interrogation room, we'll have a chat, and I'll find out what this is about. Depending on who and what they're after, I'll figure out what I say.

As many times as I've ridden in police cars, this is my first time in a tactical truck and my first time in custody. I've been handcuffed a million times, so that's nothing new.

Still, Officer Hiller tightened them more than my brothers did when we were kids and practiced a big arrest.

Tracking our progress through the city, I wonder where they'll take me. If this is more about Da or one of my brothers, likely the SIU headquarters in Mississauga. If it's more about me, I'm guessing an OPP detachment.

That might be faulty logic, but it's a start.

A right turn onto Keele sets us northbound. That tells me nothing. The 401 would be how they get to either station for either law enforcement branch.

Catherine Lent looks back at me a couple of times during the trip, but otherwise, they leave me to my thoughts. As she studies me, I scrutinize her right back. Retired law enforcement as well as forensic investigators and civilian advocates make up the SIU. Catherine handles herself like a woman with experience within the law enforcement sector.

When we pull out of traffic and into a parking lot, I'm relieved to be at an OPP detachment. The idea that they were going after one of my brothers or my father is unacceptable.

Let them come after me.

Catherine Lent opens my door and steps back for me to get

out of the truck. There's no sense being difficult. They're doing their job like anyone else. The sooner I get inside and figure out what the hell is happening, the sooner I'll be done and able to go home.

With a hand clutched around my elbow, I'm marched inside and led through the bullpen area of cubicles to a meeting room in the back. In truth, it's the same painted box setup that the local PD uses for interrogation.

There's no jazzing up an interrogation room. This one is a ten-by-ten square with wainscoting walls, blue on the bottom, gray on the top, with a rectangular table and three chairs.

"Take a seat." Hiller points at the single chair side of the table.

"Take off the cuffs." I turn to give them my back. "I've been compliant since you identified yourselves and you've secured me in the interrogation room. This is a detainment, not an arrest. Until it escalates to an arrest or I give you just cause to believe I will hurt you or myself, you have no right to keep cuffs on me."

Hiller arches a brow at Lent, and the woman unlocks my wrists.

Rubbing the red flesh, I sit and rest my arms on the table. "Now. What's this about?"

"You tell us," Hiller says. "We've been watching you and your family for months. Why don't you tell us how things got to where you are now?"

I roll my eyes. "Seriously? Everyone in my life is on the job. Do you not think I've been schooled on the protocols of leading a suspect during interrogation? Let's skip forward to why we're here."

"You think you're pretty smart, don't you?"

"I'm honestly not being a smartass. I want to hear what you have to say and clear up whatever this is. Just tell me. I'm not going to crack and spill a tale of things that didn't happen. Honest and direct will be your best approach."

"This is the part where you learn how little you know."

I shake my head. "No. This is the part where the law states the detainee is promptly informed of the alleged complaints against her."

Hiller scrubs a hand over the dark stubble of a square jaw. "Stay there. I'll get the files."

The atmosphere in an interrogation room might set some people on edge, but for me, it's home-sweet-home. Every time I needed to talk privately with Da when he was at work, he took me into an interrogation room. We had many heartfelt father-daughter chats in rooms like this.

Officer Hiller steps out, and Catherine Lent stays to babysit. She drops my bag inside the door, crosses her arms, and proceeds to hold up the wall. Having her stare at me doesn't bother me. Whatevs.

She's not the first person to try to figure me out.

Like the saying goes: I am who I am, and that's all I'll ever be.

"I can't decide if you're so arrogant you think you're going to breeze out of here, or you're so familiar with procedure you think you can snow everyone."

I chuckle. "How about, so confident I haven't done anything to be worried about that as soon as you lay things out, it'll get cleared up, and I'll be filing a claims form to have the cost of my SUV window replaced."

"You tried to run. We had every right to use force to secure you."

I chuckle again. "A man tried to grab me on my way to my vehicle. He didn't identify himself or his intentions. I evaded and tried to flee from physical harm."

"You're sticking with that, are you?"

"The truth, you mean? Yeah, I tend to lead with that."

The two of us sit there a long while before Hiller comes back with a thick file folder in his hand. After unbuttoning his jacket, he takes one of the seats opposite me, and Catherine Lent takes the other.

When he points a remote over his head, I look up to where the light on the wall turns from red to green. I smile at the black mirror lens of the camera pointed straight at me.

"This is Officer Spencer Hiller of the Ontario Provincial Police, badge number 4674, and Agent Catherine Lent of the Special Investigations Unit interviewing Fiona Cumhaill." He goes on to give my address, the date, time, and location, and we're set. "Where should we start?"

I hold up my palms and shrug. "At the beginning is probably a good place."

He sits back and points at the folder. "All right, let me paint a picture for you."

I sit back and match his pose. "Go for it. I'm all ears."

"There's this family. From the outside, they seem like real upstanding folks, working the streets, dedicating their lives to the blue, real role model types. Then, something happens, and all that changes."

"Uh-huh, and what was this family catalyst to darkness?"

"One of them gets gunned down by gangers and killed while on the job."

I flinch at the mention of Brendan, and he catches the reaction. The side of his mouth turns up. Crappers. He'll be like a dog on the scent of a bone now.

"My brother died a hero. Everyone knows that. He saved a woman and her daughter from being attacked in a street assault. He stepped in front of bullets meant for innocents."

"Are you sure about that?"

"Yes."

"Willing to stake your freedom on that?"

"In a hot minute. All-in. Whole enchilada. Brendan was a great cop and an amazing person. End of story."

"So, it must've rocked the foundation of your family when he ended up dead in the street." He slides a set of glossy photos out of the folder and pushes them in front of me. They're the crime scene shots of Brenny's shooting.

I press my hand against the swirling eddy in my stomach.

"Have you seen these before?"

I pull my watery gaze from the horror in those pictures and swallow. "No. Why would I want to see him like that?"

"I expect it makes you angry, right? That he ended up like this."

I read his expectation, and he's way off.

"Not angry—sad. It makes me sad. Brenny was fun and loving and a great guy. He died for his principles of what is right. I'm proud of him for that, but also sad to lose him."

"Am I safe to say the other members of your family have suffered the same range of emotions?"

There's no way in hell I'm bringing my family into this conversation. I gather and stack the photos in front of me without looking at them and flip them upside down. "That calls for speculation on my part. I couldn't say."

"But as police officers, they must've felt—"

I hold up my hand. "Let me stop you there. I will only speak to my feelings and my actions. Sorry-not-sorry. Get to your point. The language describing my rights is very clear. 'Promptly' explain why I'm here. That losing my brother made me sad is not a crime. Have you got anything you want to ask me?"

His smile is easy, but I catch the twitch at the corner of his eye. "All right, let's fast forward to a few weeks later." He takes out another array of photos and sets them in front of me.

It's a bloody scene of death and dismemberment, and I wrinkle my nose. "Ew...that's grisly."

"Funny you should use that phrase. These three men were mauled and killed at Seton Park the night of your brother's wake."

"Oh, that's them? I heard about that the next day. It was big news. That was an animal attack or something wasn't it?"

He nods. "That's what it was declared. Don't you think it's strange that in a city where we've never had even a sighting of anything larger than a nuisance black bear, that three men were brutally killed by what forensics deemed an unprecedentedly large grizzly bear?"

"Circle of life, my man. I can't explain it."

"What's weirder, forensics also found that the bits of claw debris found in the wounds dated back hundreds of years. Now, I don't know a lot about bears, but I know they don't live centuries. What do you think about that?"

"I'm not an anthropologist, but honestly, I think that's pretty cool. Next question. What do *you* think about that?"

"I think it's unlikely that an ancient, geriatric bear came back to life and targeted three men from the gang that killed your brother. So, I'm searching for how that happened."

"Hey, never discount karma."

"Was it karma? Or was it something more intentional?"

"Are you asking my opinion on the intent of a wild bear? How can I possibly answer that?"

"Good point. Okay, let's go back further into the summer." He cracks open the file, selects a police report, and slides it in front of me.

I check the date and see my signature. "Yep, Kady and I were mugged at the back of a bar after close. What about it?"

"Can you read your description of the attacker, please?"

I lean forward and skim through my account of that first night and read. "Tall, six-foot-two, medium brown skin, dark, chestnut eyes, and ebony hair. He was Tyson Beckford good-looking, wearing expensive, shabby-chic clothing, and spoke with a thick Irish accent."

Hiller nods and pulls out yet another set of pictures.

"Quite the little shutterbug, aren't you?" I say, leaning forward to—*oh, poop.*

I see where this is going. In front of me sits a selection of shots of Sloan and me. The two of us driving down my street, us picking up a pizza at our local shop, and kissing outside Janine and Mark's place last night. "So it was *you* in the black SUV down the road. We totes made you."

"So, you don't deny you know this man?"

"How can I deny it? Your lens might not be able to pick it up, but he has his tongue in my mouth in this shot."

He points at what looks like a black and white security shot of Sloan at Pearson Airport. "I think this photo is the most interesting."

I tilt my head. "You think a man at the airport is more interesting than a voyeuristic moment between my boyfriend and me? To each their own, Hiller."

"No. What's interesting is that Sloan Mackenzie arrives from Ireland and the next night, a man exactly matching his description allegedly attacks two women at the back of a bar."

I chuckle. "Are you saying that because he's black and Irish that he must be a mugger? Dude, that's racial profiling, and it's very wrong. Ethnicity isn't a one size fits all package, and I'm sure Sloan Mackenzie isn't the only black Irishman in Toronto. It's offensive for you even to suggest it."

He gives me a droll stare. "It's interesting too that he bought a one-way ticket and has been here all this time without a VISA."

Uh-huh...I can't say he *poofed* home. "I'm guessing that's a clerical error. I know for a fact he went home. I saw him over there with my family in September."

He nods and pulls out a picture of me from the same airport camera angle. "Yes, we have you flying out with the whole family and arriving in Ireland. Strangely, you never used your return flight, and there's no record of you flying home."

Okay, this is getting old. "Well, obviously I did because here we are."

"Yes. Here we are." This time he gathers the photos and sets them aside to get the next bunch. "And here you were less than a month ago. The local authorities in Blarney, Ireland provided these photos. Even though there's no record of you traveling there, this is you and Mr. Mackenzie coming out of the collapsed remains of a building with two of your brothers—who also have no travel documents to suggest they were there."

Dayam, Hiller's been a busy guy.

"Another unexplainable hop across the pond, and this time six women died. What's this about, drugs, illegal import-export, money laundering? Did you intend for the death toll, or was that collateral damage?"

I stop with the banter and lean forward. "I am horrified those women died, but I had nothing to do with it. You see, that's me after being pulled out from under a collapsed wall."

"What were you doing in Ireland?"

"Visiting family."

"Your family lives in Kerry. Why were you in Blarney?"

"My brothers wanted to kiss the stone, and I wanted to look at the sweaters at the Blarney Mill. They're famous."

"How did you get home?"

"From the Mill? We drove."

"No. Home to Toronto."

"Oh, private travel."

"What kind of private travel?"

"The kind that's private."

He sits back in his chair and shakes his head. "Private travel that leaves no records might be considered suspicious."

"If you have a suspicious mind, maybe."

He holds up his hands and smiles. "All investigators do."

"Fair enough. So, what exactly do all these statements of nothingness mean to you, and why is the SIU involved?"

"The SIU came to us. You see, when an officer dies and three of the people responsible turn up dead, the SIU wants to ensure we aren't dealing with a vengeance spree."

I chuckle. "If you spend ten minutes with anyone in my family you'll know how ridiculous that is. My father and brothers live by a code. They will absolutely take down those responsible, but they'll do it through the system."

"Agreed." He gestures. "That's the determination we came to as well."

"Then are we done here?"

"No, because there's still you to account for."

"Me? What? You think I killed three gangers in a park with bear claws I stole from the museum? As you said, it was the night of my brother's wake. I can give you a hundred names for my alibi, and they'll all be cops. I had nothing to do with it."

"What do you do for a living, Miss Cumhaill?"

I sigh, remembering at the last minute that I can't say I work at the bookshop because he'd never be able to find it. "I work part-time at Shenanigan's pub, but mostly I tend to our household."

"So, you're not a main breadwinner for the Cumhaill clan, I take it."

I chuckle and roll my eyes. "No. I have a bit in the bank and pick up shifts and odd jobs when I need extra money."

"Extra jobs like what?"

"I don't know. Aside from the bar, I help in a soup kitchen and sell Celtic jewelry on Etsy...stuff like that."

"Again, you're not pulling in any considerable money."

"You're giving me a complex. What's your point?"

He looks over at Catherine Lent, and she leans forward and tosses a bank card onto the table. "Can you tell us what this is?"

I blink at him. "It's a bank card. Wow, Hiller, you need to take a day off now and then."

"That *is* your name on it, isn't it?"

I reach across the table, examine the raised gold lettering, and frown. "Yeah, but it's not mine. I don't bank at BMO."

"Well, we found that card zipped in the front pocket of your purse, so you must know something about it."

"In the front pocket of…" It hits me then. The other day before the Guild emergency meeting, Garnet gave me that card and said my Guild pay would be deposited monthly now that I took the oath. "Oh, yeah, it's new. I haven't used it, and totes forgot about it."

"You forgot about it?"

"That's what I said."

"Did you forget how much money is in this account?"

"No, because I couldn't tell you. As I said, it's new."

"So, you're saying you don't know the balance."

"That's what I'm saying."

"I find that very strange. I can tell you how much I have in all my accounts."

"Bully for you. I'm a bit of a hippie that way. Money doesn't mean much to me beyond whether or not I can afford the good cheese this week at the grocery store."

"Oh, I think you can spring for the good cheese this week. Don't you, Catherine?"

Catherine nods. "Definitely."

I yawn and chuckle to myself. That was perfectly timed, and I didn't even need to feign being bored and tired of this nonsense. He pulls out a bank transcript and slides it over for me to look at.

"What the fuck?" My eyes nearly bug out of my head. Ten thousand dollars? How the hell is there—I remember Nikon laughing when he said Guild Governors get paid well to endure the bullshit.

I scan the line items on the bank transcript. I got five thousand at the end of September and another five- thousand at the end of October. That means another five thousand will be deposited for November within the next week.

Holy crapamoly.

"I honestly didn't know anything about this."

"Funny thing, I printed the card before I came in and pulled two sets of prints off it. One was yours, and the other belongs to this man. Do you know who he is?"

He sets a mug shot of Garnet out in front of me.

Dammit. Garnet Grant is practically enemy number one in Toronto law enforcement circles. Now I've been tied to accepting large sums of money from him.

"Where are you going with this? You know what? Don't answer that." I stand up and look into the camera on the wall. "I'm done playing this game. Either charge me with something, or I'm leaving."

Catherine stands, turns off the camera, and faces me.

Her eyes flash from hazel to a brilliant glowing amber and her expression breaks into an eerie smile. "Lady Druid, you don't get to quit my game."

With a wave of her hand, Hiller's neck snaps and he slumps forward onto the table.

I scream and stumble back. "Discord."

Her grin widens. "My identity you discerned well. It doesn't excuse your sentence from Hell. Blood was promised, payment due. If not from him, it falls to you."

I call Birga to my palm and activate my armor. "If it's blood you want, you got it. Your blood curse killed innocent people. You've killed even more. Enough. Go back to wherever you came from."

"Marriage pledge, a sacred oath taken. It must be paid. Cannot be forsaken. What am I?"

Okay, that one's easy. "A vow."

"You didn't make it. You cannot break it. Contracts bind and blood signed."

It worries me that I'm starting to understand this guy-girl-thing. "I get it, Salem made a blood vow to Asmodeus in Hell, and

I interfered. But he still wants the payment so I'm on deck for the suffering."

The thrill in her expression tells me I'm right.

The books I read today liken Discord to a trickster god but say nothing about immortality. I have to try.

I slice Birga through the empty air. I spin from where the woman had stood to where she appears on the other side of the room.

I Bo Duke it over the table and launch to pierce her with my spear. Again, she dissolves into nothing and reappears unharmed.

"I'll figure out a way to stop you," I snap. "I'm not a pawn, and I'm not playing your game."

She laughs and passes a hand over her face. The pristine visage of the female SIU officer morphs into a woman battered and bloody. This time it's her that screams as she throws open the door and staggers out of the interrogation room. "Help! Officer down! Our prisoner killed Hiller."

Fuuuuck!

I race around the table, slam the door shut, and press my palm against the jamb. *"Secure Seal."*

Shitshitshit. What do I do?

I look at the downed officer, and by the angle his head is hanging, yeah no, there's nothing to be done there.

Grabbing my bag from the floor by the door, I rush to the table. I rummage around the books, find my purse, and grab my phone.

Bam, bam, bam. Someone's pounding on the door. "Open up. There's nowhere to go!"

I debate my choices for a few racing heartbeats before I hit the call button.

"Red. What's up—"

"Nine-one-one, Nikon. I need an emergency evac. 2682 Keele Street. It's an OPP station. I'm in interrogation room two."

There's a muffle on the other end. Then I hear Nikon running. "Timi. Google Map me 2682 Keele Street."

Bang. Bang. The fist-pounding on the other side of the door continues. "Open it, or we'll bust it down."

"Hurry, Greek."

"It's loading. What the hell happened?"

"Discord framed me for the murder of a cop in his station."

"Fuck. Okay. I got you. I'm on my way."

The call drops, so I grab all the files Hiller had and stuff them into my bag.

"Face down on the floor, bitch," someone shouts from the hall. "We're coming in, guns drawn, and will drop your ass if you so much as blink."

Bam. They piledrive the door with a ram.

The thud shakes the entire room.

I curse, run behind the door, and crush into the corner.

C'mon, Nikon.

Bam. They ram it again, and the door blasts off the frame.

CHAPTER TWELVE

The interrogation room door shatters and swings off the top hinge. Unable to withstand the force of a tactical breach, it tilts and flies toward me at an odd angle. The instant shouting of men and the thundering of footsteps drown out the clamor of my heart in my ears.

As the incursion begins, Nikon grapples me, and the air *snaps*. A blink of a second later, we're standing in the grand entrance of a white marble mansion.

I crumple to the floor and try to restart my heart. Lying on my back on the polished tiles, I stare straight up the three stories to the visible dome high above.

"Cut it kinda close, Greek."

He drops beside me and smacks his chest. "Dramatic exits are my specialty."

"I'd laugh if my life hadn't just gone up in a fiery bag of flaming dog shit."

"Yeah, there's that." We lay there for a while, catching our breath and settling our nerves before Nikon looks at me. "What the hell happened?"

I consider sitting up, but my hands and legs are still trembling, so I abandon the idea and accept being a puddle of nerves. "How about we gather the troops and I tell the grand tale one time?"

"Okay. Do you want me to take you home or shall I bring everyone here?"

There's a buzzing in my head like a runaway semi is barreling down the highway of my mind. "I can't go there. That's the first place the cops will look, and it will compromise my family. Can you flash them here? I stole the files and pictures the cops collected, and it looks bad. I don't know how to make this nightmare go away. I'll need Garnet too. This is bigger than us."

"Let me change my boxers, and I'm good to go." He rolls onto his side and offers a sympathetic smile. "Garnet knows where I live. While I round up the Cumhaill clan, you can text him to come here."

I let my head loll. The marble tile is cold on my cheek, but I'm still way too shaky to get up. I clasp his hand and squeeze. "Thanks for the save, my friend. I was about to be thoroughly taken down by some very angry and misled cops."

He squeezes my fingers, and we lay there for a few seconds longer. He manages to gather himself way before me. "Okay. Clan Cumhaill, the bear, and the Irish lover boy. Does that cover the invite list?"

"I think so. And Greek...thanks for letting us invade your house. I won't jam you up. I promise. I'll leave before that happens."

"You're not jamming me up. *Mi casa es su casa.*" He sits up and pulls me to my feet. "Bring your bag, and we'll set up in my man cave. The girls won't bother you in there."

"The girls? Does that mean your harem of tartlets or your sisters? Please say your sisters."

He chuckles. "Yes, my sisters. Don't worry. The harem of tartlets is only here from Friday night to Monday morning. As long as we sort this out by tomorrow night, you won't cramp my style."

"That's a relief. A maniacal fae trickster derailed my entire life. I'd hate to be a cock-blocker."

He wraps a strong arm around my shoulders and kisses my cheek as he leads me through an opulent mansion. "You're a considerate girl."

He leads me through the front part of the house, and I'm overwhelmed by the fifteen-foot ceilings and massive rooms.

"So, this is your house."

He looks around and shrugs. "Yeah, one of them."

My mind is officially blown—one of them? "It's funny. I always forget the whole story of you being an immortal. In my mind's eye, you're a twenty-something goofball like the rest of us."

His grin is so genuine and warm that it makes my heart ache. "Thanks, Fi. That's honestly the nicest thing anyone has said to me in more than a thousand years."

I laugh. "Like I said—goofball. Now, I need to talk to Da and the others. This is bad, Greek. Like, really bad. Like, change my identity and disappear forever bad."

He squeezes my wrist and points into the room he led us to. "Set up on the war table and pour yourself a drink. I'll be back in a flash. We'll figure it out, Fi. If there's one thing I've learned from hanging out with you and your family, it's never to underestimate Clan Cumhaill when the shit hits."

I smile. "Damned straight."

I head inside Nikon's man cave and take in the room. Oversized couches, projector wall, gaming tables, and a stunning mahogany bar running the length of the back wall. I drop my bag on—oh, crappers—what looks to be an actual ancient war table. It's pitted and aged and beautiful. "Sloan will lose his mind when he sees you."

I scan the rest of the room and chuckle. "The boys will lose their minds when they see you." I head toward the bar. It's almost as long as the one in Shenanigans and flashes some fancy labels I've never heard of.

"Impressive, isn't it?" I turn and meet the gaze of his sister Andromeda. She's stunning in a floor-length, shoulderless gown, her long, blond hair cascading down her ribs. Her attention shifts to the brunette woman on her right. She's not quite as tall, with a Mediterranean look about her and dressed in more modern slacks and blouse. "Timi, this is Fiona, the one I went to speak to last Saturday night after she killed our brother."

Politimi arches a smooth brow, her daggered gaze piercing me straight through the heart. "A spear through his chest, wasn't it?"

My mouth drops open to respond, but I haven't got any explanations left in me. What could I say anyway? It wasn't my fault. I didn't mean to. It was a horrible accident.

All those are true, but it won't change what happened.

The truth is that if Nikon weren't immortal, he'd be dead right now. Gory images of him bleeding on the forest floor with my spear sticking out of his chest overwhelm me.

I killed their brother.

The grisly images of Brendan shot in the street fill my head next. It doesn't matter how sorry or weary or sad I am about what happened. A brother's death shatters your heart.

The disdain in Politimi's gaze is real. She has every right to hate me.

Sloan's parents hate me.

Half the empowered in Toronto hate me.

I swallow as bile burns in my mouth, vomit pushing at the back of my throat. Maybe it's karmic justice I'm wanted for murder.

The crunching *snap* of Officer Hiller's neck echoes in my skull. His head flopped to the side like limp celery left in the fridge too long.

How could people think I did that to a cop?

I would never.

The images of Brendan lying dead on the sidewalk are back. With his birthday this week, I was barely holding the glued, broken pieces of my heart together. Then it happened—I saw it.

Now I can't unsee it.

It was bad imagining it. Now I have the real images in my memory. A sister's love is fierce.

I want to tell Nikon's sisters how sorry I am, but I choke on the words, my throat clogged. Tears break loose, and I can't look at them. I grab a bottle of something golden and sink to the floor behind the bar.

"Shit, Fiona. Don't do that."

It's too late. The dam has broken.

I uncork the bottle, bring my knees to my chest, and take a long swig. The beauty of drinking straight liquor is that you only have to get through the taste bite until its liquid sedation takes hold. Then you're good to go.

Usually. This stuff is liquid gold from the first gulp.

Reaching up, I grab a bar towel and pull it over my head. I don't want to see anyone right now. No. That's wrong.

There *is* someone I want to see.

Someone I *need* to see.

I take another couple of long swigs and close my eyes. Focused on receding out of this reality, I retreat inwardly. As the hardwood floor of Nikon's bar area fades, I find myself lying on a patch of moss in my grove. Brendan is lying there with me, and I curl in against his side.

"Hey, baby girl." He wraps a strong arm around me and pulls me in tighter. "Hard day?"

"Mhmm. I need to hide from the world for a while."

"Okay by me." He presses his lips to my hair and hugs me tighter. "I have you. Feel free to shatter. You and I can put all the pieces back together after."

I set the hurt free, trusting that he can Humpty-Dumpty me back together again. The world has been too much for the past week. I need to be with Brendan.

"I love you, Brenny."

"I love you too, baby girl. Forever and always."

I close my eyes and let the healing energy of my happy place grove wrap me in a protective blanket. Despite what people think, I'm not tough. I'm a girl trying her best in a scary and dangerous world that can be too much some days.

Today was definitely too much.

Time out.

I rise from the depths of my retreat once my soul is patched and healing. I might not have filled all the cracks in my heart, but I've wrapped enough duct tape around them to hold things together for now. Sometimes, that's as good as it gets. My cheek is drool-slick and stuck to the leather of Nikon's sofa. Sloan is sitting on the floor, his arm over me, his unfocused gaze clouded with dark storm clouds.

"That bad, is it?"

His attention shifts to me and emotions swirl in his gaze. There's a flare of relief, then it's gone, and his dark and broody takes over. "I was thinking of the adage, 'Life never gives you more than you can handle,' and hoping it's true. From where I sit, some days, I can't imagine it is."

"Are we talking about you or me?"

"Who do ye think? I hate it when ye suffer."

"Nothing an ugly Oprah cry and a good bottle of booze can't handle." I sit up and scan the room. We're not in the war room anymore. By the massive sleigh bed and the lack of knick-knacks, I'd guess we're in a guest suite.

"I'm sorry for my part in yer troubles today." The pained look he flashes me is full of guilt and self-recrimination. "I know it hurts ye that I haven't shared my plans. It isn't because I don't want ye to be part of them. I just didn't want to say anything before I got it sorted. I didn't want to jinx it."

"Your parents did that for you." The hurt of that convo comes back in spades. "I've now been elevated from unworthy, unskilled, and uneducated to the likes of a money-grubbing whore. That blindsided me. I don't enjoy that happening."

He curses and shakes his head. "I can explain."

"Please do. I'd love to understand why you changed your arrangements to make the girl you've been dating less than two months the recipient of your financial trusts. It astounds me because…hello…we've been dating less than two months."

I run my fingers through my hair and fight not to lose my mind. "Sloan. I adore you, but I've been really clear. My focus is on stabilizing my life as a druid. You said you understood and would support me. Now you're living here and making me your beneficiary? That's the exact opposite of giving me time and space to figure myself out."

He nods. "I knew that's how you would take it."

"That's why you didn't tell me?"

"No." He gets up off the floor and sits on the couch facing me. "Making you my beneficiary wasn't about you. It was about me."

"I don't want your money."

"Exactly." He holds up a finger, cutting off my protests. "Please, let me explain."

I draw a deep breath and exhale. "Fine. Go for it."

"Last month, when Moira and her coven took me—"

I freeze. Up until now, he's refused to talk about what happened during the time the dark witches had taken him prisoner. All I know is that they infected him with a fester bug, and it wasn't a good time for him.

"—there were times during those hours that I considered my mortality. I wondered about my estate and realized my parents have determined what I wanted. Since then, I started to think about what's important to me."

"That's sweet, but even if I'm important to you now, it doesn't mean you change your legal directives. That's crazy."

"No. Leaving my *parents* to decide what I want is crazy. They don't know me, Fi. They don't respect me or my wishes. I didn't make ye the beneficiary because I want ye to inherit my money. I made ye the beneficiary because I trust ye to be the executor. If something happens to me, I want Manx taken care of. There's land I want to preserve and a few properties I want to be designated to the people who care about them the most, and there are some relic and antiquities projects I want to continue supporting. My parents think it's stupid."

"If it's your money, they don't get to decide your wishes are stupid."

"Exactly. That's why I wanted to change things. I see how yer family carry themselves and how ye honor what ye think Brendan would want to do with the money ye inherited. It struck home that I needed to take the reins of my life."

I draw a deep breath and exhale. "So, it truly has nothing to do with you leaving me money?"

"Not a thing. What would be the point? Ye'd hate the gesture, and it would make no difference to ye in the end. Money isn't yer thing."

He smiles, and a few more cracks in my battered heart heal.

"Yer not sure of things yet. I understand that. I'm not tryin' to rope ye in. I'm tryin' to follow yer lead and figure out who I am and where I stand on things. That's all."

I rub my palms over my jeans and nod. "Okay. I can live with that."

He slides closer on the couch and brushes his fingers against my cheek. "Seein' ye grow into the person ye want to be, showed me how little I'd done in the same pursuit. I'll work on myself while yer workin' on yerself, and we'll see where we end up. No pressure. No expectations."

"Deal." I hug him and ease back. "Thank you for not leaving me your money. You're right. I'd hate that."

He nods. "That's why yer the perfect person to be in charge of it."

"Your parents aren't happy, and I doubt they'll let it go."

"Myra told me they called and insulted you. I'm sorry about that. I thought confidentiality laws would give me more time than it did."

"Haters gotta hate."

He hugs me again and stands, offering me a hand. "What do ye say, shall we move on to the next disaster?"

"When you say disaster, you mean my life in general, right?"

"I do."

"Yeah, that's what I thought."

Sloan and I decide to take the long way back downstairs. We weave our way through Nikon's mansion, descend the grand staircase, and find the whole gang buzzing in Nikon's man cave. When we enter the room, the gathered turn to greet me. Politimi is noticeably absent.

"I shoulda been there, Red." Bruin pushes his boxy brown head against my chest. "I'm sorry."

I wave that away. "There was nothing you could've done except keep me company while the shit swirled the drain, buddy. No harm done. How's little Imari?"

"Och, she's a delight. I'm her official nap partner now. Myra said so."

Garnet steps in next and squeezes my shoulder. "Myra sends her love and support."

Love and support are something I have in endless supply. Once I've hugged Dillan, Emmet, and Da, we get to the point.

"Start at the beginning, *mo chroi*." Da points at the photo arrays and reports spread out over the table. "What happened today with the OPP, and what have they put together?"

I start from the moment I left the bookstore and end with Nikon saving my butt and flashing me out as the door blew off the hinges.

"All hail the Greek!" Emmet says.

"Fo shizzle, dude." Dillan bows with his palms in the air. "Nice save."

"Och, *mo chroi*," Da whispers next to my ear. "The things ye deal with are unfair and unkind. I'm so sorry."

I cling to my dad longer than a grown woman should, but he makes no move to separate, so neither do I. I absorb all the strength he offers, and when I step back, I shake off the last of my weariness. "Okay, that's the end of Fiona's mental meltdown ten thousand and twenty-three. The end."

Dillan chuckles. "You're not that bad. There's no way you're at anything over two thousand and eighty-four."

"Thanks, D."

While the men start a discussion about how best to handle Discord framing me, Nikon and Andromeda move in. "My sisters are assholes, Fi. I'm sorry they broke you."

Andromeda takes my hand and squeezes. "He's not half as sorry as I am. It was a harrowing day for you, and Nikon's right —I *am* an asshole. I forget how to interact with regular people at times and missed the cues you had reached the end of your rope."

"It's fine. Nothing an inward retreat and a high-end whiskey can't take care of."

Nikon chuckles. "I gotta hand it to you, Fi. You picked a good bottle to drown your sorrows. That's a two-hundred-year-old single malt you cracked open."

My jaw drops. "Ohmygawd, I'm sorry."

He waves that away. "No biggie. Two hundred years is a blip to an immortal. Besides, it's open now, so let's enjoy it."

Andromeda laughs. "Don't let him make you feel guilty. He has three stocked cellars full of aged alcohol."

"Fi." Da waves me over. "If yer finished discussing Nikon's liquor supply, we're in crisis mode here."

I meet Da's gaze and head over to the table. "Sorry, avoiding my imminent destruction is much more appealing than facing this mess."

Scanning the glossy photos spread out over the massive square table, I'm relieved they omitted the ones of Brendan. None of us needs to see those. Da watches me inventory the materials and sends me a private wink.

Thanks, Da.

"The way I see it," Da says, "our best chance of ending this is to prove Fi left before Officer Hiller's murder. Since she wasn't in the room when they breached it and the camera was off, the claim she killed him is hearsay."

He looks at Nikon's sister, Andy. Whether he's seeking corroboration or for her to challenge his idea, I don't know.

Either way, she nods.

"It would introduce plausible deniability. It would be even better if we had a video recording of her leaving the OPP station before the murder occurred."

Garnet pulls out his phone. "I have a tech team that can help with that. They're good."

Da scowls. "My daughter's future depends on them bein' more than good, Grant."

Garnet meets Da's frustration with a confident shrug. "How many times have my men and I walked out of your stations free and cleared of all charges? When I say they're good, I mean it."

By the look on Da's face, I'm not sure if Garnet's disclosure made things better or worse.

"What about Catherine Lent?" Dillan asks. "If Discord took her place, where's the real SIU officer?"

"I'm going with dead," Emmet says.

"And likely has been for a while," Da adds.

Dillan draws a finger over the photos. "It would help if we had a body and could establish a time of death. It would be easier to prove an imposter killed Hiller and framed Fi than discrediting an agent of the SIU."

Da nods. "Agreed. Find out where she lived. Sloan can take ye there to investigate."

"No." Garnet taps his phone screen to mute the call. "Anyx and Thaos will do that."

Da straightens. "Yer not in charge here, Grant. This is my family on the line."

"Exactly my point. If anyone finds your family on the scene, it won't matter what evidence they discover. The optics of you tampering with things for Fiona's benefit will taint everything that could help to clear her."

"He has a point, Da," Emmet says. "It would be way better if a worried neighbor or a concerned citizen was the one to lead the cops to a body."

"If there's a body to find."

"I think there will be," Dillan counters. "Discord doesn't seem to care about loose ends. He's more of a let the chips fall where they may kinda guy."

"It sucks balls that Fi is one of the chips," Emmet gripes.

"Ugh!" I groan. "This is so frustrating. What happened to innocent until proven guilty?"

Da sighs. "Sometimes it takes a bit to get there, *mo chroi*, but we will. Ye have my word."

"I'll help them build your defense, Fi," Andromeda says. "Leave it to us. All I need is that video and that body, and you're golden."

Nikon picks up the books I borrowed from Myra's Emporium and points at the bar. "While Andy, Garnet, and your dad work on the legal aspects of your alleged crime spree, we can work on Discord and what we need to do to get rid of our maniacal riddler once and for all."

I growl again and follow Nikon over to the bar. He pours me a dram from the bottle I opened earlier, and Sloan, Emmet, and I hop onto the swivel chairs.

"I don't know what to do." I grab one of the tomes and flip through the pages. "I asked nicely, figured out his riddles, and tried to spear him on two separate occasions. I'm not confident we *can* get rid of him."

"Oh, we're getting rid of him." Emmet lifts his glass and nods. "This will be an experiment in how to lose a trickster in three weeks or less. Sounds like one helluva screenplay."

"I'd watch it."

"Did he give you a new riddle during the takedown at the station?" Nikon asks.

"Not really."

"Maybe you didn't realize it's part of the game. He said a death each time you get a clue. So, maybe there's a clue in something he said, and you missed it."

I close my eyes and try to remember. "He—or I guess she—said, 'My identity you discerned well. It doesn't excuse your sentence from Hell. Blood was promised, payment due. If not from him, it falls to you.'"

Emmet pulls out his phone and types as I repeat the riddle. "If not from *him*? If this is tied to the wizards as you think, maybe interrupting the summoning of Asmodeus is the problem. Does the '*him*' mean Salem? You killed him before he could deliver what he promised."

"Are dark deals with demons transferable?" I ask. "I didn't sign anything to assume responsibility."

"Maybe it was in the fine print about spearing one of them to the wall before the transaction was complete."

"Rude."

"Agreed."

Sloan sips his drink and frowns. "Then what? Is that all he said?"

"No, but the next one I solved. He said, 'Marriage pledge, a sacred oath taken. It must be paid. Cannot be forsaken. What am I?'"

"A vow," Nikon says without missing a beat.

I throw up my hands and sigh. "Hey, I was proud I solved that one. Damn, Greek. The only positive thing I had from this afternoon was figuring out one of the riddles."

Nikon chuckles and tops up my glass. "Sorry, Red. You still totally get a point."

"She's not wrong, Greek." Sloan holds up his tumbler. "Yer aces at this."

"With age comes wisdom, my friends. I shudder to think about how many long, cerebral evenings I spent waxing philosophical with the sophists of ancient Greece. Those times taught me both how to speak in abstract concepts and decipher riddles. It's been a useless skill so far, but I'm thankful to dust it off for you now."

Sloan grins. "And it only took two thousand years to find a use for it."

"Right?" Nikon laughs. "Our father always says no education goes to waste. I guess you proved him right, Fi."

"Yay me."

"Back to Discord," Sloan says. "He gave you an end date for this stupid game, didn't he?"

"Yeah. He said by Yule my life would be ruined, but I think he stepped up the timeline on that."

"Unless he has more planned for you," Nikon says.

"*Duuude.*" Emmet leans back and holds his hand open. "Harsh much? I think what we're dealing with is bad enough."

"True story." I swirl the honey-amber liquid in my glass and swig it back. It slides down my throat with a sweet decadence I've never tasted before. When I swallow, I set my glass down on the bar and smile. "Hit me again, barkeep."

Nikon frowns. "I wasn't taking a shot at you, Fi. I was pointing out there is still time between now and December twenty-first for him to wreak more havoc on your life."

"Maybe the key is to stay out of the real world and away from people. Isolate and insulate."

Sloan frowns. "You mean, remove yerself from the playing board altogether?"

"Would that work?" Emmet sounds skeptical.

"No," Nikon says matter-of-factly. "Sorry, Red, but he's a shapeshifter. He doesn't need you out and about to ruin you. He can change into you and ruin you that way."

My eyes roll shut. "I never even thought of that."

"Wow, Greek," Emmet says. "You're new to the whole pep-talk concept, aren't you?"

Nikon sighs. "What's the point in shining her on? Isn't it better to know what's coming?"

"Yes, it is." I offer Emmet a smile. "It's fine, Em. I'm not going to shatter again anytime soon."

"I never thought you were." Emmet's phone buzzes and he pulls it from his pocket. "Da, Calum says the cops are outside the house. Do you still want to be there for the search?"

"I do."

"I'll come with you," Andromeda says. "It can't hurt to have an attorney present to look over the warrant. I'd also like to follow the chain of command for this operation and see who's in charge."

"Much appreciated." Da looks at Sloan. "Would ye mind, son? The upstairs hallway would likely be best."

Sloan squeezes my hand and slides off his stool. "Back in two shakes."

When they leave, I hop off my chair, grab my drink, and head over to see how things are going with Garnet. "What's the word, big guy? Have you swooped in and fixed my life?"

He finishes with the text he's typing on his phone and looks up at me. "Not yet, I'm afraid. Sit tight. I need to handle a few things in person."

He flashes out, and I'm left staring at a war table covered in the chaos of my life. Sit tight. Right.

Except I hate being sidelined, and patience isn't one of my virtues.

CHAPTER THIRTEEN

The next morning, I wake up in a strange bed and stare up at the ceiling trying to place where I am and why I'm here. That sleepy, disconnected fog where everything seems warm and fuzzy mires me. It's comforting. Something inside me says to enjoy it while it lasts. I'm still there, wondering what the day might bring…when I remember I'm at Nikon's because I'm a fugitive. "Shitballs of fire."

"That's a new one." Sloan smiles over at me from where he sits in an armchair by the window. He has his tablet on his lap and is busy typing.

"How did the house search go last night? Did anyone let us know?"

"Yer da reported everything went as well as expected."

I let out a long breath and shake my head. "I know it hurt him. To have his peers go through our lives and pull apart my character is insulting and invasive. Da's too proud for that not to upset him."

"Then I guess he's handling it as he chooses by lifting his chin and painting on a determined smile."

"That's the story of my life." I sigh, deciding I don't want to be consumed by the all-consuming mess of my life before I have to. I roll onto my side and give him an appraising once-over. "Why do you look so sexy and well put-together so early in the morning?"

"Thanks for noticin'. It could be that I've been up for two hours and attended a very successful meeting. Or it could be that I enjoy looking nice for you. Or it could be that I'm a fluke of nature and always look sexy and well put-together."

I laugh, but part of me believes it's all about the third one. "All right, let's start with the successful meeting part of that explanation. Anything you want to share?"

He grins. "Well, I signed some papers at my new solicitor's office to finish up a transaction I'm excited about. Unless something unforeseen arises, I'll tell you all about it within days to a week."

"Yay! I'm excited about that too."

He waggles his ebony brows and is practically giddy. Which, despite the spiral life has taken, I'm super thankful for. We need a little silly. "I also did a bit of holiday gift purchasing. That was fun. Manx and I borrowed yer truck and went on a tour of the city."

"Nice. Did you stop anywhere or only drive around?"

"We made a few stops. Nowhere in particular. If we saw an open parking spot, we took it and walked around a little."

"Now that you have papers for him, you two are free to roam. Remind me when things settle down that I have to get the ones for Bruin over to Dora so she can spell them."

"Am I going to build a reputation as an exotics trainer?"

"Hey, that's hot right now."

He chuckles. "Well, if it means Bruin and Manx get more time out with us, I'm game. I think even more than bein' out, Manx enjoys the reactions of people on the street when they see him."

I let out a long breath and smile. "I'm glad. I want you two to love the city."

"Och, we're a couple of fish out of water still, but we're gettin' there. I thought it would be similar to livin' in Dublin, but it's not."

"I'm glad you're taking the time to figure out how to interact with my city. I hope you love it as much as I do."

Sloan chuckles. "I'm not sure that's possible, but we'll try for a close second."

"Perfect. That works too." I stretch, sit up, and swing my feet out of the covers to dangle toward the floor. "Do I smell warm cinnamon buns?"

"Ye do. We brought ye back some of those iced rolls ye love so much from the bakery by yer house. I also picked up a large peppermint tea from yer Mr. Horton's."

I hop out of bed, move his tablet to the table, and slide onto his lap. "You know I already said yes to dating you and sleeping with you. You don't have to keep spoiling me."

He laughs. "If ye consider a cinnamon bun and a tea spoilin' ye, I'd hate to meet the men who came before me. If ye gave me the go-ahead, I'd shower ye with beautiful things day and night."

I kiss him, his lips warm and tasting of hazelnut coffee. "I know you would. Honestly, after yesterday, snuggling with you and having a cinnamon bun and peppermint tea is about as good as life gets."

"Today will be a better day, *a ghra*. I know it."

"Are you sure this will work?" I cast a wary glance at Nikon's sister sitting to my right as Anyx pulls into the OPP station. "The last time I was here, things didn't go my way."

"This will be different." Andromeda pats my hand where it lays on the leather bench seat. "This time you have me. I called ahead and made the arrangements. They know who we need to speak with, and I've assured them everything is in order. This isn't you turning yourself in. This is you voluntarily coming in to refute the trumped-up allegations against you. Big difference."

That does make me feel better, although it doesn't quell my inner pessimist for the moment.

"Best case scenario, this all goes away, and they apologize for the inconvenience. Worst case scenario, it all goes to shit, I ask for a moment alone with my client, and Anyx flashes us out of there."

I groan and stare at the officers coming out to line the walkway. "They all think I did it."

"We're here to prove otherwise. We have facts on our side. Besides, I've researched Deputy Commissioner Maxwell, and he seems like a straight shooter."

"What about the guy coming from the prosecutor's office? What's he like?"

"Jamie. He and I have a bit of a romantic history. That part will be super fun for me."

Well, at least this will be fun for someone.

Anyx opens the door and helps first Andy out, then me. When I straighten, she meets my gaze with shrewd confidence. "Remember what I told you. Head up, eyes front, don't smile but don't look intimidated."

I'll do my best. I pull up the collar of my leather bomber and shove my hands into the warm protection of my pockets. Head up. Eyes front. Don't smile but look confident.

The cold, piercing glares destroy any confidence I'm trying to project. I get it. They knew Hiller. They practically are Hiller. The fact that they even suspect me of taking the life of one of their own puts me on the enemy list.

"Ms. Tsambikos. Miss Cumhaill." A paunch-bellied officer in plain clothes holds the door open to greet us. He gestures to his right and takes the lead. "I have things all set up for our discussion. Follow me."

Head up. Eyes front.

Andromeda's advice doesn't help. Heated glares burn my flesh from all directions. The only saving grace is that my shield isn't activating in any way. Maybe Andy's right, and this won't be so bad.

"We're in here," the pudgy cop says.

I look at the door to interrogation room two and sigh. Or maybe it *will* be that bad. It's the same little table I sat behind a few days ago, except now there are more chairs.

"Seriously uncool."

"I'm sorry?" the officer says. "Did you say something?"

Andy frowns and nods at Anyx to take a position at the door. "She said it's unfortunate that you chose to flex your muscles to undermine our position. I hoped for more olive branch than a slap in the face. If you want to put us in the same interrogation room where a man was murdered, you can go that route, but it won't change the facts."

I catch my smile before it gets away from me.

Nikon said Andromeda is a force as a lawyer and I'm glad to have her as my champion.

"I see you repaired the door." I point at the frame, remembering how badly it splintered behind the force of a hand-held battering ram.

"How would you know it was damaged?"

Oops.

"Fiona has read the reports regarding the events that transpired after she was excused from her detainment," Andy says without missing a beat. "She wasn't there, but she knows what happened. Look. We came here in good faith to clear Fiona's name. If you're more interested in pinning Officer Hiller's death on her than getting to the truth, you're in for a rude awakening. I will put together a harassment and defamation of character suit that will make headlines and be all the talk this holiday season."

"That won't be necessary," another man says while stepping in behind us. He's tall and silver-haired and bears a striking resemblance to Anderson Cooper. "There's no place for intimidation tactics when searching for the truth. A meeting room is more appropriate for the size of the group."

The size of the group?

Anderson Cooper points the way as he passes us and we follow. When we get to the bright and roomy meeting room, Andy and I round the table, take off our jackets, and hang them on the back of our chairs.

"You must be DC Maxwell." Andromeda leans across the table to shake his hand. "I've heard good things about you."

He nods. "I've heard there's some confusion about what happened here the other day that left an officer dead."

"It's horrible." I press a hand against the tightening in my belly. "Honestly. My whole family is on the job. I didn't mind coming in to talk, and I respect that Hiller was doing his job. It's terrible what happened."

Maxwell frowns. "It is, Miss Cumhaill. And while I appreciate you coming in, Officer Hiller's murder has forged a lot of negative feelings toward you within the department."

I drop my chin. "That's what we're here to talk about."

Maxwell nods and leans outside to call the others in. When he takes his seat on the opposite side of the boardroom table, he shows Andy and me the remote and points at the tinted glass lens at the ceiling. "Is it all right to record this?"

Andy sweeps an elegant hand toward the device and nods. "Please. We prefer it. There's no telling when the footage might be needed to set someone straight."

Maxwell waits until the paunchy OPP officer and two other men join us before he points the remote and starts the recording.

"This is the recorded interview of Fiona Cumhaill regarding

the murder of Officer Spencer Hiller. Miss Cumhaill is here with counsel, Andromeda Tsambikos. In attendance, we also have me, Deputy Commissioner John Maxwell of the Royal Canadian Mounted Police, OPP Staff Sergeant Rick Viceroy, badge number 4331, Jamie Sharpe of the Toronto prosecutor's office, and William Halton, Deputy Director of the Special Investigations Unit."

When finished, he gestures at us. "Ladies, in your own words, please tell us what happened."

Andy takes the floor and the next twenty minutes is her being brilliant and painting a picture of what happened. "As you see by the coroner's report on the recovered body of the real SIU agent, Catherine Lent, she was dead at least forty-eight hours before she and Officer Hiller picked up my client for questioning."

"You truly expect us to believe an imposter framed Miss Cumhaill for Officer Hiller's murder?"

"I shouldn't need to expect anything," Andromeda says. "These are the facts of your case. The agent involved was dead, and her identity was compromised long before Miss Cumhaill was detained. Fiona came and answered the questions asked of her and left. The timestamp on the surveillance video has her exiting the building four minutes before the Lent imposter comes tumbling down the hall claiming Fiona murdered Hiller. Last, when you breached the room, there was no one there. That in itself should tell you what the imposter Lent said wasn't true."

The paunchy OPP staff sergeant doesn't seem to like Andy's account of things but doesn't have another explanation. "Then who is the imposter and why did she want you framed for Hiller's murder?"

A psycho trickster ruining my life for kicks.

"We have a theory about that," Andy says. "As Fiona mentioned, her entire family is on the job with TPD. Since her older brother Brendan was shot and killed in the line of duty earlier this year, her father and four brothers have been actively investigating those involved in his death. To date, they've brought six members into custody and are building solid cases against four others."

"What does them arresting gangers have to do with Miss Cumhaill?"

"Her father, Niall Cumhaill, has been warned to stop his off-duty investigations and was told if he valued the safety and happiness of his daughter, he'd drop it."

"My da doesn't negotiate with criminals," I add. "I wouldn't let him back off even if he did."

"You're saying you were targeted because your father refused to bend to the pressure of corruption?"

"That's what we believe. Until you catch whoever killed and impersonated Agent Lent, we can't be sure."

With nothing else to be presented on my behalf, Andy looks at the representative from the prosecutor's office and smiles. "Do you have any issues with my client you wish to discuss further or is she free to go with apologies?"

That earns her quite a few scowls around the table, but no one speaks up.

"All right, so we're done here. You can remove the watch patrols from her home and spread the word that not only was this a gross error on the part of the OPP, but in their haste to lay the blame on Miss Cumhaill, they let Officer Hiller's true killer walk out of this building and disappear."

I swallow and stand to get my coat on when Andy does the same. "I truly am horrified about what happened. I'm a cop's kid. My family bleeds blue. To know someone killed not only one but two members of law enforcement sickens me. It simply wasn't me. I sincerely hope the person responsible is found and held accountable."

"Thank you, Miss Cumhaill," DC Maxwell says, his gaze trained on me. "I promise you that we won't stop until the person responsible is put to justice."

With that, the meeting adjourns, and the men from all the involved departments exit the meeting room. Anyx steps inside the door and we make our way over.

"Can I have a private word, Fiona?" DC Maxwell says. "Off the record of course."

I nod at Andy, and she and Anyx step outside. They leave the door open, but Maxwell can speak without fear of being overheard. Well, he could if Anyx wasn't a Moon Called lion with heightened hearing.

"What can I do for you, DC Maxwell?"

He steps between me and the door and smiles. It's not a threatening pose, but I don't doubt the man, in his lifetime as an officer for the RCMP, has seen enough violence that he is far more lethal than his leather loafers and spiffy suit suggest.

I look up at him and aim for a look of calm, respectful confidence.

"I believe you when you say you didn't kill Officer Hiller or Agent Lent. I also believe you when you say you want the person responsible brought to justice."

"I do. Wholeheartedly."

"I also took the time to study the case file the two of them put together on you. Hiller and Lent might not be able to finish their investigation, but their questions are solid. You have a strange connection to questionable people and money and events that make me wonder what we're missing. There is more here than you explained away."

I swallow and lift my shoulder. "Honestly, there's nothing you or any of the other branches of law enforcement need to worry about. I may not be a cop like everyone else in my family, but I *am* one of the good guys."

His gaze narrows and the corner of his mouth pulls up in a crooked smile. "I hope you're right. I'd hate to see your bad choices take down the reputation of your father and by extension, your brothers."

I wave that away. "Then we're good because it ain't gonna happen. I live by the same code of right and wrong they do. My father and my brothers are proud of me and how I live my life. S'all good."

He nods. "Time will tell. You've piqued a lot of curiosity. That won't go away any time soon. If I were you, I'd lay low and stay out of trouble, Miss Cumhaill."

Trouble? Me? "Yes, sir. I'll do that."

Even with Maxwell's warning about members of the force not being satisfied, it still surprises me each time I see cars parked up the road. It's not only the house they're surveilling—they're following me too. I notice the same car pulling into my grocery store parking lot three trips in a row, and the tingly sensation of people watching me never quite goes away.

In the end, Nikon gives me refuge from the attention for a few days and takes me in. During that time, I keep myself busy researching Discord while Garnet, Da, and my family weather the fallout of my popularity with the police.

"How is staying with Nikon?" Myra hands me a box of crystals from the afternoon order.

"Nikon's been great. With me comes Sloan and by extension Bruin and Manx, so he's been invaded. He hasn't seemed to mind. Still, I'm glad to get out today and give him a break from us."

"And his sisters?"

"Andromeda's not home much but comes and goes and keeps us up to date on any developments. She's damn good at her job and doesn't need money, so she's very selective about the cases she takes on."

"Dora said she's an impressive woman."

"Oh, yeah. I admire her a lot. Beyond the obvious asset of her being a resplendent beauty, she's also tough and smart and driven."

"And the other one?"

I haven't seen Politimi since my moment of emotional crumble that first afternoon. "Nikon says Politimi is antisocial to begin with. The moment it became apparent people would be coming in and out of the house, she packed a bag and went to one of the other houses."

Myra giggles. "Oh, really? One of the *other* houses. How many are we talking?"

I laugh. "After questioning Nikon a bazillion times, he said they number in the sixties."

"Sixty houses!" Her mouth drops open. "How can someone need sixty houses?"

I finish pricing the display for the meditation crystals and sort the gemstones to go into their slots. "It's a mystery, but I suppose with rising housing markets and the opportunity for rental income, s'all good."

"Are they in Toronto?"

"I asked him. Aiden and Kinu are still having trouble finding a place in a neighborhood they like in a price range they can afford."

"Does he have anything?"

"Sadly, no." I finish sorting and reach over for the last box. "Not unless they want to move to Majorca."

She raises her hand. "I'd like to live in Majorca."

"I know, right?" We work independently for another twenty minutes before I break the silence. "Thanks for letting me work today. I was going stir-crazy sitting around doing nothing. Being Brendan's birthday, I couldn't spend the day idly sitting around."

Myra chuckles. "You don't have to thank me for letting you work, duck. I love it when you're here. Are you guys getting together as a family tonight?"

I nod. "The boys booked it off, and Nikon is letting us use his man cave and bar for the evening. Kinu and the kids, and Liam and Auntie Shannon will be there for pizza at six. They all need to leave early for bedtimes and to run the pub, but we'll be together for the important stuff."

"I'm sure it'll be quite a family affair."

"I'm looking forward to it."

"I wish you all healing vibes and happy memories."

"Thanks. We'll need an infusion of the former and have lots of the latter. Still, I think I'll buy," I count on my fingers, "fourteen cleansing stone sets."

"I'll put them together for you if you know what you want in them."

"I was thinking, jasper to nurture our spirit, turquoise to balance emotion, citrine to release negative energy, amethyst for healing, and moonstone for new beginnings.

"Lovely. Do you want them in the net bags or the velvety ones?"

"The velvety ones—purple if we have enough. Purple was Brenny's favorite color."

"We should. I have more in the back." Myra leaves to search for the purple gemstone bags and returns a few moments later dangling a new package. "What time is Sloan coming back for you?"

"I told him I'd be ready at four o'clock."

"How's he doing with his stuff these days? Is he laying his roots?"

"I think so. It's hard to know with him. He's been quiet and broody when he's alone and remarkably positive when he knows I'm watching. I've decided that's him doing his best in a bad situation."

"Doing his best is a good thing."

It is. "We talked a few days ago, and I realize he's figuring out the drastic changes in his life the same as me. I wanted space to do that so I can figure out how I want my future to look. I have to give him the same consideration."

"That's very mature."

"I know, right?" I hand her the three empty boxes and smile. "Now, if you don't need me, I promised our little bear in the back that when I finished, I could go color."

Myra chuckles. "You're excused."

CHAPTER FOURTEEN

With my newfound windfall of Guild Governor money, I want to pick up the pizzas and beer for Brendan's birthday bash. Da nixes that, pointing out my assets might still be tracked, and everything I do is under scrutiny. He doesn't want me touching money that could be traced back to Garnet Grant.

I don't think it can—Garnet's too smart for that—but I see his point. Garnet has a dark and sordid record with the TPD. Knowing the whole story doesn't change that view. Not that I think for a moment he's a "good" guy.

Nope. I've seen him in action, and he's more than a little rough around the edges. So, it comes down to a case of "pick your battle." In this instance, I'm not willing to dig in and cause tension on Brendan's birthday.

It's only pizza.

So, Da picks up the tab for everything and with a couple of trips by Sloan and Nikon, the gang's all here, and we're stocked for the night.

Liam hugs me when he arrives and chucks my chin. "Hey, shweetheart, how's life on the lam?" His Bogart impression is awful but hilarious.

"I'm no longer a wanted fugitive."

"Yay for that."

Yeah, yay for that. "Da thinks in another week or two, the disgruntled agents will get sick of shadowing me and will dwindle."

"Good. I wish you peace and privacy."

"Thanks, me too."

"Hey, listen." He pulls his phone from his pocket and waves it between us. "Aiden and I put together a playlist of Brendan's favorites for the occasion. Are you good if we take over the music for the night?"

I laugh. "It's not all Shakira, is it?"

"Not all of it."

I shake my head, laughing. "Classic 70s rock to Shakira. Hilarious."

"That's our boy."

Yeah, it is. "Hey, Nikon. Can you help Liam cast a playlist of Brenny's favs to your home stereo system?"

"Sure. Not a problem."

Aiden, Brendan, and Liam were the "older boys" while we grew up, and the three of them were tight.

Calum, Dillan, Emmet, and I were the "kids" dragging on their coattails. It evened out once we were in our late teens and they were in their early twenties, but for two decades, they were the trio of trouble.

They miss Brenny as much or more than I do.

Although I can't imagine how that's possible.

"Pizza's here, bitches," Emmet says as he and Sloan *poof* in with seven large boxes and two bags filled with wings and dipping sauces. "Everyone grab it while it's hot."

"Then I want to make a toast." I head to the bar.

While they get their plates sorted, I pour a line of Guinness pints and start passing them out. When everyone is ready, I hold up my glass and smile at my fam jam. "Brendan was a man of simple tastes. Pizza and wings were considered gourmet dining, and if you paired that with a dark stout, he was in his glory."

"A man of exquisite taste," Dillan says.

There's a rumble of laughter; then I get to my point.

"He was taken too soon, but a crusty fae friend of mine recently said, 'Death leaves a heartache no one can heal; Love leaves a memory no one can steal.' I think that's very true. Brendan was strong and principled and—"

"A giant pain in the arse," Liam adds.

"True story. As well, he was love and laughter and a safe place to rely on. I think I miss that most of all."

"I miss his pranks," Emmet says. "Even if I ended up the butt of his jokes more often than not."

"I miss Friday Fails," Dillan says.

Oh, Friday Fails. I laugh, thinking about all the times Brendan entertained us with the crazy and stupid things he'd seen that week on the streets. The streakers. The drug-addled antics. The people who tried to run.

He truly was one in a million.

"So, here's to Brendan Owen mac Cumhaill," I say, swallowing to clear my voice. "The man, the hero, the beloved brother, and friend." I lift my glass higher and smile at the faces of my family. "*Slainte mhath.*"

"*Slainte mhath.*"

Booze, laughter, and dragging up every memory we can resurrect about Brendan devour the next few hours. At some point, someone thought it would be a good idea to play a few rounds of Flip Cup. That went off the rails pretty quickly. Thankfully, Sloan and I were knocked out early.

"Sometimes it's more fun to watch the drunken chaos than to be part of it," Sloan says.

"Especially the next morning."

"Someone should follow yer family around for one of those YouTube streaming shows. Ye'd make a killing, I swear." Sloan's gaze is glued to the final round. It's between Kevin and Dillan for the title, and the gloves are off.

"I bet a bag of Skittles on the Dillmeister." Emmet holds up the red bag of candy.

"I'll see your Skittles and raise you two packs of Rolos." Calum winks at his boyfriend. "I have your back."

Kevin laughs and eyes the six cups awaiting the start of the last round.

"K versus D," Emmet says, with his fingers curled into a pretend microphone at his lips. "Two very different strategies in play. Kevin prefers to drink each cup, then flip it. Dillan prefers to drink all his cups first and flip them all at once. Which approach will take them to the winner's circle?"

Da laughs from his perch at the bar, and it does my heart good to see him enjoying himself. It's the first time he and Shannon have been a couple in front of us, and it's oddly comforting to see them happy.

Brendan would've approved.

A riotous uproar at the table announces Kevin as the grand champion of the evening.

I go over to congratulate him, and the room spins in a lovely fuzzy haze. "Well done, Kev."

"Thank you, Lady Cumhaill." Kevin rips open his winnings. "Skittle?"

I consider the colorful candy and the slosh of alcohol in my tummy churns a little in reply. "Pass, but thanks."

"All right, folks." Liam sets down his glass and gathers his phone. "You're in charge of the music from here out. Can Mom and I get transported to the pub by one of you magical fellows?"

Nikon stands and raises his hand. "I have this run, Irish. You took Aiden and his family home. Just give me two minutes to hit the washroom before we go."

I chuckle. "You can't snap through time and space with a full bladder?"

"Something like that."

I kiss Auntie Shannon and hug Liam before they go. "Love you guys. Thanks for being here."

Shannon goes down the line, hugging everyone. "There's no way we'd miss the night to celebrate Brendan. I think it should become an annual event."

"That's a great idea," Da says. "Maybe next year we can have it at the pub."

"If there's not a warrant out for Fiona's arrest." Dillan winks at me. "You never know with her and her new trouble magnet."

I laugh. "True story."

"All right, good to go." Nikon jogs back in from the hall. "Everyone ready?"

When Nikon takes their hands, and they snap out, I set the last splashes of my drink on the bar and wrap my arms around Da's waist. "How are ye holding up, oul man?"

"I still get up every mornin'. Some days that's all I can manage, and that's a chore itself."

"I hear you."

Nikon jogs back into the room and looks around. "Where'd they go? Did I miss my fare?"

I straighten. "Who? What do you mean?"

He chuckles. "Liam and Shannon. Did Sloan *poof* them to the pub? I wasn't gone that long."

Sloan and the rest of the guys stop talking.

"Nikon. You were just here. You took them. You came back from the washroom, and you snapped out."

He shakes his head. "No, Red. I didn't. That wasn't me."

Panic seizes me as I meet the panicked gazes of my family. "Was it Discord?"

"Fecking hell," Da snaps and jumps off his chair. "Sloan and Dillan, go to the pub and check on them. Hurry."

Sloan takes Dillan's hand, but before he *poofs* out, he stops. "Or *this* is Discord, and he's tryin' to clear the room."

My mind stumbles on that, but yeah, that's a possibility too. "Nikon, snap from there to the pool table, please."

"What? Don't be stupid. Discord kidnapped your aunt."

"What word did Xavier use in the meeting that we thought should get added to the dictionary?"

"Why are you playing parlor trick games with me?"

I take a step back and call Birga to my hand. "You're the one playing games. Nikon would've answered me without hesitation. What do you want, Discord? Why are you here?"

Nikon—the real Nikon—flashes back and is standing fifteen feet from his doppelgänger. "What the actual fuck?"

"It's Discord."

Three arrows whiz across the room at the same time two daggers fly in from the opposite direction.

The incoming projectiles are about to converge on the trickster when Discord screeches and dissolves. He reforms as a fox on the pool table and pulls his muzzle back to growl. "You're not in the game, brothers. You don't get to play. Don't kill the messenger. Isn't that what they say?"

"Except this messenger kills everyone else," I snap. "How is that fair?"

"Not your loves, your boundary lain. Innocent deaths and strangers' pain. To the rules, I hold true. A death each time you get a clue."

Oh, shitters. "Nikon, go check that the staff and your sister are still breathing."

Nikon curses and snaps out.

"I assume someone in this household is dead, so why don't we speed things up a little and get to the clue part?"

The fox swishes his bushy red tail and wraps it around his

feet. "I tear when you twist me, bend when you thrust me, and without me, everything would go your way. What am I?"

I look at my brothers, but they look as blank as me. Dammit, our riddle guru just snapped out of the room. "I don't know. What else have you got?"

"The blood vow owing must be paid. During Yule tidings sacrifice made."

"You need to stop this, Discord. If you—"

Before I finish my sentence, he dissolves and disappears.

Dillan rushes forward, his daggers clutched in both his palms. "That furry fucker is riding my last nerve."

"Boys, stay with yer sister a moment." Da looks murderous. "Sloan, if ye wouldn't mind, I'd like to check on Shannon and Liam myself."

Sloan glances at me, and I give him my blessing. He *poofs* out, and I'm left standing with Calum, Dillan, Emmet, and Kevin.

"So that happened," I say.

"Leave it to us to attract a maniacal party crasher," Emmet growls. "I hate that guy."

Nikon snaps back into the room, and he's practically vibrating. "He killed them. That weasel motherfucker came into my house and killed four of my staff and my sister."

I close my eyes and press a hand to the pressure in my chest. "I'm so sorry."

Dillan pulls me against his chest. "Not your fault, Fi."

I swipe at the tears escaping and fight to pull in oxygen. "Maybe not, but people are dead who wouldn't be if I wasn't here. I endanger people."

"You don't. Your sister will be all right, won't she?" Dillan asks. "She'll resurrect in Greece and come back?"

He nods. "She will."

"But the others won't," I protest.

"No," Nikon agrees, "the others won't. Still, Fi, you're not going anywhere. If Discord is determined to kill the people around you, the best place you can be is in the home of immortals."

"Or at home with us," Emmet says. "He's respecting your boundaries about killing us."

"How far does that umbrella of protection go, I wonder?" Dillan asks. "Myra? Dora? The staff at Shenanigans?"

I can't think about that. "We need to figure out where he came from and how to send him back. If he escaped during the rip in the Hell rift in the funeral home basement, then let's open that sucker back up and punt him through."

Emmet offers me a patient smile. "Love the visual, but I'm not sure opening a rift to Hell is the best way to correct a problem. It kinda feels like using kerosene to put out a fire."

I flop down on the couch and throw up my hands. "All right, what's your plan?"

Emmet grins. "Thanks for asking. As it happens, I *do* have one...but it won't be popular. Gather 'round, and I'll dazzle you with my brilliance."

"Och, are ye a total eejit? That's a terrible idea." Da makes a face at Emmet when we replay the conversation and catch him up on what he missed.

I hold up my hands. "I admit, I wasn't a fan at first, but honestly, I've been telling Garnet we need people in the hierarchy of the police department for weeks. If we didn't have to hide everything—if there could be someone running block for us—we might get further faster."

"Wouldn't that be a refreshing change?" Dillan says.

"Of course, but when yer talkin' about involvin' agents in the upper chain of command, ye should be talkin' about puttin' empowered people in those positions. The entire point of the magical sector remaining hidden is the hidden part. We can't walk into the office of the Commissioner of the RCMP and say, 'It wasn't me, sir. It was a fae trickster.' How do ye think that will play out?"

I look at Garnet, who seems equally opposed. "Think about the wider impact. There are fae communities all over the world. What you're suggesting affects everyone."

"It doesn't have to."

"If you tell someone in the upper echelon of law enforcement, then that person will share the information, and it will spread through governmental agencies. It's not solely the Toronto empowered you'd expose. You'd be outing the entire fae world."

"And they'll kill ye for it," Sloan snaps. He's been opposed to the idea since Emmet laid it out to us. "Ye think yer havin' a rough ride now? Imagine yer life when the vampires and the hobgoblins and the dark witches and wizards of the world find out ye spilled the beans. That's even if ye have a life. What's the sense of fightin' to restore yer good name if the cost is yer life?"

"Okay, but we don't have to spill *all* the beans. Maybe we open the jar and let someone see a couple of the less alarming beans so we can gain a little leeway when shit hits."

"So tell them about a fae trickster who's collecting a blood vow but not mention Hell or Asmodeus or the wizards who unleashed this nightmare?"

"In theory, yeah. Obvi we'd need to decide what to share and not share, but we don't have to out everyone."

"It's a nice thought in theory," Da says. "I see where yer comin' from, and it would be grand. It's just not realistic."

"Andromeda thought the idea had potential," Emmet says. "She and I were talking about it this afternoon. She thinks if we find the right agent with the right connections in the right agency, maybe we could assimilate him."

Dillan frowns. "We're *not* Borg. Assimilation doesn't mean this person will suddenly become part of the collective and become one with us. It's risky."

I nod. "I get that, but—"

"It's *too* risky," Garnet says, talking over me. "I'm sorry, Fiona. I'm vetoing this. Sloan's right. It's dangerous for you from both the human and the empowered side of things. You could get screwed by the humans and skewered by the empowered. Then we'd not only be exposed, but your family would be caught in the crosshairs of both worlds."

Well, I certainly don't want that.

I sigh, reading the room. There's no way I'll win them over on this. "Okay, fine. What other bright ideas do we have to bring Discord down?"

CHAPTER FIFTEEN

"The Toronto Santa Claus Parade has been held since 1905 and is the longest-running children's parade in the world. How's that for history, hotness?"

Sloan chuckles. "Is yer intention to rattle off dates of old buildings and long-lived traditions of your city for the rest of our lives?"

"Maybe." I pull the lid off the Rubbermaid bin that holds our winter gear and smile. "You expressed being unimpressed by my city being so young. It's my duty as a loyal Torontonian to ensure you're aware of the error in your judgment. I must school you until you acknowledge our greatness."

He catches the gloves and scarf I toss him and frowns. "Is this bin of warm clothes a community grab basket?"

"Yes. Does that offend your snobbish ideals?"

"No, but I'm capable of buying winter accessories."

"No need. We have a whole bin right here."

"I was fine for the night of Hide-and-Seek."

"That was almost two weeks ago. Temperatures change. You'll thank me after an hour of sitting on a cold curb waiting for the floats to come."

"Why do we have to go so early if it's cold?"

I laugh. "I don't think you grasp how busy this event is. There will be hundreds of thousands of spectators lining the city's streets. If we want Meg and Jackson to get close enough to see the clowns and catch candy, we need to scope out a good spot and hunker down."

"Are ye sure it's just them excited to get a good slab of the sidewalk?"

I wind a red and black scarf around his neck and pull him against my chest. "Don't rain on my parade, broody. This will be a great day. Myra and Garnet are bringing Imari and meeting us. It's happy holidays time."

"Yer brothers are working the parade?"

"Yep. They were either scheduled to work it or picked up the extra duty to cover the event. They'll all be there."

"Maybe we should stay home where it's warm, and one of yer brothers could nudge one of the street barricades when we get there."

I frown at him. "Parade nepotism? Shame on you. If Santa sees us do that we'll be on the naughty list."

Sloan snorts. "If Santa sees half the stuff we do behind locked doors we're already on the naughty list."

I grin and waggle my eyebrows. "Hells yeah, we are."

Twenty minutes later, Sloan and I *poof* into the bookstore, let ourselves out, and walk along Queen Street until we come to University. "There they are." I point over the heads of the crowd to where Myra and Garnet set up. They have a bench sitting right on the edge of the curb and a stack of blankets. "Wow, they do things right."

"How do we get there from here?" Sloan eyes the congestion of the street before us. Manx is drawing more than a little attention, but it seems people are torn between keeping their distance from the wild cat and wanting to touch him. "I could portal us."

"That wouldn't stand out in this crowd at all."

"Ye'd be surprised at how oblivious non-magical humans can be."

"And you'd be surprised how many people in this crowd have their phone up and their video recording. After my recent stint in the spotlight, I'd rather not go viral for *poofing* magically into a busy crowd."

He scowls at the crowd in question. "People really do come out and wait hours in the cold for the perfect spot."

"That's what I've been saying. The barricades go up first thing in the morning and set the areas where people can sit, walk, and congregate."

"It's a circus."

"Yeah, but no more than it is every year."

"Where are yer brothers?"

"They're around. They started their paid duty at seven this morning. The Holly Jolly Fun Run starts at 11:45, and the parade won't start until 12:30. It'll take two and a half hours for it to go by once it reaches the points along the route."

"Wouldn't it be easier to sit at home and watch it on the telly?"

I throw him a look. "Oh, don't kid yourself. We'll do that too. It doesn't get televised right away—and it's so much more immersive to be here in person."

"Immersed is one word for it. Drowning is another."

I giggle. "Hey, Mam used to wrangle six kids down here every year by herself while Da worked it. If she can do that, we can meet up with family and friends and freeze our butts off for the cause."

"I'm not planning on freezing my butt off. That's what *Inner Warmth* is for."

"Good point, hotness. I hadn't thought of that. This is the first year with druid powers. *Noice.*"

He chuckles and shakes his head. "Ye still have moments when ye think like a civilian."

"Only because I've always been a civilian at the parade. I would've gotten there."

"I have no doubt."

"Auntie Fi!"

I turn to see Jackson's little arm waving wildly. He's pulling at the wrist harness Kinu has on him, and I giggle. I don't blame her. That boy is a runner, and there are too many people and too much going on down here to hope he'll behave—because he won't.

"Jackson! Hey, dude." I rush over to meet up with them and pick him up for a hug. "Are you all set to see the parade? Are you gonna stay awake this year and see Santa?"

He nods. "I had a nap."

"Good job. What about your sister? Do you think she'll make it until the end?"

He shakes his head. "She's a baby. She's already asleep."

Sloan chuckles and lifts the front edge of Meg's stroller onto the sidewalk so Kinu can push. Yep, my niece is lost in dreamland and all tucked in under a mound of blankets.

"Maybe she'll surprise ye, Jackson. Maybe she'll wake up and have a sudden second wind. Cumhaill women are known to do that."

Jackson frowns, distracted by a kid with candy floss passing by. "Mommy! Look."

Kinu chuckles. "So it begins. You have to wait until we find our spot and you can sit and eat your treat. Remember? We went over this on the subway."

Jackson pouts, but he knows better than to question his mom. That leads to no treats at all.

Kinu adjusts his hat so he can see properly and scans the crowd. "Where's our spot?"

"Over there. See? Myra and Imari have a bench."

"Imari!" Jackson shouts, rushing in the direction of my pointed finger, pulling his wrist harness tight.

"Jackson, stop!" Kinu shouts as the sudden pull on her arm makes the stroller swing sideways.

Meg's stroller takes a crazy hairpin turn over the edge of the curb, and I lunge to get a hold on the handle before it tips over sideways.

Kinu looks like she's about to lose her shit and we haven't even gotten started.

"Sloan and I have the stroller. You go before he pulls your wrist off."

Kinu rolls her eyes but takes my advice and dissolves into the crowd, giving her son enough bungee rope to get to his friend.

Sloan seems flustered by the whole thing.

"Hey, hotness. Why the gritted teeth? I thought you were getting used to the kids."

"Jackson and Meg, yes. It's the other thousands of kids down here that are making me anxious."

"I'd say tens of thousands at least, but I get your point."

"It's bedlam."

"Of the best possible kind."

After another five minutes of inching through excited kids, stressed parents, and people chatting and oblivious that they're holding up the entire crowd, we break through the last of the people in our way. Jackson and Imari are talking excitedly on the bench while Kinu, Myra, and Garnet stand in front of them, blocking them from the cordoned-off street.

"We made it!" I park the stroller at one end of the bench. "Great spot, you guys. Nice bench."

Garnet winks. "BYOB."

Sloan chuckles. "Very nice. It gives ye a bit more room to move in the crush of spectators."

"They help too." Myra points at the two meaty chimichangas standing guard as bench bookends. Thankfully, they don't look like they're carrying weapons. They shouldn't need to. If they're in Garnet's security team, they'll be an aggressive Moon Called animal of some species.

I scan their noticeably impressive attributes and decide they're most likely wolf shifters. By the dirty looks they're throwing me, I think I'm right. The wolf Moon Called haven't been my biggest fans since I killed two of them the first time I met Garnet.

Totes not my fault. It was self-defense.

"Are you expecting unbridled hostilities at the children's parade, Garnet? Maybe a rogue game of hopscotch or a dangerous outbreak of ring around the rosy?"

Garnet arches a brow. To others, he might look angry and annoyed, but once I learned Garnet's body language and facial expressions, I realized this is his "funny girl" look of sarcasm. "Be prepared for anything, Lady Druid. Especially when the ones you care about are exposed."

Life teaches people how to interpret the world. I think it's a little sad that girding for war is Garnet's go-to when spending a day out in public.

To each their own.

"Kitty!" Imari shouts while pointing at Manx. "So pretty."

Sloan steps closer so that Imari and Jackson can pet him.

Manx doesn't look one hundy percent sure of the attention, so I lean in. "Remember, kids, Manx is part of our family now. You have to be gentle with him and play nice."

Imari seems very taken by Sloan's druid animal companion. Jackson's attention wanders almost immediately. "Uncle Calum! Daddy!"

I follow Jackson's smiling gaze to the two handsome men in blue coming over to us.

"Is everyone ready for Santa?" Aiden shouts while waving at the kids.

"Yes!" the masses shout back.

"It won't be long now, kids. I heard on my radio that the parade has started and Santa's on his way."

There's a deafening round of cheering before my brothers come over to hug Jackson and say hello.

"Great spot," Calum says. "Funny thing. I don't remember there being a bench here. And wow! Decided to bring the lynx to the parade, did you?"

I hold my hands up to block his view. "Nothing to see here. Look away."

He laughs. "Lucky for you we're not the fun police, Fi. As long as Manx doesn't start any panics or mobbing, you're good. And the bench is a thousand times better than sitting on the concrete curb for three hours."

"I know, right? It used to take the twelve days of Christmas to thaw our butts."

"True story.

"I gotsta pee." Jackson smiles up at us.

"And there's that," Kinu groans.

"I have him, babe." Aiden lifts his son and unhooks him from the wrist harness. "There's a line of Johnnies right around the corner. We'll be back before the pipers start piping."

When he swings around, one of Jackson's boots falls off. Sloan has to dive to beat a German shepherd for it, but it's recovered and replaced without too much trouble.

When the German shepherd takes notice of Manx, I reach out with Animal Communication and settle him down.

Speaking of pipers piping...I hear the marching band drums *tat-a-tat-a-tatting* in the distance. I clench my hands and squeal. "Hurry, Aiden. They're coming."

Calum snorts and smacks Sloan's shoulder. "Who's the kid here, anyway?"

Sloan winks. "After the past week, I think she deserves a little childish pleasure."

It takes another ten minutes before the first wave of the Holly Jolly Fun Run participants pass us. I pull out ten bucks and stuff it in a Christmas stocking as a girl dressed up like a candy cane jogs by. Sloan follows my lead and I snort as he donates a fifty without blinking an eye. Good guy, Mackenzie.

After the runners go by, there's a steady wave of clowns. They wave at the kids, dipping their hands into baskets of candy and dolling out treats by the handful.

When they pass, the marching band is in view.

"We're getting close now." I point at the floats coming up the road.

Myra, Kinu, and I are sitting on the bench with Imari, Jackson, and Meg on our laps and a blanket over all of us. The weather isn't too bad, only twenty-six degrees and no wind. Even without *Internal Warmth*, we would've been good.

"How are you doing, Meggie? Do you see all the clowns?" Poor Meg got woken up by the drumming, so she's not displaying her usual rosy disposition.

"She's fine." Kinu looks over. "Once she wakes up, she'll get into it."

"How about you?" I lean closer and rub her shoulder with mine. "You're still looking tired and stressed. Is it only the prospect of moving? You know we'll be there to help, right? Clan Cumhaill is at your beck and call."

She sighs. "It's not only moving. It's the prospect of needing another bedroom and being able to afford it. And being able to afford another couple of mouths to feed."

My eyes widen. "Wait. What? A couple more mouths to feed? You're pregnant again? And it's twins?"

"Surprise." Kinu's smiling but there's way too much weighing her down for it to be genuine. "Remember in Ireland when you and Gran gave Aiden and me the afternoon off from being parents? Yep, that's when our happy little family of four became six."

"I have so many questions. Twins. Aiden must be over the moon."

Kinu rolls her eyes. "He says it was the ambient power of Ireland that made him potent enough to make a twofer."

I burst out laughing. "That's too funny."

"Yeah, he wants to name them Kerry and Ireland."

"Are they both girls?"

Kinu shrugs. "We don't know yet. He says either way."

"Okay, that's a terrible idea for boys."

"Right? That's what I say."

I side-hug her and squeal. "This is so exciting. And yeah, that's why you're tired. You need to let us help more. This is big news. Great news."

Kinu nods. "I know. It's just a lot. I'll have a five-year-old, a three-year-old, and twin newborns. Save me."

"We will." I giggle and hold up my hand, fingers spread in the Vulcan salute. "Druid's honor."

"Paw Patrol!" Jackson shouts, pointing.

Jackson and Imari squeal as the Nickelodeon float approaches and I get back into the parade mindset.

Mind blown. Twins.

I point and wave as all the favorite characters come into view. "Wave to Marshall and Rocky! Oh, there's Rubble. Do you see him?"

We're all wildly waving when I catch Sloan laughing at me. Whatevs.

"Uncle Emmet!" Jackson yells, pointing at a woodland float coming up next. The scene on the flatbed trailer is a Snow White scene with the queen of the float waving at the kids, surrounded by live animals.

Yep, Emmet is in his uniform but walking along beside the float, trailed by a line of animals walking two by two: martens, squirrels, skunks, raccoons, and rats.

"What the hell?"

Emmet looks over at us and rolls his eyes. "What can I say? My animal mojo must be dialed up today. Just call me the parade pied piper."

"Or Noah." I cover my laughter with my glove and shake my head. "Let me know where the ark is. I don't want to be left behind."

"Hilarious," Kinu says. "I guess it's better he walks with the float than have it drive off, and all the animals patrol the streets on paid duty. That might seem strange."

"Stranger than a line of wildlife following a cop down the street?" Sloan asks.

"Go sit up with the wildlife queen and the rabbits." I point at the woman sitting on a red velvet throne with a fat lop-eared rabbit in her lap, waving out at the kids. "Wait. Is that supposed to be Mother Nature?"

Emmet nods. "I think so."

"Not even close."

"Where is dat bunny's wings?" Jackson points as the float rolls slowly past.

I smile at Kinu and Myra, and we all chuckle. Kinu leans closer to Jackson and smiles. "He's a normal bunny, not a special Ostara rabbit like the ones in the grove."

Jackson frowns. "I likes bunnies that fly."

I wink. "Me too, buddy."

I'm still watching Emmet and his band of merry followers continue up the street when the end of the woodland float passes by.

"Can your bear come out?" Imari shouts. "He'd like to be in the parade."

I blink and look around. Thankfully, there are way too many people chatting and too much excitement in the air for anyone to pick up on what Imari said.

I press my finger to my lips. "Bruin's a secret, remember, sweetie?"

"But those bears get to be in the parade."

I follow her gaze to where a dozen people in wildlife conservation uniforms walk between the woodland float and a giant Pikachu float coming up next.

The walkers wave to the kids with one hand, and in their other hand, each of them holds the lead to a wild animal. There are two bears as well as four bobcats and a half-dozen deer.

"I love the conservation message, but does anyone else think this is a bad idea?" As if to answer my question, one of the bears pulls at his harness and growls in discontent. The sound agitates the other bear, and he grumbles too.

The cats are agitated, breathing with their canines showing and their mouths agape.

"Don Valley Conservation Authority, what the hell were you thinking?"

The animal handlers struggle with their charges as they pass and we wave goodbye to them. "Bye bunnies. Bye bears. Bye deer," I say, encouraging Meg and Jackson to do the same.

"Bye foxy." Imari waves at a bushy red fox sitting on the back edge of the float.

My breath catches as the animal finds me in the crowd and his eyes flash amber as he smiles.

"Discord."

Sloan frowns and follows my gaze. "Feckin' hell. Here?"

I shift out from under Jackson and walk the street's curb, keeping pace with the float. I glance over my shoulder and Garnet, Sloan, and Manx are right behind me.

Discord is watching me, and his message from before seems horrifyingly clear. "'The blood vow owing must be paid. During Yule tidings sacrifice made.' So, would you boys consider this as Yule tidings?"

Sloan glances around at the girls dressed up like evergreen trees dancing and twirling around us and scowls. "I would."

It's tough to walk along with the float. We're getting in the way of the people trying to watch the parade. I dodge a woman with two kids in her lap and curse, pointing into the procession. Sloan understands immediately and joins the walk, waving to the crowd as Manx trots along at his side.

Bruin, I need you to spirit yourself around this float and see what you can learn from the fox. He might be here to mess with me, or he might be here to claim more blood for the broken vow.

On it.

I draw a deep breath when Bruin flutters in my chest and release him in his spirit form.

With Sloan on my right and Garnet on my left, we pace ourselves, remaining a safe distance from the fox on the float. We're behind the bears and bobcats, but ahead of the evergreen tree dancers and Pikachu.

When I see Dillan laughing at Emmet up ahead, I pull off my glove and press my fingers under my tongue. I let out a shrill whistle. It turns heads as I meant it to, but it also startles the bear and the bobcats. I flash the wildlife guys an apologetic look, but I don't have time to do much more than that.

Dillan and Emmet fall back and join us at the back of the wildlife procession. When they toss me an inquisitive gaze, I tilt my head, indicating the fox staring at us from the back of the float.

Dillan's brows crease. "You don't think he'd try anything here, do you? Not with all the kids."

Emmet curses. "That would be too vicious, right?"

"He's not vicious—he's ambiguous. If he doesn't care one way or another about the blood spilled, why would he care if he takes out women and children?"

Garnet casts a worried gaze over the crowd. "How do we figure out what he set in motion so we can foil his plans?"

Sloan groans and shakes his head. "That's it."

"What's it?"

"Foil."

I shake my head. "Still not with you."

"One of the riddles we hadn't figured out yet. I tear when you twist me, bend when you thrust me, and without me, everything would go your way. What am I?"

"Foil. Okay, so how are we any better off knowing that?"

"We're not," Dillan says. "Riddles are stupid."

"Agreed. Seriously pointless."

Emmet shrugs. "I don't know. It's kinda fun knowing we're meant to foil his plans."

I cast a sideways glance at my brother and his furry followers and roll my eyes. "All right, Em. How do we do that?"

Emmet's got nothing.

I look at the others, but they look as blank as me.

Yep. That's what I thought.

CHAPTER SIXTEEN

While we trail the float, I text the sitch to the family WhatsApp group and send a quick one to Nikon too. A few minutes later, Nikon jogs in from somewhere down a side street, and Aiden and Da join us after the next block.

"What's he waiting for?" Aiden scowls at the fox grinning at us from up on the flatbed truck.

"How far are we from the end of the parade route?" I ask. "Maybe his plan kicks in once we're back at the readying area. Maybe this time it's not about the biggest chaos bang for the buck."

Da *harumphs* and frowns. "I think yer reachin' on that, *mo chroi.* If playing games is what our wee furry bastard is about, having us wait and wonder will be hittin' his funny bone. I don't for a moment believe he'll give up the bloody punchline."

"Aren't you a breath of fresh air today," I say.

There's a device under the float. Bruin says on our private communication channel.

"What kind of device—like a bomb?"

All eyes turn to me, everyone waiting for confirmation.

No. I don't think so.

"No? Then what do you think it is?"

It looks like that portable box with buttons Emmet uses to play music in the grove in the summer.

"It looks like a wireless stereo?"

"Bombs can look like anything," Da says.

I frown. "My shield isn't tingling."

"That doesn't mean it's not a bomb. That could just mean it's not activated and causing danger yet."

True. "Bruin, are there any lights or sounds or smells on the device that might indicate that it's turned off or on?"

We're coming up to a corner when the wild bears start grunting and shaking their heads. The handlers grip the ropes with both hands, but it's obvious the bears aren't open to being placated.

"Emmet, go talk to them. Find out what's wrong."

Manx lets out a throaty *mrowl* and shakes his head. He's pulling against the harness, and it all becomes clear.

"Maybe the stereo is emitting something that's upsetting the animals."

Before any of us get a chance to weigh in on that, one of the bears bats his handler across the road. The guy goes flying, getting air, and lands in a heap. The free bear roars and books it straight at the crowd, his lead rope waving in the air behind him like a scarf in the winter wind.

"Emmet, get that bear and calm him down."

Emmet bolts off, leaving his animal friends confused. The martens follow, but the raccoons, skunks, squirrels, and rats scramble.

Cue crowd panic.

The other bear gains his freedom, and in the length of time it takes for me to say holy shitters, we have a wildlife riot like you read about.

Emmet's chasing down the first bear. Sloan is tending to

Manx. Garnet goes after the second bear. I guess that leaves me, Calum, Dillan, and Da on bobcat and deer duty.

The deer I'm not so worried about.

Bobcats are quite a bit more troublesome.

"Someone jam the transmission," Emmet shouts. "It's hurting their ears and making them crazy."

"*Silence Assault*," Sloan shouts, straightening from Manx. "It's working on Manx."

I leave my family to work on their spells and race to the back of the float. Gripping the nylon skirt, I flip it up to duck under the truck.

The hit comes fast from above.

I crash to the asphalt hard, and my head snaps back. The world spins for a second while I shake off the light show going off in my cranium. The road is cold against my spine, and I call forward my armor.

I know I shouldn't be seen by normal citizens covered in the fretwork of leaves and bark, but if Discord cracks my skull or gores me, I'm no good to anyone.

"Are you having fun, Lady Druid?"

I shift to roll to the side, but somehow I'm pinned. The wild scuffle of animals and my brothers and conservation workers and panicked citizens race past us, threatening to trample us in its wake.

Pressing my palms to the bits of ice and snow on the road, I call on nature for help. "*Sleet Storm.*"

I close my eyes as a bitter and biting wind swallows the two of us. The moisture in the air hardens to sharp pellets, and I bombard Discord with my assault.

He turns his head from the blasting ice, and I press my palms to the snow on the road. "*Ice Dagger.*"

He doesn't notice the influx of magic, and I wrap the fingers of both my hands around the hilts of the magical ice daggers. I might not be able to get up, but now that he's distracted by the sleet, I can move my arms.

With a scream, I arc both arms over my body and catch him by surprise. The blades sink deep, and a baleful wail tells me I've struck a significant blow.

He's gone in the next split-second, and my shoulders and hips are no longer locked to the ground.

"*That* was fun." I roll onto my knees, but when I sit back to continue to fight, he's already gone. "Wily little sucker."

"Fi, look out."

Strong arms cage my shoulders and roll me to the ground as a wild bear barrels past.

I smile up at Calum and roll to my feet. "Thanks, bro."

"No problem. To protect and serve and rescue my sister from the latest mayhem."

"I know. That's a full-time job." In the moments since I was tackled and pinned, the float has gotten away from me, and we're about to be trampled by forty dancing Pikachus.

Calum and I rise to our feet and bolt to catch up to the woodland float.

Behind us, marching bands continue to do their thing. The horn section is wailing *Jingle Bell Rock,* and if there were time to laugh, I would.

Seriously?

Is there a "the band plays on" clause I don't know about?

When angry bears are loose, you get to break formation, people. I shake my head and rejoin the parade riot and scan the carnage. Emmet and Da have the two bears corralled in a bus shelter, and everyone seems to be calm.

Garnet is growling and intimidating the hell out of one of the bobcats. Sloan, Manx, and Aiden have another bobcat encircled. Nikon and Dillan are working with the conservation guys to get the other two.

"I'm going under the float," I shout to Calum as I run for the skirt. It's dark under there, and I release the glamor on my eyes to flip to the fae sight I gained last month. I don't know that I'd call it a gift, exactly, but it's not the curse I once thought it was. "There you are, my precious."

I crouch-run, being careful to keep my head from hitting any of the metal obstacles on the underside of the bed of the truck. I see the thing Bruin told us about, and it seems to be activated now.

My shield still isn't flaring. At most I have a tingle, but that's it. Does that mean there are no hidden dangers if I want to dismantle this sucker and end this craziness?

I hope so.

I take a moment to examine it, wondering about the wires and the speaker output and a million other stupid things before I hear Sloan's taunting words. Think like a druid.

Right. *"Heat Metal."* I hold my hands against the sides of the amplifier and let the inferno flow out of my palms and into the chunk of junk that is ruining my day.

When the whole thing melts to a puddle at my feet, I turn and run toward the tailgate again. After the skirt passes over me, I straighten and smooth my hair. The scene is much calmer now. Without the shrieking call for insanity transmitted to the animals, they settle right down.

Emmet helps the wildlife guys get things under control while Da and the rest of my brothers work crowd control and triage the civilian injuries.

Sloan and Manx rush over to check on me, and I hug them both. "Everyone okay? Manx, are you okay, buddy?"

The long black tufts on his ears bounce as he nods. "Och, once Sloan cast his spell to block out the sound, I was fine. I'm sorry I succumbed to the chaos of the moment."

"Not your fault, puss. It was Discord all the way."

Sloan casts a glance around us and frowns. "Where'd the bane of our existence go, anyway?"

"Hopefully, to crawl into a cave somewhere and bleed out.

Honestly, I don't know. One minute I was impaling him with two ice daggers, and the next he was vapor."

Sloan sighs. "Unfortunately, I doubt that's the last we hear from him. Something tells me he won't die that easily."

"You're right. I get the feeling he's like a cockroach but with fur. Okay, let's see if we can help clean up this mess."

"And a good time was had by all." I drop my coat on the floor, toe off my boots, and go into the family room to flop on the couch. "Taking one of my favorite childhood moments and tainting it with twisted games is just plain rude."

Sloan hangs my coat, sets my boots on the mat next to his, and passes the family room to start the kettle. "Aside from panic and a few scrapes and broken bones, I think we got off lucky that no one was hurt worse."

"Agreed." I pull the blanket off the back of the couch and snuggle up. "It was still rude."

"No argument."

He comes in a moment later carrying two piping hot chocolate escapes in mugs. "Manx and Bruin, I poured some Irish whiskey and the morning's coffee into the roasting pan in the kitchen if ye'd like to enjoy yer own celebratory drink."

Bruin flutters in my chest, and I release him. He waddles toward the hall and looks back over his wide, muscled shoulder. "Much obliged."

"*Slainte.*" Sloan raises his mug and hands me mine. "I think while everyone is busy with the aftermath of the parade debacle, you and I take our hot drinks out to the hot springs and soak in the grotto for a bit to unwind."

I arch a brow and sit up. "Bathing suit or no?"

"I was thinking of bathing suit optional."

I stand and fling off my blanket. "Boys, we're going skinny

dipping in the hot springs. Mommy and Daddy need some privacy."

There's a long, loud groan from the kitchen.

"Why do ye have to paint pictures like that, Red?" Bruin snaps. "Just sneak off like every other couple."

I giggle. "Because it's more fun to hear you grumble."

He growls again.

"Just do what I do," Manx says quietly. "I hide in the closet so I don't have to see or hear what they're doing."

"That will never work, sham," Bruin says. "I don't fit in the closet. I wish I did."

"We can hear you," I say.

"Didn't you say privacy time? Don't we deserve the same considerations?"

I laugh. "I think the kids have told us off."

Sloan grins. "Then let's take our exit."

After a glorious hour of Sloan and I enjoying some alone time in the hot spring grotto the boys made to keep our grove warm through the winter, I feel refreshed and more myself than I have in weeks. The police mess is dying down. We stopped Discord from his quest for blood today, and hello…I'm skinny-dipping with my guy in the most incredible place in the world for me.

Glass half-full moment. Life is good.

"Do you think we could get away with hiding out here for another hour?"

Sloan grins. "I'm all for another hour, but I doubt we'll make it through without being interrupted. The shift yer brothers took to cover the parade ended ten minutes ago. I expect they'll be anxious to wrap up their day and come home to check in and warm up themselves."

I sigh. "I was afraid you'd say that. It was fun while it lasted though, eh?"

"It was." He trails his finger down the line of my neck and across my collarbone. Goosebumps burst to life on my skin and spread down my arms. "Have ye ever considered gettin' yer own place, *a ghra*? I mean, to have the freedom to walk naked in yer home and enjoy an afternoon delight in the kitchen without the fear of yer brothers walkin' in on ye?"

"Been there, done that," I giggle. "It's one of those 'moments that shall never be mentioned' in our family history. If Dillan's ever really grating on your last nerve, ask him about walking in on the guitar player and me in the kitchen."

Sloan arches an adorable ebony brow. "Yet another thing I missed out on by not having siblings."

I push across the surface of our steamy little oasis and settle on the smooth stone seat across from him. Lifting my feet, I lean back while he takes the hint and gives me one of his magical, healing foot rubs.

I groan and let my head drop back. "Oh, sweet baby Groot, that's so good."

"Ye haven't answered my question," he says, amusement thick in his voice. "Do ye picture yerself livin' here with yer brothers underfoot yer entire life?"

I hear genuine curiosity in his voice and give his question some thought. "I'd never move far. I love Toronto, and I love being in the everyday pulse of my brother's lives. But yeah, I've done the math."

"What math?"

"Well, Aiden and Kinu are pregnant again and—"

"They are?"

"Oh, yeah, she told me at the parade. Twins conceived in Ireland in September."

"That's wonderful news."

"It is, but it means even if they come to stay with us for the short term, within six to eight months, they'd need three bedrooms minimum. Renting a three-bedroom house in Toronto is costly. If they got a four-bedroom and one of us moved in to offset the costs, it would help not only financially but also by taking on some of the load with the kids."

"So, yer thinkin' ye'd like to move in with yer brother and his family?"

"Oh, hells no." I laugh, waving that away as water drips from my fingers. "I love the kids like crazy, but I'm home too much for that. I like being Auntie Fi. I don't want to be their second mom. I was thinking Emmet or Dillan."

Sloan chuckles. "Do they get a say in this plan?"

"It makes sense. They'll be the last to settle and come and go when needed. They could help but also work enough that Aiden and Kinu could still be their own little family."

"Ye have given it a lot of thought considering ye only found out a few hours ago."

He finishes with one foot and sets it in his lap to massage the other. "I found out she was pregnant today, but I've been thinking about it for weeks. It's hard not to. They're both stressed about finding a place, and I hate it when one of us is stressed about something."

Something is dancing in those eyes of his. "What? What have you got up your sleeve, Mackenzie?"

He lifts his arms and chuckles. "I'm afraid I haven't got any sleeves. Don't know what yer talking about."

I giggle and flutter my feet. "Okay, less talky, more massaging. Then, once I'm mush, we *poof* inside and dry off. I'm getting pruney."

The two of us are barely dry and dressed when the doorbell rings. I jog down the stairs and smile at Bruin and Manx curled up napping together on the family room rug. So sweet.

I'm still smiling about that when I open the door and find—"Deputy Commissioner Maxwell. What are you doing here?"

He shakes his head and gives me an assessing once-over. "I'm not exactly sure, Miss Cumhaill. May I come in?"

I glance behind the door and the straight sightline into the family room. "Of course. Can you give me one second?"

He catches my glance and smiles. "If it's about the bear and the cougar in your front room, I already saw them through the window when I came onto the porch."

Busted. Well, crud. "All right then, come in."

As he's coming in, Sloan jogs down the stairs. He looks at our guest and the family room and scowls.

"He already saw them from the porch."

Sloan finishes his descent and extends a hand. "Sloan Mackenzie, and you are?"

"Sorry, hotness. This is DC Maxwell from the RCMP. I mentioned him to you after Andy and I got back from our interview at the OPP station."

Sloan nods. "Deputy Commissioner. To what do we owe the honor of a home visit?"

He takes off his black knit cap and folds it into his pocket. "Too many things aren't adding up. Would it be all right if I come in for a cup of coffee and sit down with you for ten minutes?"

I shrug. "Should I call my lawyer?"

"No. It's nothing like that. This is an unofficial visit. Everything will remain off the record. I'd simply like to talk a few things out that have been keeping me distracted."

"All right, please come in. Sloan can grab us a coffee. What would you like? We have pretty much any pod flavor ever thought of."

"A hazelnut with milk?"

Sloan excuses himself and heads back into the kitchen.

Maxwell slides out of his boots and coat and collects a small electronic tablet from the inside pocket of his jacket. "I confess, Miss Cumhaill, I'm not one for tracking down people of interest and inviting myself into their homes."

"But for me, you made an exception?"

"It seems so."

I gesture for him to follow me past the slumber party in the family room and into the dining room. His gaze is locked on our furry friends snoring away, and I'm not sure what to say about that. "We have papers for them. Sloan is a trainer and does commercials."

He takes a seat at the dining room table and gives me a patient look. "Miss Cumhaill, there is no way you have papers for a grizzly bear to be loose in your home. For one thing, exotics are banned within city limits. For another, even if you had a reason for having a grizzly bear, there are no safety measures in place."

"We don't need safety measures. Bruin is a sweetie—"

He raises a hand and stops my ramble. "Before you tell me he does exactly what he's trained to do, remember the bear attack on those three gang members and your declaration that you have no knowledge of how that could've happened."

My mind spins with the implications. Denial and evasion will only get us so far. "What I said was that I knew nothing about it at the time and only learned about it from a news story the next morning. That is one hundy percent true."

Maxwell reaches up to accept the mug offered to him, and Sloan places the coaster caddy on the table. I take out three and set us up.

Once we're all settled, he taps on the screen of the tablet. "What was the last thing I said to you before you left the station, Miss Cumhaill?"

"Lay low and stay out of trouble?"

Sloan rolls his eyes, and I know what's coming even before he pulls up the footage of the parade gone wild.

"That was not my fault. I was there as a spectator when all hell broke loose. As a concerned citizen, I stepped in and did my best to help in a bad situation. And, from what I've heard from the follow-up reports, no one was seriously hurt."

He raises his mug to his lips and takes his time before answering. "I've spent most of the past two hours looking over the footage. From what the television cameras caught and the phone videos submitted, I pieced a great deal together."

Cat crap on a cracker.

"Oh? What do you think you figured out?"

"I think Hiller and Lent got a lot of things right. I think you're involved in an unnatural amount of deadly situations, and I think you're hiding a great many things that could lead us to the truth about their deaths."

"I would never kill them or have them killed. It goes against everything I believe in."

"I believe that. You see, where Hiller and Lent erred was to consider you as only a vigilante. I don't see that in you."

"Cool, because I'm not."

"But you could be." His gaze narrows. "You know the law, share the moral code to expect justice, and understand the people and your surroundings well enough you could make it work for you."

"Are you flirting with me? You're far nicer than anyone else at that meeting."

He runs a finger around the rim of his mug and smiles. "In a long career of investigation and apprehending criminals, my instincts grew quite keen. I trust my gut, maybe more than most."

"What does yer gut tell ye about Fiona?" Sloan asks.

He tilts his head as if considering that. "There's a great deal more going on than I know about. One minute, you're sitting on a bench enjoying the parade with your nephew on your lap, and the next, you're trailing the float as if you knew the animals were about to go feral."

"How could she have known that?" Sloan asks. "As ye said, she was sittin' on the bench with the kids havin' a family day at the parade."

"How indeed," he says, his grin growing. "Then there's you, Mr. Mackenzie."

Uh-oh. So far the investigation and suspicions have focused on me. I don't want that to spill over on Sloan.

"Here you are, walking alongside Fiona with your pet cougar."

"Lynx animal companion," Sloan says. "Manx is not a pet. He's an intelligent and valuable member of my family. If ye want to understand us, start there."

"My apologies." He runs a finger over the elapsed time bar and stops at a part during the wild animal bedlam. "There's a moment when it looks like he too is suffering from the shared agitation, then you calm him, and then it seems like he's following your direction and trying to help corral and contain the wild bobcats."

"That's cray-cray," I say, my voice a little too high-pitched to sell it. "He's a very well trained cat but—"

"Fi—Nikon's snapping me to Ireland in an hour. Wanna visit Gran? And guess what—I bonded with a marten. I'm naming him Doc. Get it!"

My mouth falls open, and I see the curiosity pique in DC Maxwell's eyes. "Emmet! We have company."

Emmet rounds the corner holding a large brown marten with a cream face and two round, ebony eyes. He shifts sideways to stand close to the doorway and moves his arm so he's hiding the chunky weasel behind the wall.

I roll my eyes. "Don't leave him dangling. That's stupid. Emmet, this is Deputy Commissioner Maxwell of the RCMP."

"Well, fuck. Isn't this a kick in the sprouts? Nice to meet you, Deputy Commisioner. Sloan, can you fix this for me, please?"

I roll my eyes as my brother shifts back and forth on the balls of his feet. "Okay, so, I'm outtie. Buh-bye."

He runs away like the little weasel he is, and I think he and Doc marten have a lot in common. I turn to meet Maxwell's gaze. "So, that's Emmet. He's a bit of a goofball. We ignore half the stuff he says."

"More than half." Sloan backs me up. "Sometimes we don't even pay attention to any of it."

"Good point. Let's not even pay attention to anything he said. Now, what were you saying?"

Maxwell chuckles. "What does snapping to Ireland mean? Is this part of the private travel you mentioned to Hiller? And what does bonding with a marten mean? How did he want Mr. Mackenzie to fix his blunder?"

I turn to Sloan. He's much smarter than I am. Help!

"Snappin' is what Emmet calls Skypin'. They're plannin' to Skype Fiona's grandparents and tell them about the excitement at the parade and likely him getting' a new pet ferret."

"That wasn't a ferret. It was a marten."

"Och, but was it really? Hard to be sure. Looked like a pet store ferret to me. What about you, Fi?"

"Yep. Sure did. Funny story. My Gran and Granda didn't even know how to Skype and Gran called it snapping, so we went with it."

Maxwell's smile dims. "And here we were having such a lovely conversation. Up until this pile of bullshit, you were straight with me. I know you're intentionally leaving details out, but what you said was truthful."

I swallow. Damn, why do I feel like I should be spilling the beans—or, as I suggested to Garnet, at least letting him get a peek at the beans. "I'm sorry, Mr. Maxwell. The truth is I'd love to tell you everything, but I can't. And I hate to rush you, but Sloan and I do have plans, and you said ten minutes. If you don't mind…" I tilt my head toward the hall and thankfully, he gets the hint.

"It's been illuminating, Fiona."

Well, poop. I hope not too illuminating.

I struggle with how to end the convo the entire time he's getting back into his coat and boots. When he straightens, he makes no effort to hide that he's noticed Bruin and Manx are gone from the living room.

Likely, Emmet woke them and got them upstairs.

When he looks at me, I hand him his tablet. "Please know I *am* my father's daughter. I live by the same values he and my brothers do. Yes, I seem to get tangled up in more messes than most, but I'm one of the good guys. I do my best to serve the people of Toronto and protect them when I can."

"I'd like to believe you, Miss Cumhaill, but you're not giving me much to go on."

I run rough fingers through my hair and sigh. "And if it were up to me, I would. It's just not my story to tell."

He slides the tablet into his jacket and sets it into his inside chest pocket. When he pulls his hand free, he hands me a card. "If and when the messes get to be too much for you, call me. I think you'll find I'm better as an ally than an enemy."

I take the card and nod. "I have no doubt that's true. And thanks…for not making this a pissing match."

When he steps out onto the front porch, he turns back and dips his chin. "I'm giving you the benefit of the doubt here, Miss Cumhaill. Don't make me regret it."

"I'll try my best not to. Honestly, it seems the forces are against me more often than not."

He chuckles. "Why do I get the feeling there are some very interesting stories behind that comment?"

"I hope one day I'll be able to tell you about them."

Sloan and I watch from the family room window as Deputy Commissioner Maxwell climbs into a blue SUV and drives off.

"Well, that could've gone better," I say.

Sloan chuckles. "Who are ye kiddin', Fi? It also could've gone much worse."

CHAPTER SEVENTEEN

"Gran, Granda, we're here!" I unzip my jacket and Sloan helps me shrug free of my sleeves. "Hello, the house."

"Come here to me, my darlin' children." Gran rushes to greet us at the door, her full skirt swishing from side to side as her heels click on the wooden floor. "How have ye been keepin' yerselves? I was so pleased to get yer message."

I hug Gran and wave to Granda coming up the hall. "I wish it were merely a social call, but things are getting tricky at home, and Sloan thought Granda might have something in his library to help figure out what to do about this trickster that's become a royal pain in my butt."

"Not to mention all the people he's killed," Sloan says.

"Yeah, I suppose they got the worst of it. I don't know how to deal with him. It's not like he's a villain with a specific motivation we might be able to track and end. He's all over the place having fun at my—and the victims'—expense."

Granda hugs me and pats Sloan's shoulder. "Where's Emmet? I thought Lara mentioned Emmet comin' too."

"Nikon took us all to Blarney, and Sloan *poofed* us from there.

Emmet has a little love affair heating up with that white witch Sarah Connors we met last month."

"Och, my fingers are crossed for him," Gran says, grinning wide. "White witches are lovely folks, and we'd love to see him with an Irish lass."

I giggle. "You think if we all hook up with Irish mates we might move here, don't you?"

"Me? Och, ye give me too much credit."

I laugh. "I doubt that very much. Oh! Big family news. Don't say anything to Da and the boys because they don't know yet, but Kinu is pregnant with twins."

Gran squeals and claps her hands together. "Oh, luv, that's wonderful news. I'll start knittin' now. Twins. That's doubly exciting."

The men don't seem as enthralled by the baby convo, so I shift it back to the reason we're here. "Sorry, Granda. We were talking about you having an idea what to do about Discord, and I got distracted."

Granda grabs his coat and points at a packed picnic basket on the floor. "I pulled a few books at the shrine. How about the four of us take yer Gran's little care basket and head straight there?"

"Sounds great." While I shrug my coat back on, Gran laces her arm through the handle of her woven picnic basket, and we all join hands. "Where's the new shrine?"

Granda winks. "It's in the old dragon lair. Patty and the Queen offered it to me when they vacated. See, I even have a dragon portal band, same as yers."

Granda shows me the infinity dragon that wraps his wrist. It's the same as mine, except mine is on my upper arm.

Oh, cool.

He grips the portal band, and the queen dragon's power *poofs* us four hundred feet below the Cliffs of Moher. When we settle, I look around the vacated cavern. It seemed huge when the dragons were here, and Patty's gold took up most of the main chamber. Now it looks even bigger.

"Look at this place." I wander around, staring out at all the vast space. "It's cray-cray."

A familiar snort down the hall has me turning toward the nursery wing. The flutter and shuffle of blue scales and wings excitedly flapping make my heart swell. "Dart! Dude, I'm so glad you're here."

I jog to meet my Western dragon and hug him. The last time I saw him was a month ago, and I likened his size to a Malamute dog. I'm relieved and surprised to see he hasn't grown much since then.

"Why are you here, baby boy?"

He nuzzles me with his snout, and I scrub my knuckles over his three little horns. The purr he lets out is the sound of utter dragon contentment.

Gran comes over and gives him a loving caress over his wings. "I mentioned to Patty ye were comin' earlier when he picked up a stag hit on the highway. He must've informed yer wee man."

"Is that it?" I hug him again, thrilled to spend a little time loving up my boy. "Well, I'm glad you were allowed to come to visit for a while."

"*Allowed* is stretchin' it thin." Patty stomps out of the nursery. "He was supposed to wait until I escorted him here. The queen hasn't signed off on the kids taking solo trips yet, and the wee man knows it."

"Uh-oh." I make a face at Dart, and he snorts again, white smoke rising out of his nostrils. "Are you AWOL?"

"He is," Patty snaps. "Or at least he would've been if I hadn't noticed him missin' and covered his scaly blue arse with Her Graciousness. And yer lucky I found ye here safe and sound. I'll not tell yer mother about this, young man, but don't let it happen again."

Before Patty can get too worked up, I bend down and hug him too. "Good to see you, my friend."

Patty rolls his eyes and winks. "It's always a pleasure, Red. How's life in the city?"

"Not great at the moment. That's why we're here. It seems when I foiled the dark wizards' plan to summon Asmodeus a while back, I inadvertently either missed the release of a trickster from Hell or someone sent one for me. Either way, he's pretty much mucked up my life and is demanding the blood debt promised and not delivered."

"Is that kind of horror even transferable?" Gran opens her picnic basket and sets out a dessert spread on an antique sideboard. "It seems to me if ye were there to thwart what was happenin' ye'd hardly be in a position to take on responsibility for the dark wizards' vow."

"Right? That's what I thought too."

"What was the wording of the vow?" Granda asks. "How was the contract sealed? How did the wizards bind it?"

"No idea."

Granda looks at Sloan and points. "Start a list, lad. Ye'll need to answer those questions, to begin with."

Sloan's thumbs skim over the surface of his phone, and he looks up. "What else?"

"I took the liberty to start reading up on Discord. Fi mentioned he doesn't possess ill intent. He's simply unaffected by the moral trapping of right and wrong."

"Which is wrong in itself, isn't it?" Sloan asks.

"An arguable point, but it may work to our advantage. If we can figure out what Discord's motivation is, perhaps we can stop him that way. Ye said he's big on this playin' out as a game. He's tossin' ye into the fire and watchin' ye dance over the hot coals."

"That's exactly how it feels."

Dart stomps his clawed feet and shoots a fireball across the cave.

"I appreciate that, buddy. Heck yeah, I think you'd fry him up. Thank you."

Dart's grin is filled with as much pride as it is determination. My boy will be a real superpower one day soon.

As the conversation continues, I ease over to see what Gran packed for us. She has apple spice cake with icing, mint brownies, Irish cream dessert shots…

Yum. Yes please to everything.

I grab one of the shot glasses and a spoon and start there. The first bite nearly does me in—brownie and Baileys and whipping cream. What's not to love?

"Seriously, Gran. If you keep making things like this, I'm going to start popping in just for dessert."

"Lugh and I will take ye both any way we can get ye."

Gran is kidding, of course, but I hear the truth in her words. They miss Sloan. Unlike Nikon, who is supercharged with fae energy and can snap all over the place without draining, Sloan's wayfarer gift isn't like that. They used to see him all the time, and now that I've stolen him away, it's been a month.

I'm sure his parents miss him too.

I finish with my dessert shooter and bump Sloan's shoulder. "Being so close to home, did you want to take an hour and check in with your parents?"

He looks down at me with a mint brownie in his hand and shakes his head. "No, I wouldn't. It's kind of ye to think of it, especially when they wouldn't give ye the same consideration, but I have no interest in speakin' to them just yet."

I stretch up on my tip-toes and take a bite of his brownie. "It's called taking the high road, hotness. I do try. But don't get me wrong, I'm just as happy to keep you to myself."

Granda clears his throat and points at the textbooks. "Are ye here to flirt or work?"

I step back and grab a brownie. "I can multitask and do both, but fine Mr. Crankypants, let's figure out how to stop a fae trickster from ruining my life."

Sloan and I finish in the dragon lair, escort Gran and Granda back to the grandparents' Shire, and get back to Toronto using his wayfarer *poofing* power.

"I wish we could've stayed longer." I hang my jacket on the hook and move my boots to the waterproof mat. "Have I told you lately how incredibly grateful I am for your ability to portal?"

"Not in so many words, but I see the smile on yer face when ye get to pop in and see Lugh and Lara. That says it plain enough for ye."

I step close and raise my arms over my head, linking my hands behind his head. "Not good enough. I need to say it more often. I treasure the freedom your abilities allow us, and I think you're pretty much the most talented druid I know."

He chuckles. "Are ye drunk? How many of those dessert shooters did ye have?"

"More than my share, but the only drunk I am is drunk on Sloan Mackenzie."

"Fucking hell, stop that," Dillan shouts from the family room. "Your sappy sweet is making my midnight snack revolt. If you don't want me to barf on the rug, end the sappy shit now."

I roll my eyes. "Remember when you asked about me moving out? Moments like this I think it's a stellar idea."

"Wait. What?" Calum rushes out to the hall and does a *Risky Business* sock slide to stop. "Moving out?"

I wave my hand to stop the panic. "That was taken out of context. No plans. We were chatting this afternoon about Kinu and Aiden moving in here with the kids and how that would look."

Kevin steps out to join us in the hall. He's carrying nacho

snack dishes and passes us on his way to the kitchen. "I don't know why he's acting so surprised. We've talked about him coming to live with me before."

"But that's *me*." Calum looks shocked. "Fiona holds this household together. I can't imagine these walls without her in them."

"Aw, so sweet." I kiss Calum's cheek as I head into the family room. The knotted strap of my bookbag slides off my shoulder, and I pull out what little we were able to find about Discord and set it on the coffee table. "We think we've found a couple of ways to end the trickster's taunting. One, wait him out. He said it would end by Yule, so odds are it will."

"That's still two and a half weeks away," Calum says.

"So much time, so many people to kill," Dillan adds.

True story. "Two, we address the broken vow angle. What did the dark wizards promise Asmodeus? What was the wording of their oath? How do I break it?"

Sloan sits on the ottoman against the wall and reaches to scrub Manx's ears. "If we can negate Asmodeus' claim on Fiona being responsible, yer Granda thinks Discord might move on to a new game."

"If Asmodeus is behind it."

"There's that too."

"What about killing the weaselly little fucker?" Dillan snaps. "I think we should go that route."

I shrug. "Not gonna happen, I'm afraid. All the descriptions consider him 'god-like.' I'm pretty sure he's immortal."

"Fucking A." Dillan tilts his head back on the couch and looks up at the ceiling. "So we can either wait him out or break the vow, or what? Is that it?"

"No. The third idea is to turn the tables and meet his riddles with riddles of our own."

"Will that deter him or make him more engaged in playing with you?" Calum asks.

"That was my point." I hand over a couple of the examples we came up with. "I think solving his riddles and creating new puzzles will only make him more interested in me as a playmate."

"Hard pass on that one," Calum says.

"Agreed. Our fourth idea is to bribe him with something he wants more than to torment me."

"Which would be what?"

"No idea."

Dillan scowls, rolling his eyes. "Thanks for playing Don't Know Shit with tonight's special guest, Fiona Cumhaill."

I raise my eyebrows and smile at Dillan. "You're crustier than usual tonight. What's up?"

"Nothing. Just my normal sunshiny self."

"Pants on fire," Calum says. "Liam confessed he's been seeing Kady and they're going to make a go of it as a couple."

I sigh. "Aw, I'm sorry, bro. I know you liked her."

Dillan strangles the neck of his beer and presses the bottle to his lips. After a long swallow, he forces a smile. "Doesn't matter. S'all good. Here's to the happy couple. It just means more popping bottles with models for me."

Poor Dillan. Sometimes the ones who seem to have no feelings have the deepest feelings of all.

"Maybe I can cheer ye up, Dillan," Sloan says. "If yer game to bend the rules a little."

Dillan sits up straighter in his seat. "What are you thinking, Irish? I'm game. What rules? How far do we need to bend things? I'm feeling pretty flexible tonight."

Sloan looks surprised at the enthusiasm, but he doesn't know Dillan as well as the rest of us. Avoidance and stirring up trouble are two of his key coping mechanisms.

"What have you got in mind, hotness?"

"Why don't we move this nachos and beer party next door? I may not feel right about stealing the pool table and bringing it over here, but I've been in that basement, and the house is empty. There's no reason we can't go there and play a few rounds. I can portal everyone out fast if we're discovered disturbing the peace."

"Done!" Dillan raises his beer and jumps over the coffee table. "I call first break."

I don't know what expression Sloan's reading on my face, but he shrugs, looking guilty. "What? I'm tryin' to cheer up yer brother."

"By breaking and entering?"

Sloan chuckles. "We're not breakin', and they won't even be able to prove we're enterin'."

Da comes through the back door after having a pint at the pub with Shannon. He seems sober and steady, so I hope that's a sign that he's getting his train back on track. "What's this about breakin' and enterin'?"

"Dum-de-dum-dum," Calum says. "Busted."

Sloan straightens and meets Da's curious gaze. "Dillan's havin' an off night. I suggested portalin' everyone to the basement next door to play some pool. The house is empty, and I thought it would be fun. Are ye game to join us?"

Oh, dayum. He went for it.

My boyfriend totes invited Da to break the law. Sad face. I liked him too.

"Sounds fun. I call the first game."

Cue the dropping jaws around the room. What the hell?

Sloan stands and smiles at all the shocked faces. "Then it's set. Everyone grab yer bevvies and snacks of choice and meet back in the hall. The poolroom portal leaves in five."

My mind is still tripping on that when Manx bounds into the hall and sits, ready to roll.

I scratch my head. "Da? Are you really cool with this?"

He glances over at Sloan and shrugs. "Why not? Yer only young once, right?"

"Who are you?" Calum gives him a sideways glance. "What have you done with our father?"

Da chuckles. "I'll have ye know I jumped my fair share of backyard fences to take a dip in the neighbors' pools."

I snort. "Your neighbors were miles away and likely didn't have pools."

"But I had culchie friends who lived in town. Believe me or not, I think it'll be fun to live on the wild side for a change. What would Brendan do?"

Now we're all laughing. Brenny was our wild child. No ill-advised idea passed him by if somebody challenged him. But that's Brendan, not Da.

"WWBD," Calum says. "I think 'What would Brendan do?' should be our new litmus test."

I'm still staring at my father. My hamster has fallen out of his mental wheel and is now caught in the inertia, flipping and flopping like a limp noodle in my head. "Okay, someone grab me a cooler while I run up and change into comfy clothes. Back in a flash. If Da's up for family B and E, I'm certainly not going to miss it."

I hit the stairs running, pulling up the hem of my shirt as I reach the top.

Da chuckles in the hall below. "Last one into the portal circle cleans up at the end of the night."

I'm halfway through my bedroom door with my shirt over my head when my brothers start yelling, "Not it."

"Aw, Da! That was rude."

CHAPTER EIGHTEEN

Sloan, Calum, and I meet Garnet and Anyx on the wide, sheltered driveway of Garnet's home the next afternoon. The Grand Governor of the Lakeshore Guild owns a pricey property in a swanky part of mid-town Toronto. That's not where he really lives. Empowered folks he invites are transported to an African compound when they step through the brick archway.

Non-magical or folks not invited, simply pass through the same archway to the home inside and find no one home.

Talk about screening your guests.

However, today isn't a social call. We're not even going inside. Sloan *poofs* us onto the driveway, and the five of us climb into Garnet's massive black Navigator.

I press my hand against the flutter in my chest, and Garnet takes notice. "Are you well, Lady Druid?"

"Yep. Bruin is excited to head back to the funeral home. He enjoyed smashing bad wizards doing bad things last time around and hopes for a repeat performance."

Garnet arches an elegant brow. "I hope for questions

answered without a bloodbath this time if that's all right with your bear."

Nothing wrong with a good bloodbath now and then.

I smile at Bruin's response, but Garnet is right. "I hope we can figure out what the deal was with Asmodeus and how I got roped into being Discord's target."

"Do you think they'll cooperate?" Calum asks as the truck leaves the driveway. "They aren't part of Fiona's fan club. Won't they want to see her suffer?"

"Harsh, bro."

"Likely, yes." Garnet's not one to protect feelings. "The trick will be to convince them to tell us despite the animosity they hold toward your sister."

"Can't we all just get along?" I add, smiling. "Make peace, not war." Garnet rolls his eyes, so I give up the flower child approach. "Have they picked a leader to replace Salem?"

"No, and I hope that works to our advantage."

"How so?"

Garnet turns around in the shotgun seat and looks back at the three of us. "Even though they don't like you, they understand the significance of having the Guild's support behind them."

"Ye plan on playin' one against the other until we have what we want to know."

Garnet nods. "More than a pretty face."

I smile at Sloan's pretty face, thankful every day for him crashing into my life. "So, if we agree they all hate me, should I try to blend into the background?"

Garnet chuckles. "If only that were possible, Lady Druid. I'm afraid that in a room filled with powerful, morally ambiguous empowered folks, you don't blend well at all. In truth, your fire for justice burns so hotly you practically ignite those around you."

I bark a laugh. "That's poetic. It's also crazy. I'm bumbling along like everyone else most times."

"From the outside looking in, no one can tell that."

I hope that's true. I sink deeper into the plush leather of my seat and stare out at the passing city. "What about the hobgoblins and the necromancers? How are they doing at reestablishing things?"

I've left a swath of damage through the empowered community since my arrival. It was never my intention, but hey, best-laid plans, amirite?

"I spoke to Droghun. As you've probably noticed, he hasn't been at the past few Guild meetings."

"I noticed. It's been heaven."

Garnet pulls his phone from the pocket of his black trench. "I assume his absence has been partly wounded pride, and partly him reconsidering their druid status."

"Because they aren't druids."

"So you've mentioned."

I grin. "Sorry, carry on."

"I received an email from him this week restating their principles and practices so there is no confusion in the future."

"No confusion at all. They siphon blood and power from innocent fae and other empowered folk and consider themselves clever and powerful for doing so."

"Tell us how you really feel, Fi," Calum says. "And when I say that, I'm kidding. We all know how you feel."

I roll my eyes. "Fine. Droghun's finished regrouping and knows what they represent. Bully for them. What about the hobgoblins?"

"There have been some updates there as well. Not every male warrior was in attendance in the subway tunnel when Kartak of the Narrows tried to have you killed. They too are regrouping and have chosen a new leader. Ginsheer of the Caverns."

"Do you know him?"

Garnet shakes his head. "The only two things I know about him are that he wasn't a fan of Kartak, and he's reached out for help to support the women and children left behind after the sudden bloody demise of all the war-waging males of their community."

They deserved it, Bruin says directly to me. *They shot at you and almost killed Liam.*

Agreed. No argument here, buddy.

Anyx turns onto Bloor, and we head toward the West Village. It's December, so the commercial shopping in the area makes things even busier than normal. Thankfully, funeral homes have parking lots, so we don't have to circle the block waiting for a place to park this behemoth.

Seeing only three cars in the sizable lot, I take that as a sign that they don't currently have a funeral to tend to.

That's a good thing.

Anyx pulls Garnet's beefy black truck in between two white lines and flips the shifter into park. "This stop, cowards, crybabies, and corpses. Everyone out."

I burst out laughing. "Was that a joke, Lion? Good one."

Garnet pegs me with a look. "My right-hand enforcer doesn't joke. Stop tainting my staff. I face enough insouciant banter from you. I don't need it from any other sources."

I catch the amusement in Anyx's gaze in the reflection of the rearview mirror. "Understood. Leave your staff members morose and focused. Got it."

I pull the handle on the door and drop out of the truck. A gust of wind hits and I pop the faux fur collar of my jacket. "So, the questions we need answered are, what was the wording of the vow they made with Asmodeus? How was the contract sealed? And how did the wizards bind it?"

Garnet rolls his alluring purple eyes. "Not my first rodeo, little girl. I'm focused on the task at hand."

When Garnet turns to lead the way, I make wide eyes at Calum, and we fall into line like schoolchildren.

. . .

The electronic door chime goes off the moment we open the front door of the funeral home. As we step inside, the first thing I notice is that it's nothing like the last time. They've modernized the décor and changed the picture over the mantle to a commemorative oil painting of Salem Markdale—sadly without Asmodeus swirling in an evil rift in the background—and there is now a beautiful ebony grand piano off to the side of the main foyer.

"Andreas Markdale." Garnet gestures at a lanky man with a dark skull-trim buzz cut and a newly stitched gash under his eye. "Horacio Baynes," he sweeps his hand to a bulky, roid-droid guy with tats and dirty blond, shoulder-length hair, "This is Fiona Cumhaill, her brother Calum, and their associate Sloan Mackenzie."

We nod to each other in turn, and I meet the gaze of the first man introduced. "Markdale. You're related to Salem?"

Andreas's gaze isn't as cold as I expect. He eyes me up and down and lifts his chin. "First cousins."

"Well, for what it's worth, I'm sorry to have taken him down. I tried to reason with him, but his spell was getting dangerously out of control, and he wouldn't listen to reason. When he attacked, I defended and ended it."

A hint of a smile curls the man's thin lips. "That a little girl so easily ended him speaks more about him than you, Fiona Cumhaill. I have no quarrel with you."

Well, that's a first. I wonder if he'd repeat that so I can get it on video. "I appreciate you saying so."

Garnet gestures toward the meeting rooms. "If I could have a private word with the two of you before we begin, it would be appreciated."

I didn't know about this part of the plan, so assume it's Guild business and not vow business. Either that or this is his way of ensuring I blend into the background.

He takes the two men vying for High Priest of the Toronto Wizarding Council into one of the family meeting rooms to chat.

The door clicks shut, and leaves us most definitely on the outside.

"Well, this is anticlimactic," Calum says. "Why do I feel like we just got seated at the kid's table?"

"Because we did." I frown at the closed door, and Anyx shrugs where he stands guard.

I'm not good with being benched. *Bruin, feel free to spirit yourself and snoop around. Do you remember what the spellbook they were using looked like?*

I do.

I release my battle bear and smile as the two solemn ushers smile politely from beside the main doors. "Excuse us, gentleman."

Sloan, Calum, and I step over to the piano.

"Very pretty." I run my fingers over her perfect shine and smile at the fingerprints I leave in my wake. "Oops."

Sloan sits in the center of the bench seat and sets his fingers on the keys.

"You play?" I ask.

"I do."

"Well?"

"Of course." Sloan winks at me as his fingers start moving over the keys and he plays us the most amazing song. The notes float in the air creating an upbeat yet passionate rhythm. As I watch, I swear I can almost see the magic of the notes rising into existence around us.

I pull out my phone and discreetly video him. I want to keep this moment for posterity.

"You took lessons," Calum says, equally impressed.

"I did. With a local lady who taught out of her home near to where I lived, then picked up some tips from Niall Horan if ye believe it."

My eyes bug out as my jaw drops. "Shut the front door! You're shitting me?" I scowl at Calum. "Did one of my asshole brothers put you up to this?"

Sloan frowns, and the music stops. "Put me up to what?"

"To name drop. Niall Horan."

Sloan chuckles. "Yer ridiculous. Niall and I are the same age and both support philanthropy. We're both football and golf fans, and the fundraising circles aren't that big in Ireland."

I shake my head, but it still feels fuzzy. "You seriously know Niall Horan?"

"I seriously do. Why? Yer a fan, I take it?"

Calum laughs. "A mindless teenager, screaming superfan. She played One Direction songs until the five of us considered starting up a Cumhaill cover band because we knew all the words. Then there's the fact that he's her wedding singer."

Sloan laughs. "He sang at yer wedding? Did I miss the part where yer married?"

"Didn't I tell you?" I laugh and wave that away. "No. I told them since I was fifteen that I want Niall Horan to sing at my wedding."

Sloan flashes me a cocky smile and laughs. "Well, choose yer groom well, and that just might happen."

Calum is laughing now. "You never know, Irish. That might be enough for you to clinch the win."

"Have an edge then, do I?"

"A big one."

I ignore the teasing banter, my mind awhirl. "Play me something. Do you know any of his songs?"

Sloan starts playing *Slow Hands*, and I'm in my glory.

When Anyx steps into view and signals for us to join the conversation, I'm momentarily at a loss. I've lost focus and forgotten why we're even here.

Right. Demon vendettas and my murderous stalker.

"We're not done with this, hotness. I will spend all my Guild money and buy you a piano if you play me Niall Horan songs."

Calum laughs and pats Sloan's arm as we stand. "You're about to get *soooo* lucky, Irish. Seriously, this is your angle to take home the gold. Congrats."

"Come in," Garnet gestures at the vacant seats when we file into the beige room. By the binders lined up on the little credenza against the wall and the box of tissues on the table, I guess this is where the grieving families make their selections for upcoming funerals. It kinda sets an ominous tone for the discussion to come.

Calum and I sit.

Sloan stands at the open door with Anyx.

Garnet leans forward in his seat and folds his hands on the table. "A moment ago, I asked Andreas and Horacio about the terms of their pact with Asmodeus. They assure me that no terms were set and your troubles with Discord are unrelated. I can scent a lie and find no reason for them to deceive us."

"Okay, let's say that's true. Then why did the trickster first contact me through the bloody virus set to work its way through the wizarding ranks?"

Horacio opens his palms to me and smiles. "Merely a coincidence, I'm sure."

"I'm sure," I lie.

Fi, I've found the spellbook. It's locked in the basement ritual room where you faced off with Salem. There's a false wall behind a blue cabinet. There is all manner of spine-chilling things back there.

Is there anyone down there?

No. No one.

I'll text Sloan. He pulled me from that room so he can poof in there. Then you can show him.

Okay, I'll wait down there.

I discreetly slip my phone out of my pocket and hold it under the table. "I'm sorry for the losses of your fellow wizards. That virus was nasty."

Andreas frowns. "It certainly was. The way those men perished was almost more devastating than the deaths themselves."

I'm not sure what that says about the bonds of wizards but keep that to myself.

Horacio seems less torn up about it than Andreas. Or maybe it's just that his buzz cut, muscle-builder, tough-guy image is harder to read. "The randomness of those deaths is regrettable."

I lean back a little while Garnet engages the men in conversation and text Sloan what Bruin found. After I hit send, I ease back into the convo. I don't think anyone noticed except Calum beside me. "If you allow us to look at the spell as it's written, it might help. If we had the wording of the vow, we could figure out how the contract sealed and what happened to bind it to me."

I hold the focus of the conversation as Sloan excuses himself to go to the men's room.

Neither of the men rallying to be the next Grand Wizard seems eager to share the spell.

"I'm sure you understand, Lady Druid," Horacio says unapologetically. "There is power in possessing certain information. To simply surrender it weakens our position in a very competitive community."

"So, you won't let us look at the spell because you want to hog it? Is that what you're saying?"

"You make it sound like this is some kind of schoolyard rivalry."

"Isn't it? You have information that could save not only my life but dozens or even hundreds of lives of innocent people. The responsible 'community' thing to do would be to allow us to examine the language of the spell so we can understand how to break its hold."

Andreas shrugs. "I'm sorry, Miss Cumhaill. Even in this time of transition, the edicts of our cohort are clear. Wizards do not share spells outside of our community. I wish we could be of more help."

"What if we hadn't figured out the intent of the virus and ended the spread so quickly? You would've lost many more members of your cohort. I would think you'd be grateful for the sharing of information whether it comes from wizards or druids or nymphs. The point is, we're *all* members of the Lakeshore Guild of the Empowered."

Horacio chuckles and looks at Garnet. "Where did you find this one? She's ready for pep squad. Give her a short skirt and let's watch her shake her pom-poms."

My hair stands on end as the glamor on my eyes burns away. Standing, I call my connection with nature and let my freak flag wave. Electricity arcs in the air as the wind starts to swirl around us.

"Don't mistake my age or my gender for weakness, Mr. Baynes. If you talk about me like that again, I will call a lightning strike and fry your tiny boy balls while you beg me for mercy. Or have the earth swallow your home while you sleep. Sinkholes are a mysterious thing."

Horacio stands and plants his palms on the table. "Are you threatening me, Lady Druid? Wizards have power too, you know."

I grin. "When you or Andreas finally figure out who's boss, I'll welcome you to the Guild Governor's table. I'll wave to you from the far left from the seats of power. You haven't been there yet, so you don't know the kind of power *I* have. Maybe you should ask around before you burn those teensy balls of yours."

Sloan steps into the room and holds out his hand to me. "Time to go, Fi. Ye can fry the man's testicles next time, I promise. This is gettin' ye nowhere."

"Did you get it?" I ask Sloan the moment Anyx pulls the truck out of the funeral home parking lot. We merge with the coming traffic and are on our way out of the wizard domain.

"Get what?" Garnet turns in the shotgun seat and pegs me with a look.

I pat the flutter of my bear in my chest. "Bruin had a little look around for the spellbook Salem used. When he found it and told me where it was hidden, I sent Sloan to take a screenshot of the spell so we can see what we're dealing with."

Garnet frowns. "I'm not thrilled you made that call without my input. What if they agreed to take us down to look? We would've looked stupid if they found Sloan down there already snooping around."

"Sorry. It was a time-sensitive decision, and I figured since you and I had their attention, it was the perfect time to have a peek. Sloan can *poof* out at a moment's notice."

Garnet seems to accept that without offense. "What did the spell say?"

Sloan tilts his head from side to side as if considering that. "Andreas was telling the truth. There was no vow written into the spell and certainly nothing that could've transferred to Fi when we terminated the summoning."

I sigh. "Poop. I thought that spell might help us figure things out."

Sloan's cocky grin ignites a rush of hope. "*That* spell didn't tell me much, but I did find a log sheet for other spellbooks and did a little snooping."

"And?"

"Horatio signed out *Summoning, Ensnaring, and Ensorcelling Powerful Beings.*" He pulls out his phone and shows me a list of books with notes. "It's one of the books Myra suggested might hold answers. She didn't have a copy, but being a Fae Historian of books, she knew it was one possible resource to find an explanation for Discord's arrival."

"How's that?" Garnet asks.

"Because it contains a powerful summoning and enticement spell for tricksters."

I scrub my forehead and try to put the pieces together. "You're hurting my brain. Are you saying Discord isn't here because Asmodeus wants blood at all?"

Sloan nods. "That's what I'm saying. I think Horatio summoned Discord and set him on you to A) get back at you for killing Salem and stopping their Asmodeus plans for power, and B) to take out the wizards who support Andreas as the next High Priest."

Garnet frowns. "That's a serious accusation based on the title of a book the man signed out of the wizarding library. There must be dozens of spells in that book."

Sloan nods. "I'm sure there are, but if we could locate the book, Dora could call up a tracking record for it and tell us who cast what spells most recently. She could tell us if I'm on the right track."

Calum grabs the headrest of the seat ahead of him and leans forward. "If a spell in a book summoned Discord, is he like a genie in a bottle? Can he be released from his task? Can we set him free and end this?"

"That's a simplistic way to put it, but yes," Garnet says.

Calum slaps Sloan's leg. "Nicely done, Irish."

I couldn't agree more. "Okay, now all we have to do is figure out where Horacio has the book so we can swipe it, track it back to him, and fry his balls. *Noice!*"

CHAPTER NINETEEN

"This place is warded up the ying-yang." Sloan leans in the open window of the truck when he and Anyx come back from their intel gathering. "We don't know enough about wizard magic to counter it and gain entrance into his house."

"But we know someone who does." I pull out my phone. "Should I text her and see if she's game?"

The four of us all look at Garnet for his thoughts. "Go ahead. If Horacio is behind this mess, I want to know."

My thumbs glide over my screen as I check Dora's interest in helping us out. The response comes back almost immediately. "She says yes. She's at the bookstore visiting Myra. She's good for a pickup."

"I'll go." Sloan pushes off the side of the truck.

Garnet and Anyx nod their agreement, and he checks his exposure and *poofs* off.

He's back in a flash with Dora in tow.

I've noticed a change in Dora since she's been more involved in owning her past and magic. She's still over-the-top glam, but not so outrageous. Today she's fabulous in leopard print pants and a tight, ivory angora top. "Hey, baby." She winks a gold glitter-dusted eye. "How can I help?"

I catch Dora up on Sloan's theory about Horacio being the one behind Discord and not Asmodeus as we first thought. "We now think it's all part of his plan to get back at me and secure his spot as High Priest."

Dora pushes out her full, glossy lips and sighs. "I have to hand it to the man. If that's true, it was a solid plan. Eliminate the competition, punish you, and all the blame falls on a Greater Demon trapped in the Hell realm."

"Neat and tidy, isn't it?"

"Except, I think Fi figured out the blood curse faster than he anticipated," Calum says. "He probably thought he could take out more of Andreas's followers before we contained the contagion."

Dora narrows her glittery gaze. "That death toll almost included me. Speaking as one who watched an innocent woman die because of it, I'll tell you he has his coming."

I think of Imari's mother, Nathan, Endor, and the cleaning ladies and Nikon's staff, all the chaos at the parade, and I'm with Dora. "He has treachery to answer for. This isn't going to end well for him if he's responsible."

Garnet steps out of the truck. "All right then, let's find out one way or another."

Horacio Baynes lives in a modern, white brick house with lots of glass and chrome. With the size of his home and the neighborhood, it would carry an easy two-and-a-half-million dollar price tag. To make it even more impressive, it's almost as close to the natural setting of High Park as my house is to the Don Valley greenbelt.

"All right, folks." Dora raises her hands to assess the warding. "Let's see what Mr. Baynes is hiding."

While Dora works on the warding, I release Bruin to have a look around. "Let us know if you see or hear anything we need to worry about, Bear."

Will do.

Sloan *poofs* in beside us with Dillan at his side.

My brother has his green cape on and pulls up his hood with a grin. "Did somebody call for a ranger adept in finding hidden clues? Well, look no further. I'm here."

I roll my eyes. "And you're so humble."

"Hey, there's no need to be humble if you're da bomb."

I shove his shoulder and point toward the side of the house. "All right, hotshot. Go find us something astounding and earn that reputation you're trying to establish for yourself."

"Watch and learn, sista. I shall return with something mind-blowing shortly."

When he leaves, Sloan steps closer and whispers into my ear. "Is his conceit growing, or has he always been like this?"

"Nothing new. Although, to some degree, he's not wrong. With the hood of his cloak up, he's remarkable."

"That's the cloak's magic, not his."

I shrug. "The cloak chose him and bonded with him. There has to be something to that."

"If you say so."

I chuckle and go back to watching Dora.

Dillan might come off as cocky and broody, but when it comes down to it, he has a heart made out of the sweetest, gooiest honey of anyone *evah*. That's why it hurt him so deeply that Kady and Liam are getting closer. He cared for her but knew his life of being a danger-lover wasn't something she'd ever be comfortable with.

If you love something, set it free, right?

He'll find his perfect match. And hey, with the empowered world opening up for us, there's no telling who or what she might be. Life has gotten a whole lot more interesting.

"There, that should do it." Dora lowers her hands and gives Anyx a thumbs-up. "Give it a try, cookie. You should be good to flash in without resistance."

Anyx vanishes, and a moment later opens the side door of the house, letting us all in.

"Quick and dirty, people." Garnet strides in and heads straight toward the back of the house. "We don't want to be here when Horacio gets back."

I'm not all that concerned about Horacio having a tantrum about us invading his space. I do agree, though, that it's good not to be at the scene of the crime when the bad guy comes home.

Sloan pulls out a couple of his druid stones and starts a scrying spell while I head over to the bookshelf and start searching.

I don't take it for granted that the title on the spine is what the book is about, so I pull them out and have a quick look through each one before replacing them. Horacio seems to have eclectic tastes when reading.

There are science journals and texts on ancient culture and modern DIY books on how to build hunting blinds and land-scape them to blend in.

"Anyone getting anything?" Garnet asks, coming out from the back.

Sloan is standing in the center of the house staring down at his pendulum. "Unless he spelled it to remain hidden—and I'm not detectin' any spells—it's not here."

I walk around looking at the pictures, trying to get into this guy's head. "If he was going to summon Discord, would he do it in his home? Do wizards have a Bat Cave? Could there be a hidden room in the basement or something?"

Dillan shakes his head. "No. I've been all through this place, and I don't sense any secret shelves or passageways or hidden doors. There's nothing here that feels wizardy."

"Then where does he practice his magic?"

Dora shrugs. "If it were me, in the old days, I would've had a place hidden in the nearby forest. I was especially fond of caves."

I think about the books I've read about Merlin and remember Mary Stewart's book about *Merlin in The Crystal Cave*. How accurate were the stories? One day, maybe I'll be brave enough to ask. Today is not that day.

I point out the window. "What about High Park? It's not exactly a wild forest, but it's a natural setting and almost a square mile of trees and water and animals."

Sloan nods. "How about the Cumhaills and I move the search to High Park, Dora puts the wards back up, and while she's doing that, Garnet and Anyx continue to search? Then, if Horacio comes back, ye'll be able to flash her out."

Everyone seems good with that plan, so the four of us leave and head across the road to High Park.

Toronto's High Park is similar to the idea of New York's Central Park; only it's a third the size. There's a forested area, paths, a café, gardens, a children's zoo, and a meditation labyrinth painted in a large circle. It's a lovely green space to give people a chance to absorb nature in the city setting.

"Where would a wizard hide his den of darkness?" I scan the area.

Calum points to our right. "Likely in one of the more remote, treed areas would be my guess."

"Horacio had books on building wildlife blinds and landscaping. Maybe they have something to do with this. Do you think he built a nature screen to hide his wizardy ways?"

Calum chuckles. "I think it's more likely than him getting camo'ed up and waiting for hours in a blind to shoot a deer. From what we saw today, I doubt he's the type."

Sloan heads toward the trees, his strides much longer than

mine. "We can cast *Detect Magic* once we find a private spot. Maybe we'll get lucky."

Dillan snorts. "I don't know about you two, but Calum and I don't want to be anywhere near you two while you're getting lucky. Poor choice of words, Irish."

I stick my tongue out at him. "Don't make things weird."

"I make things awesome. Point me in the right direction, and I guarantee if the wizard's clubhouse is here, I'll find it."

I giggle and pat Dillan's arm. "I never have to worry about you having a confidence problem."

Dillan grins. "Why would I? I'm fucking fabulous."

"That you are, brother mine." The four of us find a little treed area not far from the edge of Grenadier Pond, and while Dillan stalks around with his hood up, Sloan closes his eyes and casts his *Detect Magic* spell. When he makes no effort to stride off in any given direction, I figure it isn't an easy win.

"Something's blocking the spell," Sloan says, looking miffed. "Maybe we can divine the location."

"Or maybe there's nothing to find." When everyone hits me with a wave of stink eye, I surrender. "I believe we're on the right track, but it never hurts to be an advocate for the other side of an argument. How about a divining rod?"

"You have to hold it," Calum says. "I'm not letting you do to me what you did to poor Emmet."

Vibrant images of Emmet bouncing over forest obstacles and poison ivy with his pants getting pulled down and his shoe flying off crack me up. "You guys are just mad you weren't there to see it."

"Hells yes we are, but I'm still not holding your sadistic wand of torment."

"Fine. I'll do it myself. I did it successfully in Ireland last month. I'm sure I can do it again."

Calum, Sloan, and I search for a forked branch from an oak or ash tree or a yew shrub. "I should keep one of these for moments like this. It seems I need to divine things more often than you might expect."

"Nature provides, *a ghra*. When ye need it, ye'll find it."

"If you build it, they will come," Calum says.

"Is this heaven?" Dillan cracks a smile.

"No…it's Iowa," I answer.

Sloan looks at us like we're nuts.

I hold up my hands. "C'mon, hotness. Seriously?"

"Ye realize yer family speaks its own language? Ye think it's common knowledge, but it's not."

"*Field of Dreams*, Irish," Dillan says. "If you build it, they will come. Kevin Costner, James Earl Jones, Amy Madigan…are you with us now?"

"I grew up studying the fae world and the natural world. My parents didn't put much importance behind American entertainment."

Calum frowns. "Well, this is serious. We'll have to go right back to basics. You'll have to be schooled not only in the classics but the fringe films too."

Sloan looks at me as if I'm going to save him.

"Don't look at me. I'm one hundy percent with them. We're going to put together a list of all the best movies and begin your training. It could take years."

Sloan's bewilderment eases and his mouth curls up in a crooked smile. "So, ye see me in the picture fer years to come, do ye?"

Dillan snorts. "Now you went and made it weird. Weren't we out here looking for a stick?"

"No, *we* are looking for a stick," I say. "You're supposed to be using your goddess-given gift to find Horacio's hideout without a stick. Come on, Mister Fabulous, do your thang."

Dillan tilts his neck from side to side releasing a subtle *pop-pop-pop* of his vertebrae. After he shakes out his arms and runs on the spot for a few seconds, I'm busting a gut.

"Now you're being an ass."

"What? You don't unleash what I have going on without warming up. I might blow something important."

"Blow it out your butt and get to work, goofball."

Dillan mumbles something about being grossly misunderstood and tromps off. I turn to catch up with Calum and Sloan and find Calum sitting cross-legged in the frost-bitten scrub with a skunk in his lap.

"Um…hello? Earth to Calum…you have a skunk sitting on you."

"Shh." He waves me away. "She's a little scared, but she's sweet." Calum brushes his fingers along the little white stripe on her head. "She's not happy here. The other skunks and forest animals are mean to her."

I blink and look at Sloan. "What is happening here? He doesn't have Wildlife Communication, does he?"

"No, but he won't need it if she's his animal companion. The druid bond will allow them to communicate without a natural strength in that discipline."

Calum is bonding to a skunk? This should be interesting.

"I promise, little one. Go ahead and show us." Calum sets the little ball of fur onto the brittle grass, and she waddles off deeper into the trees. "Daisy knows the wizard and will show us where the hideout is. In return, I told her she could live in our grove where the other animals won't bully her."

We strike off, following the little stinker and I can't help but ask. "Why do the other animals bully her?"

"She says she's sick. When she has one of her spells, she can't control her spray. She lets out her musk without warning, and the other animals in the forest don't like it."

Hubba-wha? "You thought a skunk that can't control her stink spray should live in my beautiful grove?"

"It's *our* beautiful grove, and I said I'd help her. No one should be bullied or made to feel bad about themselves for something they have no control over."

"I agree, but—"

"No buts, Fi. I gave Daisy my word. I'm helping her."

He strides off in a huff and leaves me with a dazzled Dillan. "Did he just bond with a skunk that sprays without warning or control?"

"Yep." I take Sloan's hand and look up at him with a pleading gaze. "Please tell me there's a spell we can use to stop her spray problem from happening."

"I would if that were possible. If it's a natural occurrence, there won't be anything a spell can do. We can look into medical treatment though, depending on what type of spells she suffers from. We might find something by going that route."

"Might?" I throw my hands up and sock that argument away for another time. "Awesome."

"Good girl, Daisy." Calum picks up his skunk companion and sets her safely out of the way while Dillan and Sloan assess the opening of what seems to be an underground cavern. "That was excellent."

I text Dora and Garnet and give them our location to the best of my ability. A moment later, they tromp through the trees.

"What are we looking at?" Garnet studies the stone slab we found when we moved a large rock and pulled away the drape of grass and scrub below.

I cock my head. "I'd guess a magical stone slab to block the entrance to a wizard's evil lair."

Garnet gives me a droll stare and looks at Dora. "Can you get this open for us?"

Dora winks at me and chuckles. "Surely."

"Don't call me Shirley," Dillan says.

The three of us look at Sloan, but he has nothing. I sigh. "Add *Airplane* to the list."

Garnet snaps his fingers. "Hello? Can we focus, please? I swear, put three Cumhaills in a room, and you're suddenly living an episode of *Who's on First.*"

Dillan smiles. "Then our work here is done."

I grin at the stern censure of our Grand Governor. "Love you too, Garnet." When the warning growl of his lion rumbles all around us, we straighten up. "Okay, point taken. We're focused. Let's get inside."

CHAPTER TWENTY

I've decided to stop imagining what I'll walk into because I'm terrible at it. When I think something will be creepy, it's upscale and polished. When I believe someplace will be fine, it's uber gross. I figured Garnet's place would be metrosexual modern, and it was a home in the African savanna. That's not even close. Like I said...I'm bad at it.

Horacio's hidden wizard lair feels more like a Starbuck's lobby than a clandestine chamber of criminality. I study the white tile floors, the long wooden counter with a glass display, and a coffee maker in the back. It's not even small or cramped... it's not dark at all.

"Is anyone else weirded out that this place is so upscale?"

Calum's checking out the coffee station and laughs. "He has a French press. Who sets up a French press in their evil den of debauchery?"

"Right?"

"Focus, children," Garnet says. "Find the book."

"Right." The five of us who came in spread out to look. Calum starts opening doors and drawers, Sloan heads over to the work-

243

table, Dora lifts the corners of the area rug, and Garnet and I meet over by the apothecary cupboard on the far wall. "So, what happens if we prove Horacio is behind this? Does he go to wizard jail or something? Does the Guild have a penal system?"

"We have a containment facility for those who are deemed worthy of rehabilitation and a second chance. Otherwise, we put down the most heinous offenders."

Harsh. "I suppose capital punishment is an effective deterrent for people veering too far out of their lane."

"In most cases, yes."

"You make sure the guilty are guilty, right? There's no way we're killing people if they could've been framed or coerced?"

"We don't take the sentencing of death lightly, no. It's only in extreme cases and if we're entirely certain of the perpetrator's guilt."

That makes me feel a little better. I don't want to be a cog in the wheel of tyranny.

"I have it." Sloan holds up a textbook. "Dora, if ye don't mind, yer up."

Garnet and I move over to where Sloan sets the book on the worktable. Dora twists toward me and pulls up the hem of her shirt. I recognize the brooch tattooed on her hip before she calls it forward.

When it's in her hand, she holds it over the spellbook.

The words she uses aren't anything I understand, so I simply wait and watch.

After she speaks her spell, the air builds with the potential of power to come. The hair on my arms stands on end, and the flutter in my chest isn't my bear settling this time. I lean to the side to get a better view.

A soft hum in the background builds to a buzz and gains strength to become a rumble.

Sloan is so intently focused on what Dora does that it's remarkable. That's why he's great at what we do. Where I have a boatload of gifted skills and generally shoot from the hip, he studies and learns and becomes proficient.

I should try to be more like him.

"Here it comes." Dora steps back.

Garnet moves forward to stand at her side as a swirling orange cyclone of magic rises from the book's cover. It lifts into the air until the tiny windstorm hovers above the table. The spellbook's cover *clacks* against the surface as it flips open and the pages flap and flutter until they settle.

The orange cyclone magic turns black, and we're looking at a holographic image of Horacio bending over the book and reading out the spell.

"Help me, Obi-Wan. You're my only hope," Calum says.

I manage to keep a straight face, but I was totally thinking the same thing. "You were right, hotness." I squeeze his arm and smile. "You figured it out. It's much less scary to be targeted by a duplicitous wizard than it is to think a Greater Demon from Hell is after me."

"I think we all agree with ye there. Now that we have the bastard dead to rights, all we have to do is figure out how to counter the spell."

Dora closes her hand over the brooch and returns it to its inked state. I'm pleased to know she's keeping Morgana's talisman close, but at the same time worry about having such a powerful object internalized.

I know from personal experience how deadly dangerous that can be. It sucks ass.

Still, Dora is much stronger than I and the brooch isn't nearly as dark as the grimoire was—maybe it'll be fine.

"Irish." Dora closes the book and tucks it under her arm. "How about the two of us put our heads together and go through the spell line by line? I have some reference materials back in my loft that might help."

Sloan shifts his gaze to me, and I nod. "I couldn't be in better hands. I want to ride this out with Garnet and see Horatio's face when I nail him to the wall."

"Time to fry his tiny man balls?" Sloan says.

I grin. "Go, team."

He winks, reaches for Dora's hand, and the two of them *poof* out.

I look around the room and smile. "I for one, feel good about this. With the druid dream team set on the task, I'm sure we'll be done with this Discord stuff before we know it."

"Easy peasy, guaranteedy," Calum says.

I widen my eyes. "Guaranteedy?"

"Too much of a good thing?"

"A little, yeah. Besides, don't jinx us—"

"The wizard approacheth," Dillan shouts from above.

I frown at Calum. "That is completely your fault. You jinxed us."

"My bad."

Calum and I take the lead, and Garnet follows behind. By the time we climb out of the underground workshop, Horacio is barreling at us with three of his friends.

His hands are up, and magic is crackling when he spots Garnet and changes tack. "What's going on here? Why have you trespassed into my private space?"

"Private?" Garnet gestures at the woods around us. "This is a public green space, and in our dedication to saving lives, we were led here in the search for the truth."

Horacio looks from us to the open doorway into the ground and scowls. "What truth?"

"That you're the douche-canoe behind all the Discord mayhem ruining my sister's life," Calum says.

"As well as killing innocent people," I add, which I find more alarming and disturbing than the crap I've had to deal with. "We have you, dude. We found the spellbook, magic-redialed the caster, and guess whose face popped up?"

Garnet looks at the three sidekick wizards and grins. "You three would do well to step away now, boys. Things are about to go very badly for your friend Horacio."

The men seem to consider that for a moment but soon abandon any show of solidarity. "Grand Governor," one of them says and bows his head before backing away and turning to leave. The others follow close on his heels.

"Then there was one," I say.

Garnet nods. "Anyx and I will escort Mr. Baynes— "

"Watch out!" Calum tackles me as Horacio's arm swings, and a bolt of energy singes the tree next to my head.

We hit the ground and roll as the stand of trees we're in erupts in a magical firefight. Those three friends double back and bring more friends.

We're outnumbered.

"Tough as Bark." I push off the ground and call Birga, releasing Bruin. "Have at it, Killer Clawbearer."

Bruin's roar of excitement reminds me that we're in High Park. While Calum and Dillan engage, I erect a cone of silence over the fight to keep anyone from hearing the battle and being curious enough to check it out.

Thankfully, Sloan has cast it enough times in the past month that I have it memorized.

Air around us stay silent and still,
No whispers shared, no secrets to spill.
Nothing is heard beyond the quiet,
Our actions here remain private.

The slight popping of my ears means it worked, and I give myself a mental high-five.

A brute tackles me and knocks me onto my back. With my armor engaged, I barely feel the impact. Taking a move straight out of the Ninja Turtles movie, I roll onto my back, get my knees up between us and launch him off.

Gripping a handful of snow, I throw it. *"Ice Dagger."*

My magic takes hold as the projectile releases. What starts as a snowball morphs in the air into a finely-tipped dagger. My attacker dodges, but the blade catches his cheek, and he goes down, clutching his bloody face.

Regaining my footing, I call Birga and crack him over the head with the blunt end of the staff.

My guy is down for the count.

As I spin to assess the fight, two arrows fly by and catch a skinhead wizard in the chest center mass. He grunts and drops to his knees, faceplanting into the brittle scrub.

A groan to my left shifts my attention to Calum going down with a wizard pressing a glowing palm to his forehead. Whatever he's zapping Calum with sends my brother into convulsions. His body shakes violently, his limbs flailing out of his control.

I grab Birga and—

The wizard reels off my brother at the same moment I get bombarded with fresh musk. "Oh, gross."

Daisy drops from her handstand and climbs onto Calum's chest. While she nuzzles his chin, I go for the disgusted wizard. The guy is big, another tatted-up baldy, this one with a scar through his lower lip.

I'm about to harpoon him when the air vibrates between us and he portals out.

I groan. My protective side wants him to pay for hurting Calum. "You okay, Calum? Talk to us, bro."

I block a hit from the next opponent.

When nothing comes back to us, my panic rises. "Calum? Give me something here."

Still nothing. I drop to the ground and sweep the feet of the wizard I'm facing off against. When I get back to my feet, Dillan is there, repositioning himself.

"You go. Bear and I will cover you. Bruin!"

I don't wait for Bruin to get there. I know he will without a doubt. Instead, I rush to check on Calum and drop to my knees on the forest floor.

His body has stopped convulsing, and now he lays much too still. "Calum, wake up, bro. I need you to look at me."

Nothing.

"I tried to protect him," Daisy says.

I pat her little head. "I know you did, baby girl. You got that man off him before any of us could get to him. That was great work."

My eyes are stinging with tears, and I'm not sure if it's panic over my brother or the skunk spray—both are incredibly strong. Even if the wizard was her target, Daisy is a potent warrior.

I brush my hand across Calum's throat and feel for a pulse. It's there and seems strong and steady.

Thank the goddess for that.

"Okay, so you got your eggs scrambled, and now you're taking a time out? Is that it?" I swipe at the tears that escape, at a loss for what to do. "That's cool. Take the time out—as long as that's all it is. Garnet, help. I don't know what to do for him."

Garnet's long, ebony hair flows wild behind him as he rushes to close the distance between us. He pushes in beside me, kneels, and presses one hand on Calum's chest. With his other, he reaches up, and I clasp hold of it.

In the next moment, we're on the floor of a medical clinic and Garnet is barking orders.

I grab Daisy off Calum's chest and step back. "It's okay, sweet girl. They'll figure out what's wrong and fix him. I know they will."

I recognize the two Guild doctors in lab coats from when Imari's mother exploded down here. They're hustling around Calum and making me dizzy.

As the adrenaline from the fight drains, I feel woozy.

I remember seeing plastic chairs in the hall last time and figure sitting is better than falling. "We'll wait out here and let them work."

"Fi!" Dillan says a few minutes later. He's jogging up the sterile corridor with Birga in his hand. "How is he?"

Tears tingle in my sinuses and whatever hold I have on my emotions slips. "I don't know. They're working on him."

Dillan sets Birga at my feet and pushes into the medical room. The door hisses back into place in slow-motion, and I watch the polished tiles of the clinic room get swallowed up inch by inch.

I press my fist against the tightness in my chest and look at Daisy. "Kevin should be here. That's Calum's partner. We need to call him."

Deciding that makes me feel a little stronger.

Glad to have something to do, I text Sloan.

911. Calum's hurt. Find Kevin and bring him to the Guild underground clinic where Imari's mother exploded.

His response is immediate.

On it.

I read it twice more to reassure myself. "It's okay. Kevin's coming. I bet Calum will be up and looking around before they even get here."

He's not.

Garnet's healers work on Calum and give him a clean bill of health. I'm not sure how they can say that when he still hasn't woken up, moved, or shown any sign of life since that wizard took him down. Still, they wash the skunk stink off him and make him comfortable and say they've done what they can.

Kevin spends hours talking to him.

Still nothing.

In the end, Dillan and I talk with Kevin and decide to have him flashed home to his bed. If there's nothing more the Guild medical team can do for him, he's better off at home with his family.

CHAPTER TWENTY-ONE

"How's he doing?" I ask as Kevin comes downstairs for dinner the next night.

Our blond, all-American beauty looks tired, and I wonder if he slept at all since yesterday afternoon. "No change. He seems perfectly well, but he refuses to open his eyes."

"Come have a bite to eat, son." Da points at the pot of chili on the stove. "Calum needs us to be healthy and well so when he wakes up, we'll be ready to celebrate."

I swallow a bite of sweet potato, the food tough to get past the lump in my throat. "We'll be ready. When those emerald gemstones open and he looks around to say hi, we'll be ready to raise the roof."

"True story." Dillan holds up his fist.

I meet it with a half-hearted bump.

Kevin fills himself a bowl, grabs a spoon, and heads back for the doorway.

"No, son." Da stands. "I'll sit with him for a bit while ye have a chance to eat and take a break."

"I don't mind going—"

"No. Eat first. Then come up when yer ready. This isn't yer burden to bear on yer own. We're all here."

Da goes upstairs and leaves us to ourselves. When Kev settles in, I squeeze his hand. "He'll come back to us. He'll be all rested and bright-eyed and give us hell for worrying so much. Wait and see."

"I'm looking forward to it, Fi," he says, his voice thick with emotion, "because I can't live with the alternative."

I blink fast as his glassy eyes trigger my tears.

Standing, I move to the sink and start running hot water for the dishes. Calum will be okay. He has to. Opening up the faucets lets the tides of water start to build, and I squirt in some dish soap.

Sloan's arms come around my waist, and he hugs me tight to his chest from behind. "I'll wash up if ye want to sit."

"No," I say, my tears falling freely into the sink. "I'm good. I need to do something."

The knock on the door has us all turning.

"Are we expecting anyone?" Cue the blank looks and shaking heads. "You boys eat. I'll get it."

With the dishtowel in my hand, I dry my tears as I close the distance to the front door. Before I open the door, I draw a deep, steadying breath and toss the towel onto the bench.

"Deputy Commissioner Maxwell, back again so soon?"

He nods. "A word, Miss Cumhaill? It's important."

I wonder for a moment about Manx and Bruin, but that ship has sailed. Thankfully, Daisy was content to stay in the grove until we address her unintentional spraying, and Doc marten is with Emmet in Ireland.

The coast is clear.

I push the door wide and take a step back, ushering him inside. "I'll warn you. It's not a great time for a visit. My brother had an accident yesterday, and we're not sure what that means at the moment. Emotions are close to the surface."

He pulls his knit cap off and tucks it into his pocket. "I am truly sorry to hear it, Fiona. Even from our brief conversations, I know how tight your family is and how deep your devotion."

I blink fast and draw another deep breath. I can't think about Calum right now without tearing up, so I push the emotion down. "Thank you. Would you like to come in and sit, or will this be quick?"

"I'd appreciate sitting down if you don't mind."

I do, but Da taught me to have better manners than that. "Right this way. Would you like a coffee?"

He looks at Sloan, my strong and steady shadow. "The same as last time would be wonderful if you have it. It's bloody cold out there today."

"It is at that." Sloan squeezes my wrist as he brushes past and ducks into the kitchen. "Would ye like somethin' fer yerself, Fi?"

"Tea would be great. Thanks."

I grab the coaster caddy and get us set up. Maxwell shrugs out of his jacket and lays it on the seat next to him. "I apologize for forcing myself into your family's time of trial, Fiona. Truly, I do. And I hate to sound like a broken record here, but it seems we're in much the same place we were a few days ago."

I blow out a breath and tighten the reins. "How's that?"

He pulls out the same silver tablet he had the last time he came by and pulls up a video. It's yesterday's battle against Horacio and the wizards.

Sweet mercies, can we not catch a break?

There's no sound, of course, because I cut that off, but the entire interaction is on video. Bruin tearing through people. Me throwing snow and it turning into a dagger, Calum shooting arrows into a man's chest. Dillan taking his opponents down with his dual daggers.

My mind grasps at how I can explain this away. "How did you get this?"

"Metro security measures were ramped up this year. The province put motion-activated cameras in many of the major city parks. They only come on when they're triggered, but they continue to record until things go still."

I'm watching a full replay of the fight when Sloan comes in and lets out a colorful curse.

"Agreed." I accept the tea and take a sip to settle my nerves. "If I were feeling more myself, I would spin a yarn about LARPing with my cosplay group or something equally witty, but honestly, I don't have it in me today. I will tell you this though. If you push for details, you're exposing yourself and your family to things you can't imagine."

His brow tightens as he stiffens in his seat. "Are you threatening me, Miss Cumhaill?"

I raise my hand and shake my head. "No. Not at all. I like you, Mr. Maxwell. I'm telling you that the answers you seek are held within Pandora's box. All you've seen is the tiniest of glimpses from the tiniest of cracks in the lid. If I tell you what's going on in the streets, that knowledge puts you and yours in danger."

He takes the time to consider my words and blows across the surface of his mug. "All right. Consider me forewarned. I understand you are genuinely giving me the chance to walk away, but I can't do that. Something is happening here, and it's not any kind of organized crime I've ever seen. I may not know what it *is*, but I know what it's *not*."

"And your family?"

He swallows and sets his mug down. "There's my basset hound Cooper and me. My parents are in a retirement home in Montreal, and I'm an only child. I chose the law as my mistress a long time ago, for this reason."

I sigh and sit back. "All right, then, Mr. Maxwell. What do you want to know?"

"Fi, yer not serious," Sloan hisses. "Ye can't. The Guild will have yer head. Ye'll get yerself killed."

I point at the screen. "We have two choices here. Tell him or wipe his memories."

"I think ye know they'll vote fer the latter."

I meet Sloan's panicked gaze and nod. "You're probably right, but we need help. We can do better for the city than we're doing. I know we can."

Sloan frowns and steps away from the table. "I'm gettin' yer Da. This shouldn't fall solely on yer shoulders."

After Da looks over the footage and talks with DC Maxwell, he sits back and crosses his arms. "I'm with Sloan on this, Fi. I think we clear his memories and clean up this mess."

Maxwell frowns. "First, you talk about clearing my memory as if you can actually do it. Second, I'm sitting right here. If you plan to lobotomize me, talking about it right in front of me seems like a bad idea."

"Not really," Da says, "because either she tells ye everything, and ye realize we can and maybe should have done it, or we do it, and ye don't remember us talkin' about it."

Maxwell runs his fingers through his silver hair and shakes his head. "Just tell me. What is this you're all into?"

I think about what to say and look at my father. He shakes his head. "Don't look at me, *mo chroi*. I still think we should wipe him, but yer the chosen one, and yer instincts rarely let us down."

I think about Maxwell's question. What is it?

"It's magic, Mr. Maxwell." I pause and hold up a finger before continuing. "Before you close your mind and accuse me of trying to get away with something, listen to me. There is a community of magically empowered people living within the city. Like any community, there are much more good than bad, more law-abiding citizens than criminals—but there are criminals."

"What ye see here," Da points at the tablet, "is Fiona facing off against a rogue wizard who targeted her. The man enlisted the help of a creature called a trickster who killed a lot of innocent people and would have killed more without her actions."

"Wizard," Maxwell repeats. "As in witches and wizards and Harry Potter at Hogwarts."

Da nods. "The same."

He chuckles. "All right. You know I'll need proof."

"Of course, ye will." He sits back and crosses his arms at the end of the table. "Fi, since this is yer party, I'll leave it in yer hands."

I stand and move to the doorway of the dining room. *"Tough as Bark."* My skin hardens with my natural armor, and I give Maxwell a chance to take it in. "I can call my armor for battle, and it makes my skin all but impenetrable. Go ahead. Touch it."

Maxwell joins me in the front hall and takes my arm. "That's incredible. Does it hurt?"

"No. It's part of me." I release my armor and show him the inked image of Birga. "So is my weapon."

I call Birga forward, and he starts when she appears in my palm. "Where did it come from?"

"From the ink on my arm." I release Birga and send her back into my forearm. "Magic."

He looks around at me, Da, and Sloan and notices Dillan leaning with his shoulder against the kitchen doorway. "I saw you in the video. You had two daggers."

Dillan pushes up his shirt sleeves, shows Maxwell his ink, and calls his daggers to his palms.

"Incredible." He scrubs a hand over his mouth and lets out a long breath. "Just incredible."

Da leans against the banister and smiles. "Now, Fiona was truthful with ye. It's dangerous that ye know about the magic realm at all, but there are members of this community who will kill ye in the blink of an eye for the knowing. Ye must keep it to yerself."

"As a police officer, you know I can't do that, Officer Cumhaill. If there are truly magical beings committing crimes in the city—"

"We'll handle it the best we can." I cut him off. "We have a governing guild, and there are protocols in place. There's nothing non-magical folks can do to detain or defend against some of the people we're dealing with. It'll get good cops killed to try."

He scratches the back of his neck and frowns. "Obviously, sometimes things go beyond what you can manage without being detected."

Da nods. "That's true, but that's when the folks with mind magic move in and clean the slate."

The tension that builds in the crinkles around his eyes doesn't bode well for us. "I am *not* a slate to be cleaned."

"So, the question is, are you with us or against us?"

"How can I be either? I don't know what you are."

"We're druids." I smile. "Keepers of nature and guardians of magic. We're the adjudicators of the magical world."

"Druids," he repeats, looking at me. "When I hear that, I think of old men with staffs and long cloaks."

I giggle and point at Da. "Well, he's our old man and has a staff. Show him, Da."

Da calls his staff forward, and Maxwell holds out his hands. "May I? Is that rude to ask?"

I laugh. "No. It's fine."

Maxwell studies the ancient staff. It's a solid shaft of oak with a twining twig running and twisting around its length like a protruding vein. At the top, the solid knot of a burl acts as a club. "I'm guessing this is centuries old."

"Have ye heard of Fionn mac Cumhaill?" Da asks.

When Maxwell seems to be drawing a blank, I help him out.

"You might know him better as his modern English translation, Finn McCool."

"Like the Irish pubs?"

I nod. "The Irish pubs are named after our ancestor. That was his staff, and I carry his spear. He was the leader of the Fianna warriors."

"Consider them the Robin Hood and Merry Men of medieval times," Dillan says.

"So, there are druids and witches and wizards," Maxwell says, "and what else?"

I shrug. "I won't lie to you and tell you that's all there is. I also won't open Pandora's box so wide that I get you killed. The point is, we *are* the good guys. Da and the boys police the streets as cops, and I police the magical communities and call them in when I need help."

"Like Fi said," Sloan adds, "most magical folks are good people who want to live their lives in peace like everyone else. They could be yer next-door neighbor or the man who owns the fruit stand at the corner. They simply have a connection with nature on a different level than most."

"All right, so if you're not going to clean slate me and I'm not to tell anyone, why tell me?"

I laugh. "You keep showing up at my house asking me to explain things."

"You were suspected of killing an OPP officer in his station. Of course, I'm going to follow up on that."

"I understand that, but I didn't do it. I would never do it. That was the trickster Da told you about. A dark wizard named Horacio Baynes, a corrupt politician in our community, summoned him. I got in his way, and he unleashed a creature called Discord on me."

"Where is this Discord now?"

"Still at large. But, now that we know Horacio Baynes summoned him and what spell he used, we're certain we can release the summons and send him back to wherever he came from."

"He killed people."

"He's more like an 'it,' and he's powerful and immortal. In this case, Discord was a deadly weapon wielded by a bad man. We have the man in custody. There's nothing to be gained by trying to take on the weapon itself."

"I'd like to see this Discord and speak to him."

"No, you wouldn't," Dillan says. "With psychotic fae creatures, staying off their radar is always the best course of action. He's called a trickster because he likes to toy with people. He thinks it's fun to take your worst fears and explode them in your face."

"Like framing you for a cop's murder in the station." He nods. "And targeting the innocent people at a children's parade."

"Exactly."

"Okay, I think I'm beginning to fill in the blanks."

Good. This is good. "In a perfect world, you shouldn't have to worry about any of this, but this is far from a perfect world. I think we need someone in upper law enforcement to help us. Obviously, the SIU and the OPP and likely the TPD have started noticing things."

"Well yes, they put together a rather thick file on you. And the other man you've been seen with, Garnet Grant, there's quite a lot of speculation about him."

There's no way I'm bringing Garnet into this conversation. Not my monkeys. Not my circus.

"The point is, we need someone who can flag stuff like that and help us keep the lid on Pandora's box."

Maxwell leans back against the wall and crosses his arms. "You need more than one man lingering in the distance. You need a response team that can be responsible for handling the kind of messes you seem to get into."

"We have that." I step into the dining room and reclaim my tea. "Remember, I told you we have a guild? I'm the druid representative on the Lakeshore Guild of the Empowered Ones. It's not perfect, but we've been making a lot of positive changes over the past months."

"You're telling me there aren't people in the policing community with powers?"

"I've been assured over and over that there aren't. When we've needed there to be, there's been no one we can call, so I tend to believe them."

"All right. Let me think about it." Maxwell frowns, reclaims his tablet and jacket, and shrugs it onto his shoulders. "On a scale of one to a hundred, how much of the full picture do I know?"

I think about that and make a face. Between the different races, fae worlds, summoning demons, ley lines, immortals, dragons...there's so much he doesn't know.

"Maybe five percent?"

He blinks at me. "You've told me about witches, wizards, druids, magic guilds, and a fae trickster that's immortal, and that's only the tip of the iceberg?"

I look at my father. "Da? Am I wrong? How informed do you think DC Maxwell is?"

Da shrugs. "I think five percent might be generous."

Maxwell slides back into his boots and straightens. "As I said, leave it with me while I think it through—"

"Da, how's Calum?" Emmet snaps into the front hall with Nikon, and they solidify directly in front of a stunned DC Maxwell. "Oh shit."

"Oh fuck," Nikon says. "Did we just step in it?"

Maxwell raises his hand. He looks a little pale but otherwise relatively well glued together. "No. You're fine. I take it this is the private mode of transportation you mentioned to Hiller?"

Da rolls his eyes and shrugs. "Welcome to our world, Deputy Commissioner. It's crazy chaotic at times, but we have great snacks."

CHAPTER TWENTY-TWO

After two somber, very stressful days of Calum showing no sign of coming out of his catatonia, Sloan and I fall back on the same plan we had success with when Myra was in a similar state. It gave us answers with her. I pray it works for my brother too.

"Are ye ready?" Sloan looks over Calum's still body and squeezes my hand.

I close my eyes and send a wave of positive intention out into the world. This will work. It has to.

"Good luck, Fi." Kevin is sitting on the edge of the bed at my hip, holding my knee. "Tell him I love him and can't do this everyday bullshit without him."

"I will." I meet Sloan's gaze and nod. "This will work."

Sinking into myself is like letting the world fall away and retreating to the most authentic part of my soul. My happy place used to manifest as a simple backdrop of Shenanigans, but as life became more complicated, so too did my internal safe place.

Deep in my heart and soul, it's my shelter from the harsh realities the world throws at me. Normally, I take people there with me if they're willing and focus on it. With Calum being unconscious, Sloan's abilities with the Spiritual discipline and mental manipulation make it possible.

When I open my eyes, Brendan's warm, emerald gaze greets me as he stands behind the bar. He wipes down the surface and moves to polish the draught taps. "Hey, baby girl. Back again? How's life treating you these days?"

In my head, I know this place is simply an emotional construct with the magic of Brendan's heritage spark allowing me to place him here. In my heart, he's still alive and well at least in this tiny, magical corner of the universe.

If given a choice between picking between my head and my heart...there's no question.

I sense the arrival of Sloan and Calum the moment they join me. Rushing over, I wrap myself around my brother. "I'm so glad you're here."

He looks around as though he doesn't quite understand. "Where is here, Fi?"

"My happy place. I finally got you here. Come on. Come say hi to—"

"Brenny." Calum's and Brendan's gazes lock. Calum rounds the bar to meet our older brother chest to chest. "It's damn good to see you, bro. I've missed you like crazy."

I give them a chance to catch up and take a few mental snapshots of them together. Funny how things like that matter after the fact. Sidling up next to Sloan, I step into his arms and rest my head against his shoulder. "It took you a bit to get here. Did you have trouble?"

Sloan's expression is unreadable, which in itself tells me he did, and he doesn't want me to freak out about it. "I'm not sure what the jolting of that wizard's magic did to his brain patterns, Fi, but something is definitely out of phase."

"Okay, well, that tells us something at least. Maybe that's where we start. We figure out what's out of whack and we correct it."

"In theory."

I smile as Calum and Brendan bust up laughing over something Brenny says. In a big family, relationships are the same and yet different between each of the family members. My relationship with Brendan is sibling, but it's totally different from Calum's and different again from Aiden's.

Not less or more—just different.

Some of it has to do with birth order and shared experience. Mam and Da named us alphabetically, and there aren't more than two years between anyone as they built their family, so six kids less than eight years apart.

Aiden and Brendan are over a year apart, and then two years until Calum. Dillan was born under a year later, and two years after him, Emmet arrived then me a year later. I've wondered if they would've kept going if I hadn't been a girl. Heck, they might've gotten to G or H.

"What put that silly smile on yer face?" Sloan says, watching me.

"Nothing. Just my mind wandering. Do you think him being here with Brendan and touching base with us will do anything to realign his out of phase issue?"

"Do ye want a truthful answer or a sunshine and rainbows answer?"

The fact that he asked that answers my question. "Door number two."

"Then sure. It could. Maybe he needs more connection with his family and his life, and he'll open his eyes."

I close my eyes and press my cheek against his chest. "Thanks for being a big fat liar."

"Anytime ye need me to be, *a ghra.*"

After I've delayed the inevitable long enough, I step back. "Let's spend a few minutes enjoying this. Then we'll get back to the real world and figure something else out."

"Whenever yer ready. This is yer show."

I nod and head toward the bar. If this was truly my show, I think I'd have more answers.

The family is at a loss when Sloan and I reemerge and admit we're no closer to getting Calum back than we were before. Kevin holds it together pretty well, but we all recognize he's losing his hold on his disappointment, so we vacate the room and give him some privacy. Sloan *poofs* back to Dora's to continue working on the spell to banish Discord.

"I hate this." Emmet grabs another donut from the Tim Horton's box a half-hour later. When in doubt—carb out. "We need to *do* something."

"Maybe having Daisy with him might help." Dillan grabs the regular milk and the almond milk out of the fridge and brings them over to the table so we can all refill our glasses. "I know they bonded less than an hour before he lost consciousness, but maybe she could help."

I sigh. "I'm willing for our house to get skunked if it brings him back."

"Oh, shit." Emmet jumps up from the table. He grabs his backpack from the floor at the back door and reclaims his seat at the table. "Gran sent me with stuff for the wee stinker, and I forgot. Snapping in right in front of that RCMP guy kinda blew my mind."

I chuckle. "You should've seen your face. Priceless."

"Gran says she had a rabbit with epilepsy a decade or so ago and developed this remedy to control the seizures. She says if it doesn't work, she can tweak it, but it should give Daisy immediate relief to some degree."

"Awesome." Dillan takes possession of the little pill bottle and rattles the tablets around. "I'll go get her."

While Dillan goes to the grove to fetch Daisy, I stroke Doc's head. "It hasn't been a very happy welcome for you, buddy. I'm sorry about that."

Emmet's marten blinks up at me with wide ebony eyes and smiles. "Tough times don't last. Tough people do."

I giggle. Emmet's animal companion seems to have a poetic side and an endless supply of motivational sayings at his disposal. "That is true."

"Back to the issue of the second in command at the RCMP knowing about magic in Toronto," Aiden says. "How did Garnet take it?"

I lean back in my chair and grab a chocolate glazed. "I didn't tell him. I'm not going to tell him until things settle and we see how it goes. I truly think having people in key areas know is the only way we can keep the peace and not end up looking like criminals."

Emmet's dark brow arches. "I don't want to be anywhere near you when he finds out. That man is homicidally scary."

I wave that away. "Garnet's a big pussy cat."

"Who kills people."

I tilt my head and think about that. "Okay, point to you. A big pussy cat who kills people."

My phone buzzes against the table, and I read the incoming text. "Thank you, baby carrots. Dora and Sloan have come up with the wording for the counter-spell to release Discord from tormenting me."

"Woohoo. Finally, some good news."

I shove the last bite of my donut in and wash it down. "I'm running up to get dressed. Sloan's *poofing* her into the grove in twenty minutes."

"Cool. Doc and I will go out now to check on Daisy and inform Dillan. We have a couple of hours before we need to get ready to leave for the station. Maybe we can help."

Sloan *poofs* Dora into our sacred grove twenty minutes later, and I hug her. "Thank you so much for all you do for us. You're a rockstar."

Dora winks and shrugs off her zebra print jacket. It's cool and something I might wear if it didn't have the slime green fur lining the collar, bottom hemline, and cuffs. "You don't have to thank me, Fi. I turned my back on my duty for centuries. I shall be forever thanking you for reminding me what it means to be a druid."

Now it's my turn to shrug. "So, this is a mutual admiration club. I can live with that. Now, tell me what you put together and what we're doing."

Emmet, Dillan, Aiden, and Sloan all gather around.

Dora raises her hand and sweeps the air. Hovering in the space before us, the words of a spell appear. Glowing gold and curling with a lovely cursive flare, I read the counter-spell over in my head.

"You think this will do it?"

Dora looks at Sloan, and they both nod. "We do. I'll also cast a protection spell, and I want you to drink this when you've finished the incantation."

I accept the vial of blue liquid. "I hope this tastes better than the red stuff."

"I guarantee it."

"Perfect. Then let's get started."

The six of us step out of the grove and into the back yard. Discord already knows where I live, so there's no reason not to do it here. Especially now that Janine and Mark have moved away and won't be spying on us from their property.

Reaching into my pocket, I finger through the different gemstones I carry and select the ones I want to work with. I choose the peridot Patty gave me for luck and positive results, the Ostara swirly turd for strength and grounding to my connection to the grove so close at hand, the labradorite to rise above challenges, and the green aventurine to empower new beginnings.

"All right, call up the spell. Here goes everything." After drawing a few deep, cleansing breaths to center my focus, I settle squarely on my feet and strengthen my connection with the ley power running deep in the earth beneath me. Dora flicks her fingers, and the spell appears in front of me. I swallow and focus my intention.

Discord, trickster, I call on thee
To end your summons and set you free.
The wizard's task of blood and blame
Has been exposed, his plot aflame.
Your bond to harm, torment, and play
Is ended now; no need to stay.

When I finish the spell, the last line lingers eerily in the air. I uncork the vial of blue liquid, swallow it, and...yum, raspberry. Much better. When that's down, I look around. "Does anyone sense him? See him?"

My supporters seem as baffled as I am.

"That should've worked," Sloan says, his brow deeply furrowed with annoyance. "We took the time to untangle the key binding words in the original spell and canceled out their power with deliberate intent."

"Give it time to work," Dora says. "Patience, kids. Rome wasn't built in a day."

I always liked that saying. I make a mental note to ask Nikon about the rise of ancient Rome one day when he's drunk and seems like he might want to spill his stories.

A fascinating man, our Nikon of the Isle of Rhodes.

"There. Do you feel that?" Sloan holds his hands up and casts another glance around. "My skin is tingling."

"That's called frostbite," Dillan says. "You gotta start wearing gloves, Irish. Toronto winter winds are nothing to tough out."

"It's not frostbite," Sloan snaps. "It's magic and not a power signature I'm familiar with."

"Remember." I peg them with a serious look. "No matter what happens to me, don't do anything that makes you stand out. My initial boundaries protect you. There's no reason for that to change."

"Having those boundaries in place is certainly better than not having them." Aiden searches the scene. "I know you guys worry about Kinu and the kids, but I feel a lot better knowing that Discord is keeping them off the list of victims—especially after what happened to Calum."

I don't even like to hear about it. "In all fairness, Discord didn't hurt Calum. That was one of Horatio's wizard goons."

When their gazes rise behind me, I turn to find Discord in his fox form prancing on the slope of our roof. "Goons or not, the terms declared. Those you love were to be spared. Without the rules, a game's not fun. The harm to yours shall be undone."

"Is he serious?" Emmet whispers. "Can we trust him?"

I blink, wondering the same thing. "What's the catch? Is this another part of the game?"

"There is no catch a deal we made. No harm to yours while game is played. You end it now with damage done. I make amends and restore the fun."

None of this was fun, but I'm not about to argue. "If you heal Calum, you are a true and honorable riddler. I will respect how you played the game."

"Words of praise. I accept. As a foe, you were adept. I leave you now with fond affection and add you to my friend collection."

Dillan grunts behind me, and I'm with him.

The thought of me and this psycho furball being friends is cray-cray, but why ruin a good moment with reality? "The spell has been broken. You're free to leave. If you're serious about helping Calum, he's in that bedroom up there."

Discord stands and swishes his tail. "The boy is fixed, the lovers bound. Before Yule tidings, the winner found. I leave you now, with one last word. What has feathers and flies but is not a bird?"

With that, Discord dissolves, and we're staring up at an empty roof.

"Anyone know who the crazy old lady is watching us from two doors over?" Dillan forces a smile and raises his hand to wave. "Try to look normal."

We turn to look and the woman smiles and sips her tea. Silver-haired with a crocheted shawl, the old girl is sitting in a rocking chair on the upstairs balcony two houses over.

"It's cold to be rocking outside, isn't it?" Sloan asks.

"Maybe she's not all there," Dillan says.

I wave and smile back. "How much did she see?"

"No idea," Emmet says. "Likely not much. She's old. Eyes and ears are first to go, aren't they?"

No idea.

"Is your shield weighing in, Fi?" Aiden asks.

"Nope. I've got nothing."

Aiden nods over at her and gestures to the back door. "Okay, everyone head inside. Nothing to see here."

The moment we're inside the back door, Emmet, Dillan, and Aiden take off running for the stairs, and Sloan grabs mine and Dora's hands. We poof upstairs into Calum's room, and I run and throw myself onto the love-in already in progress.

"It's true," I choke, kissing his stubbled cheek. "You're awake. Are you okay?"

Calum frees an arm from holding Kevin, and I get some loving too. I barely have time to draw a big breath before Aiden, Dillan, and Emmet join in.

"Sandwich." Emmet laughs. "It's been a lotta years since we played sandwich."

Calum lets out a breathy gasp. "I forgot how much I hate being bottom bread."

"It's not much better being the mayo over here," I gasp... although I'm not complaining in the slightest. I'll take getting squished by my brothers any day of the week over any one of them suffering. "Someone has to call Da."

"I've already sent word." Sloan shows me his phone. "He says ye promised a grand celebration, Fi, so start plannin'."

I nod. "We have to celebrate the twins, too."

The focus on the pile-up shifts, then everyone tackles and is lying on our oldest brother.

"Congrats, my man." Emmet grunts as Dillan's knee digs into his ass. "I heard the ambient fae magic of Ireland gave you super sperm."

Aiden grins, groaning as Kevin and Calum start wriggling to free themselves from the pile. "That's my story, and I'm sticking to it."

"It's a good one, too."

The rowdy celebratory hug breaks up, and Kevin and I usher Calum down to the kitchen while Sloan poofs Dora home. Emmet runs out to get Daisy and tell her the good news. Her boy is awake.

"What are you hungry for?" I start opening the cupboards, looking for Calum's favorites. "You name it, and I'll make it happen."

Calum sits in his usual seat, and it's so damn good to see him there. "I'd kill for spicy pork miso."

I close the cupboards and grab the basket of take-out menus from on top of the fridge. "Done. Even easier. I'll get a list going, and we'll stuff ourselves with ramen to celebrate."

"I wish Dillan and I could stay and celebrate," Emmet says

while handing over Calum's skunk. "But we gotsta book it upstairs and get ready to leave for the afternoon shift."

"Hey, beautiful girl." Calum cuddles his ball of black and white fur. He reaches out with his free hand and first Emmet, then Dillan meet him for a bump. "I get it. Safe home, boys. We have lots to celebrate."

"Hells yeah, we do." Kevin's voice is husky with emotion. "But tonight, we eat and turn in. I'm two days behind on sleep, and I'm man enough to admit that I need to have Calum to myself for a while or I'm going to melt."

Aw, poor Kev.

"Understood. Ramen, then everyone returns to their corners for the night." I meet Sloan's gaze as he poofs back in and smiles. "Sounds amazing."

CHAPTER TWENTY-THREE

The next morning, I wake from what feels like an almost drugged sleep. For the first night in weeks, both my conscious and subconscious minds relaxed. Discord's game is over. Calum and everyone I love is healthy and well. We have two new Cumhaill druids growing stronger every day.

Honestly, life is pretty freaking good.

I curse myself for even thinking that in my mind. As we've proven often enough, jinxing is real.

I lay there for another five or ten fuzzy minutes drifting in and out of the golden glow of morning. I listen, but the rumbled snore of my bear isn't at the end of the bed where it usually is.

I open my eyes, but it's dark—much darker than it should be, considering I feel like I've slept through until mid-morning. Rolling onto my side, I pat Sloan's side of the bed and sit up quickly. "What the hell?"

There is *waaay* more bed than there should be.

"King Henry?" I sweep back one side of the heavy, drawn curtains to let some light in. "How did I get here?"

Sloan pushes through the opening with a breakfast tray in his hands. "Prop yerself up. I've made yer favorites."

I do as told because I never say no to fruit waffles and chewy bacon. "What's the occasion, and does the reason you're buttering me up have anything to do with the reason you *poofed* us to Ireland while I was sleeping?"

He steals a berry off my plate and smiles. "We're not in Ireland. We're still in Toronto."

"You brought King Henry here?"

"I did. Last night with the help of Nikon and yer Da, we made a few trips and brought quite a few of my things so I can make my new house a home."

I almost choke on a bite of bacon. "You rented a *house*? That's exciting. I'm a little let down that I didn't get to house-hunt with you, but I get that you wanted to start laying down your roots on your terms."

"I did, but I think ye'll approve. Yer Da gave me the thumbs up. It's a good neighborhood and from what I've gathered, good neighbors too."

I peek out of King Henry's curtains and smile. "Big master. How many bedrooms?"

"Four upstairs, with a spare room in the basement that I might use for an apothecary room. Manx and Bruin picked their room and have decided to share."

"Share? Are you asking me to move in with you?"

Sloan's eyes glitter with excitement. "I am, yes. It's early in our relationship, I know, but I'll not hold ye to anythin' if it's not to yer likin'. I enjoy sharin' space with ye, and I feel like we're quite compatible."

I fork in another bite of berry-waffle-bliss and smile. "I think so too. Things are good. Really good."

His grin is too much. "So, come and see."

I'm cutting and chewing now with increased speed. "I want to check it out, but I won't waste this breakfast. This is delicious. Thank you, by the way."

"Yer very welcome."

"You rented a house…man, that *is* exciting."

"Actually, I bought it."

Okay, wow. He bought a house in my city. That's quite a declaration that he's in this. His comment about making sure he wasn't the only one all in makes more sense now. Of course, he'd want to make sure he wasn't reading too much into our relationship. This is huge.

"That's the purchase you made that you promised to tell me about?"

He nods. "It's an investment in the future. If things work out with us, it'll be perfect. And if for some reason things don't work out between us, I won't regret purchasing it. I want you to know that."

"Noted." He looks like he's still struggling to say something, but I'm not quite getting the point.

"Fi, I've never bought anything like this for myself before now. Ye know I have money."

"Had money," I snort. "Houses in Toronto cost big bucks. How much did you put down on this place? The payments are going to be brutal."

"No payments. I bought it outright."

Waffle goes down the wrong pipe, and I choke. Coughing and sputtering, I try to grasp that. "Outright? Holy-schmoly, hotness. No wonder your parents are shitting kittens. You broke the bank on one purchase."

Sloan laughs. "No, luv. I didn't. Buyin' the house didn't even ripple the pond. Don't worry about that."

I blink, trying to catch my breath after my spectacular choking spree. Didn't even ripple the pond? Holy shitballs. "Okay, I don't even want to know. Your money. Your business. You do what you want with it. Good for you."

His smile is still so tense that it's making me nervous. "While I bought this place with you in mind, it's what *I* want. I don't want you getting all tangled up about it."

"Why would I get tangled up—I'm not following."

"Finish off." He points at the last splash of juice in my tumbler before removing the tray and returning to hold out his hand. "Ready?"

"More than ready." I take his hand and let him pull me out of King Henry. I've loved his massive antique bed since the first time I saw it. That he brought it here makes my heart full to the brim. He's laying roots like Myra said he needed to.

"This is exciting." The moment I'm standing upright and look out at the buttercream walls and the wood trim it hits me. I run to the window and look outside. "It's my street." I spin around and meet his gaze. "You bought Mark's and Janine's house."

He dips his chin. "I did. Now it's Sloan's and Fi's."

I'm about to burst with questions when he holds up his finger to stop me. "I've heard all yer arguments, and I think buying this house makes sense for several reasons. We have enough space here to invite Calum and Kevin to join us. Yer Da plans on moving into yer room to give Kinu and Aiden the master. There's enough room in there for two cribs, so that should give them almost two years before they need to worry about space. If Calum moves in here, there are already two beds in that room fer Meg and Jackson to share. Ye once told me ye loved sharin' with Emmet when ye were young."

"I did."

"Ye'll only be next door, so ye'll still have yer finger on the pulse of the family. And I was thinkin' we can take down the fence between the two yards and expand the grove. Then we can add some lattice and climbing ivy to the top of the fence to next door to keep pryin' eyes from takin' notice."

"Like crazy ladies in rocking chairs?"

"Exactly."

I hesitate for a moment and let my mind catch up with things. "Wow, you have thought about this, haven't you?"

He nods. "This isn't charity, Fi. I know ye didn't want my

money to solve yer family's problems, but this isn't that. I love this house. It's old and has character, and I love it all the more because I see how much yer house means to yer family. I want that too. One day—not now or anytime soon—I want to fill these bedrooms with kids and build a family like yer Mam and Da did. I want that more than I can tell ye."

He's beginning to ramble, and I can feel the tension and worry creeping into his words.

"Way too soon to go there, but I get the point. And yes, it's amazing." I pull him into a hug. "You're amazing, Sloan Mackenzie. The fact that you've thought all of this out with my family in mind, knowing that I can only be happy if they're happy..." I cup my fingers into a heart and press them against my chest. "I heart you hard, hotness."

He sighs and sags with relief. "Ye mean yer not annoyed with me that I'm rushin' ye or readin' too much into things? Because I talked it all out with yer da. I'm not ropin' ye into a life after knowin' ye six months. I understand that we're still testin' the waters. I'm not a stalker or the like."

I giggle. "I know you're not a stalker. No. You're all good. This is a massive sweeping gesture that locks things down sooner than I expected, but the opportunity presented itself, and your reasoning is sound. I only have one revision, if I may?"

He nods. "Go ahead? What did I miss?"

"I'd like to offer the other bedroom to Emmet if you don't have any immediate plans for it. That way, Dillan will have that room to himself and Em will be included. I wouldn't feel right having an extra bedroom and leaving him to share with Dillan instead of coming to join our adventure."

"That's it? We invite Calum and Emmet, and everythin' else is to yer likin'?"

"That's it for adjustments."

"Will Dillan be slighted not to be invited too? I sorta already promised Bruin and Manx that they could have a room so they don't have to suffer through us gettin' naked."

I giggle. "No more hiding in the closet. No. Dillan won't care. He'll get a room for himself and won't have to worry about moving. It's a perfect plan. Honestly, it couldn't have worked out better. Best boyfriend, *evah*. See, I always say you're brilliant."

He flashes the brightest smile I've ever seen grace his beautiful face. "Ye hear that, boys? It's a go."

Bruin lets out a massive roar somewhere down the hall as Manx barrels past purring and sliding on his massive furry paws. "I knew she'd love it. Ye do love it, don't ye?"

"I definitely do." I smile down at my Costco slippers sitting on my bedside rug under our feet. He really does have a heart of gold, this one. "When do we tell them?"

"How about right now? I figured if ye liked the idea, everyone could be moved in and settled by Yule. A true family holiday with everyone together."

I wrap my arms around his neck and hop up to wrap my legs around his hips. He chuckles and catches my weight. "I'm glad yer happy, *a ghra*."

"Oh, I'm more than happy. We're going to go over to tell them the good news, pack my toiletries and essentials, then come back and christen this house like a boss. In fact, they can't move in until the weekend. That gives us a few days to make all the rooms in this house our own."

The next days are filled with exciting plans, packing, and getting everyone sorted and settled. Moving my stuff into the master bedroom next door is as easy as Sloan laying his hands on my dresser and *poofing* it there.

I freaking love magic.

I pull an armful of clothes off the hanging rail, and *poof*, Sloan transports me to the beautiful new master closet next door to rehang them. It's quite fun.

Who says moving is terrible?

"You haven't told Garnet anything yet?" Calum asks as I help him clean out the room he's turning over to Meg and Jackson.

"Nope. Not yet. Maxwell said he'll get back to me when he has a plan for how best this will work. There's no sense mentioning anything to Garnet and getting him all bristled up and growly when I don't have all the facts yet."

"And you're totally avoiding it."

"Hells yes, I am. That lion's gonna eat me."

Calum chuckles and finishes with the closet.

"I can't believe Sloan faked us out," Dillan says, coming into the room and heading to the pile of Brendan's t-shirts up to claim.

I laugh. "Da knew he already owned the place and had the keys. They pretended we were breaking and billiarding."

"He earned himself two demerit points for impersonating a badass," Dillan says. "Things like that can't be allowed to go unpunished."

"We should've figured it out when Da went along with it." Emmet comes in for a couple of t-shirts himself. "We were all off our game on that one."

"He did fool all of us. That's a feat."

Dillan claims a Green Day t-shirt and frowns. "Fine, he can have two points for fooling all of us."

I laugh as Sloan passes the room carrying empty boxes. "Did you hear that, hotness? You're even again."

"It's too late to put me back on probation anyway." He laughs. "I haven't given them their keys yet."

Dillan grins. "That doesn't affect me. I'm not under your thumb, Irish."

It's kind of cathartic going through Brendan's things together with the move in mind and knowing we're making space for Aiden and his family to move in.

Brenny would be jazzed to know Meg and Jackson will share the room he shared with Calum. We all still miss him every day, but this is a happy way to move forward.

The doorbell rings as I'm heading downstairs to get a bag for donations. "I'll get it!"

I open things up and scowl as a blast of polar vortex hits me in the face. "Ew gross, come in. Come in."

John Maxwell steps into our front hall and eyes the boxes. "Did I catch you before skipping town?"

"If we were, you'd never catch us." I throw him a sly look and laugh. "No. Sloan bought the house next door, and we're spreading out."

"Congratulations. I hope by your smiles, things turned around for your brother who was hurt fighting the wizards?"

I grin so wide my cheeks hurt. "They did. Funny enough, it was my trickster stalker who turned those tables. He said the game was no fun if the wizards broke the rules, so he fixed him before he left."

"How?"

"I have no idea. In this world, sometimes it's better not to ask —safer too." I realize we're still standing in the hall and gesture into the room. "Do you want to come in?"

He shakes his head. "Not today, thanks. You're busy, and I just came by to follow up on our conversation from the other day. I've given it a lot of thought and see a couple of ways forward. I agree with your assessment. I think I could help flag problems and smooth your road."

"That would be great. What do you have in mind?"

He pulls a folder out from under his arm and hands it to me. "I've detailed my thoughts in here. To summarize, I think your people should come up with a name to submit for the SIU position opened by the death of Agent Lent."

"I'm sorry she got caught up in the chaos of Horacio's game. I hate that Discord killed her and Officer Hiller."

"I know you do, Fi. That's why we must work through the shortcomings of what's in place now and build a stronger foundation for the future."

"Okay, so we submit a name for the SIU."

"This will be a real position. The person you find will need credentials in law, military, policing, or something along those lines so we don't raise unnecessary attention. I'll ensure they get the job. Then, I'll put together a special investigations team run through the federal jurisdiction of the RCMP and overseen by that person."

"Who would head up that team?"

"If he's willing, I'm hoping your father."

"Da? Would he still be a cop?"

"Of course. The task force will be an extension of the TPD, and I can't think of a better person to stand at the helm. Your father has enough experience behind him that no one will question the appointment, and since Brendan's death, it's been noticed that his focus has shifted to a lot of off-duty investigating."

"I'm not sure what Da will think about stepping off the streets to be a team leader."

"Ask him and see. I mapped out how I see things working, but after you all have a chance to read through and think about it, we should meet up and change anything you think could work better."

I crack open the file and peek inside. There are pages of notes and an org chart and some funding projections. None of which fall into my wheelhouse. "Da is much better suited to look through this. I'll give it to him as soon as he gets home."

"Perfect. So, when I drop in from now on, should I come here or go next door?" He thumbs the direction.

"I suppose there. Sloan, Calum, Emmet, and I are moving over there. Da, Dillan, and Aiden will be here. But Aiden's wife and two little kids are moving here, so it's probably best to keep the discussions away from them."

"Good enough. I think it's best if I come to you when there are issues to be discussed rather than have the kind of topics you deal with surface at a station."

"Likely a good idea." I point at the second folder tucked under Maxwell's arm. "Is that for me too?"

"Yes and no. This is for your guild leader. I sense that everyone is afraid of how your authorities will take me knowing about your world. This lays out my full professional CV and commendations as well as my background check, and my thoughts about how having a civilian in my position knowing what's going on could benefit both communities."

I accept the second folder as my chest tightens. "Maybe we shouldn't rush into telling them."

Maxwell shakes his head. "As a commander of a force, I'd rather people be straight with me and not play games. I owe the same respect to your leaders. I have faith in you, Fiona. You can sell this idea. It's a good one, and it'll work."

I hope he's right.

"All right. We're getting together for holiday drinks tomorrow night. We'll all go over what you've put together, and I'll bring it up then."

"Good luck. And Fi...don't let them clean slate me. I'm excited about what this partnership could mean to the city. I won't let you down. You can trust me."

It's crazy to have a man so accomplished and respected saying those words to me. I'm just me. "I'll do my very best. Thanks. Having all this will make it much easier."

On the eve of Yule, our family gathers in the joint backyard of our two houses. Pulling down a section of the fence was the first thing we did. Once everyone gets settled, we'll start working on the plans to expand the deck straight across and extend the grove.

"Everyone ready?" I scan the faces of Clan Cumhaill and am both excited and terrified.

"It's gonna be fine, Fi," Emmet says. "If anyone can slip into the cracks of Garnet's hard shell to get to the gooey center, it's you. You've got this."

I appreciate the sentiment, but I'm not so sure.

"What's the signal if you need to be snapped out?" Nikon winks at me. "Between lover boy and I, we can evac you across the globe and out of reach. You might have to live on the lam for the rest of your life, but I have lots of houses to hide you in."

I roll my eyes at the Greek and tuck DC Maxwell's files under my arm. We've pored over every detail for the past twenty-four hours. It's a good plan. Garnet will see that.

I hold out my hand and stack it on Sloan's to ready to leave. "Here goes everything."

"Everyone got a hold on one of our magical Ubers?" Da asks. "Have ye got a good hold on the monkeys?"

Aiden checks with Kinu and nods. "Got them. They aren't going to run off this time. They know we're going to see and play with Imari."

"Imari's my cousin," Jackson says.

I look at Aiden and laugh. "How so?"

He shrugs. "Auntie Fi has a bear inside her, and Imari has a bear…somehow that makes them cousins."

I giggle. "Okay, then. Let's go with that. It's time for holiday fun with your cousin, Jackson. I'm sure she's waiting for us to arrive."

Nikon and Sloan portal the whole family onto the private

driveway of Garnet's Toronto house. It's the first time for many of them to experience the wonder that is Garnet Grant's home.

"Clan Cumhaill et al.," I say to the two men standing sentinel blocking the brick archway. By their muscled builds and the energy I sense coming off them, I'd guess the one on my right is a wolf and the one on the left is a raptor of some kind—an eagle maybe.

They count our number, take notice of Nikon, and allow us through. "Have a lovely evening," the wolf says.

"Thank you. Stay warm, boys."

Sloan and I lead the posse through the archway and wait for everyone to arrive in the African savanna on the other side. Garnet's portal gate is a direct passageway to his African compound. Other than a slight pressure in your chest and *pop* in your ears, you'd never realize you zipped to the other side of the world.

"It's a little disorienting the first time," I say, untying my scarf and opening my jacket, "but it's worth it. How cool is this? Beautiful, isn't it?"

"It's very impressive," Da says. For once, there isn't an edge of wariness in his tone. It's a Yulemas miracle.

We remove our winter jackets and leave them hung in the outdoor hanging area. The kids kick off their boots and run around on the grass in their socks like they've been set free.

"Clan Cumhaill, welcome." Garnet strides over from the oasis grotto where several lions are lounging in the water, absorbing the warmth of the sun. He looks good in a navy linen suit with a cream dress shirt beneath. "Please, make yourselves at home. There's food in the house, a bar inside as well as under the canopy, and the water is fine if you want to enjoy the waterfall grotto."

"Can Imari play?"

Garnet adjusts the fabric at his thighs and squats down to meet Jackson in the eye. "She is very excited for you two to visit. I think she's helping Myra get the snacks ready for the kids party. Should we go see if they're ready?"

When Jackson nods, Garnet holds out his hand. Before they stride off, he meets Aiden's gaze. "You're welcome to join us or take a moment to orient yourselves, whichever you choose. We're just heading inside."

"I'll go inside with them," I say, seizing the opportunity to get Garnet alone. "You guys grab some cocktails and start the night off."

"You don't have to tell us twice." Aiden grabs Kinu's hand. "Have fun with Auntie Fi, kids."

I laugh at how quickly they disappear under the palm fronds of the waterfall grotto. Hilarious.

The boys head to the canopy bar with Nikon while Da and Sloan stick close to me. I wave to Suede and hold up one finger to let her know I'll come to talk to her in a while.

First, I must throw myself at the feet of the lion.

"Fi, there you are, duck. I'm so glad you came."

I let go of Meggie's hand and hug Myra, who's looking festive in a green and silver sequins shirt dress. "Thanks for having us. Happy holiday, Imari. Jackson and Meg are super…" I laugh as the three of them run away to go play. "Never mind. You get the idea."

A timer goes off on the stove, and Garnet grabs oven mitts and tends to it, humming to himself.

I smile at the Grand Governor of the Guild.

Score one for the healing properties of a child's love.

While he's distracted, I squeeze Myra's hand and lean in to whisper. "I did something, and Garnet will be pissed. Don't let him eat me, 'kay?"

Myra's wild and wonderful eyes widen. "I got you, luv. Whatever it is."

I nod, my chest growing tight. When Garnet's finished pulling food out to cool, I bite the bullet. "Garnet? I hate to disrupt the party, but could we talk somewhere private for a few minutes? Something happened, and I think you'll want to kill me in private."

Da's gaze narrows on me. "That's how ye want to lead into this? By invitin' the man to kill ye?"

"I said he'll *want* to kill me."

Da considers that and nods. "Fair enough. I suppose yer right."

There's a low grumble of a lion in the air as Garnet shuts the five of us into a home office and frowns at me. "I don't like the sounds of this, Lady Druid."

I nod. "Then I've set the stage appropriately. All right. I'm gonna rip this bandage off." Before I lose my nerve, I tell Garnet about the videos and Maxwell confronting me, and how I went ahead and confirmed what I didn't think could be denied any longer. I cover the follow-up conversation and the plans he brought me and end by handing him the copies we made of the files.

"This happened *when*?" he booms. "We fought Horatio and the wizards what…four or five days ago."

"Yep."

"He came to you the next day?"

"Yep."

"And you're just telling me this *now*?"

I nod. "He already knew, and he'd already secured the video. I figured he deserved a chance to show us how it could work. It's a good plan, Garnet."

Garnet bares his teeth, and the roar of his lion isn't a rumbling in the background this time. It hammers in my chest and steals my breath. "We talked about this, and I said *no*. You went behind my back, and you had no right."

No one in the room misses the fact that his eyes have flipped from purple to amber. His lion is ascending, and if he loses control, I'll be its prey.

"I'm sorry. I didn't mean for it to happen."

"But it did happen," he shouts. "You're a fucking Governor of the Guild now. You took an oath. Do you even remember what you swore to?"

"As a matter of fact, I do." I raise a fist with my right hand and press it into the palm of my left. "I swear on my honor as a citizen of Toronto and warrior of the empowered world, that I will be dutiful in the laws of our community, never cause needless suffering, and will fight until my dying breath against all persons who intend to do harm within the boundaries of my fair city."

That takes a bit of wind out of his sails.

"Calm down, Garnet." Myra grips his wrist. "Rage is bad for your complexion. You know Fi would never knowingly betray a friend. She was put in a situation and let her instincts guide where that took her next."

"Fi's instincts are usually spot on," Da adds. "I've checked out Maxwell. I think he's solid, and I'm willin' to be the team leader in place for his special unit. It could work, and it could save a lot of trouble down the road."

Garnet is focused on regaining control and closes his eyes while breathing in and out.

"I tried to do right by both communities based on the situation I found us in. Maxwell said the city would be putting up more motion cameras to record night and remote activity. We have to consider what that will mean to the empowered going forward. It might be a vampire feeding or a shifter changing forms or a fae dropping a glamor at the wrong time. It's a matter of time before one of us slips up and it's caught on video."

I set the files on his desk and tap a finger on the folder. "John Maxwell is a good man, and he believes in keeping the peace in our city. He already knew, so I thought we should at least give him the opportunity to show us his value."

Garnet curses and sits back on the edge of his desk. "There

are members of our community who will end him simply for knowing about us."

"I warned him of that, and so far, he only knows about wizards, witches, and druids."

"And the trickster," Sloan adds.

"Yeah, and the trickster." I sigh, the tension in the air not what I wanted for us on an evening of celebration. "I'm sorry, Garnet. I wouldn't have said anything if we weren't already exposed. Can we give him a chance?"

Garnet rolls his eyes and looks at Da. "You're willing to take on the position of a middleman for human investigations and exposure coverups?

Da nods. "I am."

He looks at me. "Very well, Fiona. We'll play it your way and see how things go…but if the shit hits, it won't be me standing in front of the fan. That honor will belong to you and you alone."

"Understood."

"Until we see how it plays out, we say nothing to the rest of the Guild Governors. No one knows about this except us, your family, and my people."

"Understood."

After another few deep breaths, he tilts his head back and roars at the ceiling. "You're not the little mouse who took the thorn out of my paw today, Fiona. Today you *are* the thorn."

"Understood."

When he straightens to leave I catch his wrist. "I'm sorry, Garnet. I hate that I jammed you up on this. My instincts say this will turn out fine. My shield is happy. S'all good."

"Let's hope for all our sakes, you're right. Now, let's get out there. We have drinks to consume—many, many drinks."

Garnet growls and storms out of the room.

Myra makes a face and squeezes my hand. "It'll be fine, duck. You'll see. Let him get a few drinks into him, and I'll remind him you brought us Imari. He'll forgive you."

"I hope so."

"He definitely will."

Da hugs me. "You did well, *mo chroi*. Myra's right. I think this will work out fine. How about we enjoy ourselves and go take the edge off?"

I draw a deep breath and nod. "Hells yeah. Someone point me to the bar."

Thank you for reading *A Broken Vow.*

While the story is fresh in your mind, click **HERE** and tell other readers what you thought.

A star rating and/or even one sentence can mean so much to readers deciding whether or not to try out a book or new author.

And if you loved it, continue with the Chronicles of an Urban Druid and claim your copy of book six:
A Druid Hexed

A DRUID HEXED

The story continues with A Druid Hexed, available now at Amazon and Kindle Unlimited.

AUTHOR NOTES - AUBURN TEMPEST

JANUARY 22, 2021

Thank you so much for reading _A Broken Vow_, and for continuing along with Michael and I on this amazing journey of characters and adventure.

I heart Clan Cumhaill hard.

On that note, you might be pleased to know that LMBPN has contracted me for at least 3 more books in the series and I'm excited to see where Fiona and the others take us next.

Book 6 – A Druid Hexed is written and in the hands of Michael's team for edits. Thanks to them for helping to make my books the best they can be.

As always, thank you for all the love and support the series has been given. Every morning, I begin my day by checking each book for new reviews. I read every one and take your comments to heart. Most people love the combo of family, fun, and fantasy, so that's what we aim to deliver.

More immersion into Toronto life and mayhem with Fi and her friends to come.

Wishing you all lives filled with laughter and love.

Auburn Tempest

P.S. If you enjoy my writing and read sexy steamy romance, my pen name for the books I write Paranormal and Fantasy Romance is JL Madore. You can find me on Amazon.

AUTHOR NOTES - MICHAEL ANDERLE

JANUARY 25, 2021

Thank you for reading this story and here to the back and our author notes!

As Auburn mentioned, it's the family that has so many fans loving the stories, and somewhere, I mentioned that Auburn has patterned many of the family members after her own.

I can only imagine what a big celebration with her family would look like!

As a reader, I love it when series I enjoy (and more importantly, the characters I love) continue. Therefore, I love the fact that Auburn was willing to jump on board for another three books with LMBPN and continue this series.

Like she says, I heart this group a lot.

For those who follow my escapades in the other author notes with my cooking, know that I've found a recipe to make a small (1 person) serving of rice using my sous vide Joule.

If you are interested, this is the recipe I'm looking at: https://www.cooking-4-one.com/2017/11/21/white-rice-for-one/

Overall, my "from grill (or pot), to vacuum sealed (MX Bold) and freezer, to sous vide re-heat no-muss, no-fuss" is going very well.

I get a small thrill knowing that if I fail to fetch the food at the right time...it doesn't matter. That substantially reduces the stress I feel during the hectic days as I go from beats to covers to meetings back to beats and an hour later, I go, "Oh crap, I've got something cooking." Only to find out what I have is a burnt mess.

Not anymore!

If you *loves* you some Fi and Family, please drop a review on Book 01 and let's kick the Amazon algorithm into loving the series more. Then maybe I can (eventually) get Auburn to consider books 10, 11, and 12.

Because at the end of all of this publishing business, I'm a reader, too.

Ad Aeternitatem,

Michael Anderle

ABOUT AUBURN TEMPEST

Auburn Tempest is a multi-genre novelist giving life to Urban Fantasy, Paranormal, and Sci-Fi adventures. Under the pen name, JL Madore, she writes in the same genres but in full romance, sexy-steamy novels. Whether Romance or not, she loves to twist Alpha heroes and kick-ass heroines into chaotic, hilarious, fast-paced, magical situations and make them really work for their happy endings.

Auburn Tempest lives in the Greater Toronto Area, Canada with her dear, wonderful hubby of 30 years and a menagerie of family, friends, and animals.

BOOKS BY AUBURN TEMPEST

Auburn Tempest - Urban Fantasy Action/Adventure

Chronicles of an Urban Druid

Book 1 – A Gilded Cage

Book 2 – A Sacred Grove

Book 3 – A Family Oath

Book 4 - A Witches Revenge

Book 5 - A Broken Vow

Book 6 - A Druid Hexed

Misty's Magick and Mayhem Series – Written by Carolina Mac/Contributed to by Auburn Tempest

Book 1 – School for Reluctant Witches

Book 2 – School for Saucy Sorceresses

Book 3 – School for Unwitting Wiccans

Book 4 – Nine St. Gillian Street

Book 5 – The Ghost of Pirate's Alley

Book 6 – Jinxing Jackson Square

Book 7 – Flame

Book 8 – Frost

Book 9 – Nocturne

Book 10 – Luna

Book 11 – Swamp Magic

Exemplar Hall – Co-written with Ruby Night

Prequel – Death of a Magi Knight

CONNECT WITH THE AUTHORS

Connect with Auburn

Amazon, Facebook, Newsletter

Web page – www.jlmadore.com

Email – AuburnTempestWrites@gmail.com

Connect with Michael Anderle and sign up for his email list here:

Website: http://lmbpn.com

Email List: http://lmbpn.com/email/

Social Media:

https://www.facebook.com/LMBPNPublishing

https://twitter.com/MichaelAnderle

https://www.instagram.com/lmbpn_publishing/

https://www.bookbub.com/authors/michael-anderle

OTHER LMBPN PUBLISHING BOOKS